THE SUFFERING

MJ MARS

WICKED HOUSE PUBLISHING

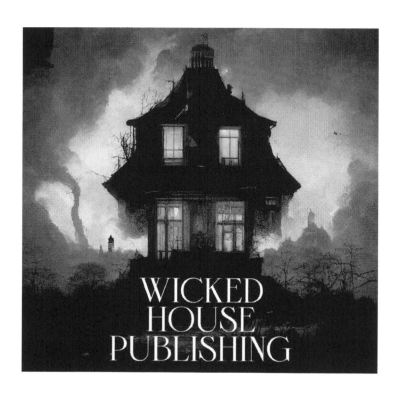

The Suffering
By MJ Mars

Wicked House Publishing

Cover design by Christian Bentulan
Interior Formatting by Joshua Marsella

Contents

Dedicated to my favourite pioneers of the paranormal
Loren Coleman, Zak Bagans, and Tom DeLonge
And all those who build empires while others stand and laugh.

"There is no exquisite beauty...without some strangeness in the proportion" – Edgar Allan Poe

Chapter 1

Halloween 2016

"Trick-or-treat! So, what's it like living in the Victorian murder house?"

Cassie laughed at the little girl peering up at her from the porch.

The kid's young mother wearily pinched the bridge of her nose and apologised. "I'm so sorry. She's extremely morbid. We have no idea where she gets it from."

"That's all right," Cassie said, reaching for the dish of sweets behind the door. "I was the same at that age."

The woman eyed Cassie's Halloween costume. It was a homemade praying mantis homage, complete with the cardboard half-eaten corpse of her mantodean husband swinging by a thread from her arm. "I can imagine."

Grinning, Cassie caught a glimpse of herself in the hallway mirror. She suited green, and it was a good thing she did—her costume comprised of lime leggings and a turtleneck sweater, green make-up painted over her cheeks, lips, and eyes. Her hair was tied back and sprayed with neon colour. Her scalp felt chalky and stiff. When she raised a hand to scratch an itch, green powder tumbled down and dusted her cheeks.

"Guess who I am?" the little girl demanded, hopping closer to Cassie and throwing out her arms. A straggly brown pigtail escaped from the red wig that sat lopsided on her head. She wore a torn blue dress with a white apron tied around her middle, and she carried a toy octopus. Her jewellery was too large for her, pooling around her hands instead of her wrists, the cords threaded with dozens of seashells.

Cassie snapped her fingers, impressed that the kid had chosen to dress as one of the ghosts from the house's history. "You're Lisa Vaughan."

"Yes!" The little girl reached behind her and grabbed her younger brother, pulling him up the steps to join her. "Guess who he is?"

The boy looked to be about five years old, adorable in a grey three-piece suit and shiny black shoes, a pocket watch swinging from his waistcoat. While his sister had come dressed as one of Brackenby House's infamous ghosts, there wasn't anything too gruesome about his outfit. Visibly disinterested in the history of the house and his costume, the little boy wordlessly held up his pillowcase to Cassie.

She tossed a handful of sweets into the sack. The suit and slicked-back hair could only mean one thing; that the kid's costume depicted the Victorian psychic who had unleashed the ghosts on Brackenby and banished them back into its walls. "Some loot for Mr. Lucius Holgrove?"

The little girl jumped up and down and clapped her hands. "You got it."

"Wait here a minute," Cassie instructed. She hurried

down the hallway and yelled into the dining room. "Kyle! Come out here a sec."

A few moments later, her housemate ambled up to her side, clutching three long, white candles. He was dressed as a Ghostbuster in a tan jumpsuit and jackboots, a plastic proton pack slung over one shoulder. Cassie pointed to the tiny trick-or-treater on the doorstep. "Look who it is. It's your Great Uncle Lucius."

Kyle looked stunned. "That's fantastic!"

"And I'm Lisa Vaughan. What's it like living in the Victorian murder house?"

"Emelia!" The mother cringed and stepped forward, attempting to herd the kids away from the house. "I am so sorry for this. Thank you for the sweets."

"Are you going to do a séance at midnight?" the little girl persisted, gawping at the candles in Kyle's hand.

He grinned down at them. "As a matter of fact, that was the plan."

"No way! Can I come?"

"Emelia! I'm so sorry...get down off that step at once and leave these poor people alone."

Emelia frowned up at her mother and folded her arms, shell bracelets sliding down to her elbows. "I'm going to have a séance all of my own. I want to talk to The Suffering ghosts."

"Emelia Grace Stone, you are eight years old. You will not be having any kind of séance in my house." The woman's exasperated voice faded as she ushered the children onto the street. They disappeared behind a row of hedges.

Cassie closed the door with a laugh. "Great kids."

"It's always nice to meet the fans," Kyle quipped.

Cassie glanced down at his nametag and hid her smirk by biting her lip. Earlier that day, Lance's cousin, Jonah, had painstakingly changed the stitching on the tag so that instead of saying Venkman, it clearly read *Wankman*. Kyle had been too wrapped up in thoughts of the séance to realise. She followed him as he carried the candles through to the dining room. He had set the huge oak table ready for the séance, and the other housemates were sat around a make-shift ouija board made up of Scrabble tiles and symbols taken from occult web pages.

Gaia untangled herself from Pete's long limbs and tumbled off the giant beanbag they had been snuggling into. She was less Halloween horror and more adorable, dressed in a petite Jigglypuff onesie, glittering pink blush shimmering against her brown skin. She leaned forward to kiss Pete, then stood up and addressed the room. "Right, I'm out of here, guys. Call me superstitious, but I know better than to fool around with a ouija board."

"You're leaving?" Cassie asked, forlornly. As the only girl in a household with four boys, Cassie enjoyed having Pete's girlfriend join the group. Even if the feeling was a little one-sided.

"Sorry," Gaia sang, not sorry in the least. She scurried from the room and closed the door behind her. Her foot-steps, muffled by the fluffy padding, creaked off down the corridor. They heard the heavy front door close.

Pete dragged the beanbag closer to the table, careful not to pierce the fabric with his Freddy Krueger glove. It had been a peculiar fever-dream, witnessing Freddy cuddling a Pokémon, but now that Gaia had left, the room looked suitably horrifying.

Lance was dressed as the Zodiac Killer. His black hooded tunic was daubed in white paint in the same way the killer had worn his symbol at the Lake Berryessa attack. He slipped the hood back to reveal his ruddy face, blond curls springing up in all directions, then picked up the planchette and tested its weight. "Wait, wait, wait. Let me just do a status update."

The group groaned and waited impatiently while Lance readjusted his hood and held the planchette up in front of him.

He snapped a few selfies then added one of them to his Insta feed, mumbling, "Hashtag what's your sign, hashtag happy Halloween, hashtag all in the game...send."

Tad had chosen to honour his Japanese roots and was dressed as a chōchin-obake, which he had described as being a traditional lantern ghost. He'd carefully crafted rice paper into elegant shapes, bending wires to make a frame that fit snugly over his head. An engineering student, Tad had built an articulated tongue that slipped from the paper mouth and flicked out when he tugged a concealed string. He had cut neat holes for his eyes and had painted black face paint across his eyelids. His dark irises scanned the table, and he considered the ouija tiles with calm interest.

Kyle fixed the candles into holders and lit them, shrugged off the proton pack and dropped it under the table, then hurried to switch off the lights. "Everyone see the table okay?"

The housemates stared down at the dimly lit circle of letters and pictures, then mumbled that they could.

"Great." Kyle sat down next to Cassie and held out his arms, theatrically presenting the board. "Welcome to The Suffering: Part 2!"

"Oh, Jeez, I hope not!" Cassie protested, shuddering as if she were suddenly cold.

"As you all know, we came to live in this house thanks to my uncle, Caleb, who charitably passed it to my mum for a fraction of its true value. She then had the bright idea of offering it to me and my friends for our student digs."

"Woop!" Lance cheered, and the housemates all lifted their glasses and clashed bottles. They knew how lucky they were to be friends with Kyle. They paid peanuts in rent, and the large Victorian townhouse was a palace compared to most of their friends' student accommodation.

Kyle continued his spiel, lowering his voice to a suitable Halloween host bass tone. "The house we sleep in each night has a sordid history, a history that dates back to 1876. Professor Josiah Grant enlisted the help of my great-great-great-grand uncle, Lucius Holgrove, a noted Victorian psychic."

Pete held his hand up. "Usually referred to as Kyle's Great Uncle Lucius."

"Thank fuck." Lance glanced at Kyle and shook his head, the hood shimmying. "The only thing more ridiculous than the idea of ghosts is trying to keep up with your ancestors."

Although Brackenby House was undoubtably creepy at times, the group tried to be as scientific and practical as they could. They humoured Kyle's paranormal enthusiasm, but none of them had lost much sleep over the home's gruesome past.

"I think I know Lucius. Is he about yay-high?" Cassie grinned, holding her hand to the height of the trick-or-treater who had turned up dressed as Holgrove that night.

Proudly presenting them with a framed picture, Kyle let

the candle's glow dance over the glass as he spoke from behind it. "*This* is Lucius. Young and kind, agreeing to demonstrate his paranormal skills as a favour to his beloved cousin, Jenna Parks. He had no idea what his powers would unleash on the party. Before midnight, 29th February—the leap year—all the household but Lucius would be dead."

"He was handsome," Cassie pointed out, earning a sharp glare from Kyle for interrupting his dramatic monologue.

"Naturally, I've inherited the Holgrove looks."

The friends broke into laughter, the tension well and truly shattered. Kyle wasn't ugly, but with his scruffy brown hair, slightly crooked nose, overlapping front teeth, and hefty frame, he didn't bear too much of a resemblance to the immaculate Victorian in the picture.

"All right, all right, let's get back to it." Kyle lowered Lucius's photograph and folded his hands on the table in front of him. "Professor Grant was in possession of an old book, a *tome*, if you like. The tome had been found chained underground in an Irish monastery during renovations. Grant had bought the book for his museum and was in the process of deciphering the ancient text. He discovered a formula for seeing his own fate. All he needed was the power of the dead. But not just *any* dead."

Pete smirked as Kyle bent forward, his enthusiasm for the local legend reaching a crescendo.

"He needed five ghosts who would capture the key components of his spell: Strength, Stealth, Frivolity, Deception, and Malice. The secret to the hidden depths of the human condition."

"Well, that's depressing," Cassie said.

Pete nodded in agreement, his hazel eyes shimmering in

the candlelight.

Ignoring them, Kyle went on. "Grant needed Lucius to bring forth the spirits who would represent each state. Po, an ancient Peruvian monster. Connor Rourke, a factory worker who had been caught stealing from the owner and had fallen through a trapdoor attempting to escape. Lisa Vaughan, a teenaged fortune teller who cursed the sailors who sought her wares. Anthony Pile, a member of the Hellfire Club who committed satanic rituals to keep his stolen fortune in the afterlife. Finally, Malice—Jarvis Rice. A corrupt executioner who enjoyed his profession so much he murdered women and framed their husbands for the killing, having them sent straight to his axe block."

"That's dedication," Pete whispered to Cassie.

"Worthy of a promotion," she blurted, bumping her elbow into his shoulder. They dissolved into snickers.

"All we know of how the events unfolded that night comes from Lucius himself, the only person to escape the house. Grant, along with his seven-year-old son, their maid, Lucius's beloved cousin, Jenna, and two of Grant's friends, perished at the hands of the ghosts that were released in the séance. Lucius managed to use his powers to vanquish the spirits, banishing them within the walls of the house. *This* house." Kyle threw his arms wide. "But the survivor guilt and the trials of what Lucius had witnessed that night caused him to descend into madness. His guilt was insurmountable. After his release from prison and a stint in a mental institution he bought the house from the Grant family, rendering himself penniless and homeless. He refused to live in the cursed house. Before the year was out, Lucius had thrown himself into the sea."

"Wait, so Lucius only escaped by banishing the spirits *inside* this house?" Pete asked, tapping a Freddy blade against the tabletop.

"Yep."

"And you want to use the ouija board tonight to call them back out."

"Correct."

"Is this really a good idea?" He looked up and scanned his friends' faces for their opinion.

Lance shrugged. "It's only a silly legend."

"Hey!" Kyle protested. "The official records show that everyone in the house, bar my great-uncle, died that night. That's not a legend."

"Well, maybe a wild animal escaped. Grant was rich and eccentric. People had all sorts of crazy shit back in those days."

"But what about Lucius's testimony?"

Lance shifted uncomfortably. He plucked back the hood to reveal his sweaty, blotched cheeks. His blond curls made a wild sprouting halo around his face. "Mate, the guy was put in the loony bin. Just saying. It's not a huge stretch that when he saw a roomful of people mauled to death, he might have invented an alternative reality. Especially since he was hired specifically to raise some ghosts."

"He's right," Tad told the group. "Legends are always based on half-truths and twisted facts. I'm pretty sure we're safe to do this."

Satisfied, Pete joined in as they all reached out to place a finger on the planchette. "All right. But on your head be it if this thing goes bad."

Kyle beamed. "Let's do this."

The group settled over the table and Kyle briefly skimmed through the rules of the board. Cassie used her free hand—free in the sense that it wasn't touching the planchette but still dangled the cardboard insect corpse—to sip from a large glass of red wine. She left green smudges all over the glass from her *galactic shimmer* lipstick.

Tad bobbed his lantern head when Kyle explained how the board should be closed after the session. Although he was a sceptic, he was a stickler for the rules.

Kyle cleared his throat and spoke to the board. "We have come together this Halloween night to call upon the banished spirits of The Suffering ritual, who were cast into the walls of this home in 1876 by my great-uncle, Lucius Holgrove. I welcome you to use our strength to break free of your spiritual shackles and come and talk to us tonight."

He stared down at the planchette, willing it to move.

"Why don't you ask a question?" Cassie suggested.

"Is anybody theeeeeeere?" Lance wailed, using his best *they're coming to get you, Barbara* voice.

The planchette slid to the left, almost imperceptibly.

"Good one, Tad," Kyle snapped.

"It wasn't me." Tad objected. He started to lift his hands in defensive protest, then quickly pressed his fingers back on the planchette. Although he didn't believe in the superstitions of the board, the housemates knew how pissy Kyle could be when they didn't follow his rules on game nights.

Kyle looked down at the planchette and lowered his voice. "If this is Lisa Vaughan and your horde of drowned sailors, show us a sign!"

The group waited, listening intently.

Somewhere, something dripped.

Lance jumped, despite himself, then gave a breathy laugh. His rosy cheeks deepened in colour. "Kitchen tap. I wish your Uncle Caleb had fixed the plumbing before he moved out."

Kyle frowned. "Jarvis Rice, executioner and murderer, if you wish to speak to us, move the planchette. Spell your name."

They waited, holding their breaths. Nothing happened. Cassie exhaled and huffed a chuckle before she wrinkled up her nose and turned to Tad. "Did you fart? It stinks!"

Kyle wrinkled his nose. A rotting, earthy stench that didn't smell like it came from a human was slowly filling the room. His eyes widened with excitement. "Is that you, Jarvis?"

Lance leaned over the board and whispered with urgency, "Jarvis...did you fart?"

Pete smirked and Cassie turned her head away from Kyle, hiding her grin. Her shoulders bounced as she struggled to contain her laughter.

Blanking them, Kyle eyed the board. "Anthony Pile, satanist and extortionist, can you come and take the coins from this table?"

Lance looked at the money Kyle had placed on the tabletop beside a printed painting of the thieving Hellfire Club member. He snapped his head back to look at the coffee table where he'd emptied his pockets earlier. "Hey, that money's mine!"

"So what? It's only a couple of quid."

"Give your own money to the ghosts is all I'm saying. You're as bad as the Hellfire guy." Lance scowled.

"Connor Rourke!" Kyle pressed on, calling for the ghost

of stealth. "You died running through the rafters of the factory you worked at. Legend has it that you run still..."

Pete rolled his eyes. Tad, expression unseen behind his lantern mask, lifted his finger, triggering the mechanism to stick out his paper tongue.

"For fuck's sake, lads. If you aren't going to take this seriously —" Kyle's anguished voice cut off as a sudden gust of cold air began to blow the candles out. All the players except Kyle pulled their hands from the planchette as the room was plunged into darkness. "Don't break the circle!"

But it was too late. Cassie scrambled across the room and hit the lights to reveal Tad sprawled on his back, the mask yanked from his face and crushed under his fist in his panic. Lance was still at the table but sat frozen with his hands in the air, fingers spread, a dazed expression on his face. Pete stood a few feet from Cassie, having had the same idea to go for the light. He, too, was statue-still, panting, and pale, the knives of the Freddy Krueger glove poised toward the light switch.

The housemates looked to Kyle for guidance.

Outside the room, above the hallway, footsteps sounded on the landing.

Cassie screamed and ran to Pete, ducking behind him.

The steps ran back the way they'd come, unmistakably human but echoing and light, too quick. Too agile.

In the next room to the right, the tap in the kitchen came on with full force, sluicing water into the plastic basin, rumbling through the old countertop.

Lance looked at the table and pointed. "The money's gone," he whispered, staring at the empty space where his change had been piled.

"Who else is left?" Tad asked Kyle, his expression cold and unreadable.

Kyle let out a shuddering exhalation, his fingers still pressing into the planchette so hard the skin around his nails had turned white. "Po."

The planchette flew from his fingers, tearing across the table and scattering the ouija tiles.

Underneath their feet, deep in the cellar, something thudded.

Cassie covered her face with her hands, and Pete wrapped his arms around her protectively, his wide eyes scanning the room.

The rotary telephone on the wall shrilled to life, causing them all to scream. Visibly shaking, Kyle stood up and moved to it, the loud jangling of the old bells within the vintage phone making him wince. As he reached out to take the phone, Cassie cried, "Don't! What if it's...one of them?"

Expecting the usual scathing barrage from the boys, Kyle looked to them, but they simply stared back, nodding, eyes wide in anticipatory fear.

"If it is a ghost it might be Lucius... He might be trying to tell us how to fix this," Kyle said hesitantly. His great-uncle was long dead, but he'd had psychic powers, after all. He'd been the one to banish the ghosts to the house in the first place.

The old phone let out another urgent vibration. Before it could ring out, Kyle snatched it from the cradle and slowly put it to his ear with a trembling hand. "Huh...hello?"

"Just what the actual fuck have you just done?" His uncle Caleb snapped.

CHAPTER 2
TURBULENCE (3 WEEKS LATER)

The plane shuddered and dipped through thick cloud cover over the North Atlantic Ocean. Kyle Birbeck tightened his grip on his seat and thought about reaching over the sleeping passenger beside him to shut the window blind. He wasn't usually afraid of flying, but he was tired and eager to get back to his housemates at Brackenby, and the reminder that he was still hours from reaching London only made the turbulence worse. The man let out a snore and shifted a little in his sleep.

Kyle reached down under the seat in front of him and tugged out his flight bag. He groped in the side pocket for his notebook. The A4, hard-backed book bulged with information about the history of Brackenby House. He kicked his bag back into place and lowered the small drinks table, before spreading out some of the papers on its surface. The pages were photocopies of an old newspaper series, the engravings similar to those depicting the timelines of the victims of Jack the Ripper. Kyle let his eyes drift from the headline; *Mystery of the Massacre at Brackenby House*, to the first image in the series. The layout reminded him of the graphic novels he liked to read. Only, he wasn't skimming through tales of the Watchmen, or a Marvel superhero. He was looking at sketches of his own great-uncle, the newspaper artist using Lucius Holgrove's court testimony to create the macabre comic spread in front of him.

The first illustration showed Lucius arriving at Brackenby House. Professor Josiah Grant peered at him over his spectacles, a speech marker questioning the young visitor; *"Have you no umbrella, man?"*

Pen-made slashes of rain lashed down in the doorway where Lucius stood soaked, the young man wide-eyed and apprehensive. *"I forgot it, sir. The newspaper forecast clear skies."*

The next image showed a heavy-set man in rich-looking Victorian clothing, a glass of whiskey in his hand. His pudgy face twisted in a sneer. This was Cillian Waverley, Kyle knew, Grant's accountant. He was depicted as being a snide and unpleasant man, but the fact he died a gruesome death that night made Kyle feel some sympathy for him.

"What kind of psychic knows not when it will rain?" Waverley scoffed.

"Most of us, I believe, sir. The spirits tend to whisper of more important things. Such as a man's future." Kyle couldn't help but smile at his ancestor's rebuttal. Although he had been young and inexperienced, Lucius Holgrove had faith in his paranormal talents. Despite his nerves, he'd had no doubt he could give the men a show.

The flight attendants moved through the aisle, trundling a small drinks trolley. Kyle asked for a Coke with ice and took the can from the crewman, who looked down at the engravings with interest. He flashed Kyle an intrigued look, then pushed on with the cart.

Kyle skimmed through the next few panels. In the pictures, Grant took Lucius to the room where the séance would be held and introduced him to the others. Attending Grant's séance that night was Lucius's cousin, Jenna Parks, who had recommended Lucius to Grant. As well as Cillian Waverley, the fat and rude accountant, there was also the baby-faced factory owner, John Lincoln. Grant's maid, Clara, had provided the guests with refreshments before disappearing up the stairs to put Grant's seven-year-old son to bed. In his testimony, Lucius had disclosed how Waverley had continued to belittle him throughout the evening. This had been a contentious point for the jury who had been torn between convicting the young psychic for murder and believing the evidence placed in front of them—the evidence that something beyond comprehension had happened in that house.

Kyle turned the page, feeling a little winded to see his own dining room sketched out in the drawing. Grant was leaning over a large book in the centre of the heavy oak table, his arms spread wide over papers scattered across the surface. The similarity between the original séance and his own ill-advised attempt at making contact on Halloween didn't escape Kyle. He frowned down at the image.

Writing spidered around Grant's picture, the professor's words taken from Lucius's courtroom accounts. *"This book, my honoured guests, was found chained and bricked into the wall in the cellar of a monastery. It was sent to my museum, where it was my duty to uncover the secrets as to why the monks took such extreme measures in its keeping. I am certain I have discovered the truth. And with Master Lucius' assistance, tonight we will crack the code of the tome. We'll unleash the spirits who will piece together the puzzle of our very own futures."*

The next panel showed Lucius staring down at the book in confusion. Lucius's full lips were parted, his eyebrows curved ruefully above eyes that were deep-set and similar in shape to Kyle's and his mother's. *"Forgive me, Sir,"* the caption read. *"But I do not understand what you ask of me."*

"You, my good man, are a conduit—a lightning rod to the spirits I require. With your assistance, I believe I have the recipe for a power unseen by human eyes. The five spirits of divination: Malice, Strength, Stealth, Deception, and Frivolity."

Kyle turned the page, taking in the artist's impression of the rogue's gallery that made up The Suffering ghosts. First was Stealth. Connor Rourke was etched running through the rafters of the factory he had stolen from. He was looking back over his shoulder, hair streaming behind him, his white worker's shirt billowing. His raised foot was hovering over a rickety trapdoor, the artist having chosen to depict the moment just before the thief tumbled to his death.

At the bottom of the drawing, Grant's guest, John Lincoln, who himself was a factory owner, was looking smug. *"Well, I dare say the vagabond deserved an untimely end! If one will steal from a paying employer."*

Frivolity was the fortune teller, Lisa Vaughan, who had been sketched standing on a dock, a boat leaving port in the distance behind her. Her long hair blew in the wind and her dress lifted to show her bare feet. The inscription explained how in the early 1700s she had approached sailors who arrived at Lancaster's port, offering them a bed for the night and a palm reading. The next day, the men would venture off on their journeys and, inexplicably, would fling themselves from the ship into the sea a few days later.

Strength was the ancient Incan monster, Po. The prospect of a three-eyed giant was probably a little too much for a Victorian newspaper spread, Kyle guessed since the panel's border cut off the top of his head. Instead, he was shown standing behind Waverley, a scene described in Lucius's testimony. The words snaked to the side of the sketch: *The brute was the first to appear—a mirage from the fires of Hell itself. The monster grunted and towered over Waverley. And I knew then that none of us would survive.*

The artist's drawing of the 17th-century Scottish executioner, Jarvis Rice, was just as subtle. The man's face was shrouded in a hood, gloved fingers curling around the blade of his axe. His label read *Malice*, in small copperplate.

Money-driven satanist, Anthony Pile, was the last of the ghosts in the series of sketches. Representing Deception, in life, Pile had embezzled, stolen, and charmed his way into a small fortune. Having used his sudden wealth to worm his way into high society, he had joined the Hellfire Club and allegedly used his newfound knowledge of ritualistic sacrifice to ensure he kept his fortune in the afterlife. He was wearing a collar-length powdered wig and a jewelled crucifix, sneering with contempt.

Beneath the bizarre set of portraits, the artist had drawn a long, thin sketch of the séance beginning. The guests held hands as Grant rang a small bell. Lucius stood with his eyes closed, mists swirling around him.

Kyle glanced out of the aeroplane window, the cotton

candy effect of the wings cutting through the thick clouds making him uneasy. The plane jerked violently, and the *fasten seatbelt* sign pinged above him.

Concentrating on the pages in front of him rather than the juddering plane, Kyle turned to the next set of images. This was a full-page spread depicting the carnage as the ghosts began to appear. In the centre of the page, Lucius's testimony was printed, describing how the séance descended into chaos.

"I told Grant, 'I see a demon!' He was elated at the news, and said, 'Surely the beast known as Po! Do you see others?'

"At his question, I could not bring myself to answer, because the room was full of sounds and smells that had been purged from another realm. Footsteps thundered through the halls of Brackenby, and Lincoln staggered to the side as the spectre of Rourke rushed past him. I caught the man in my arms, and he insisted he felt as though he were falling. I reassured him t'was not him who had fallen, but the thieving spirit Rourke in his dying moments. But it would not be long before I would come to regret those words.

"Grant decried that I control the spirits. 'Control them? You implored me to bring them to you and that I have done! Anything further is beyond my power!' I cried, helpless to do his bidding. And then a sight that filled me with more woe than any other of that night. The boy, Joseph, but seven years old, stood in the doorway. Though still in slumber, he paced with purpose to the table, and the ghosts turned their attentions to him.

"Jenna, my sweet cousin, could not bear harm coming to a child. She made to protect the boy, but the dreadful sea witch Lisa Vaughan appeared beside her. The hag gave one glance

and a flick of her hand, and I watched in horror as my cousin began to drown where she stood, sea water gurgling and spilling from her very lungs. She clawed at her throat and fell to her knees, and a score of spectral sailors arose to surround her, blocking my view. It was a scene of such insanity I can scarcely believe I am relaying it to you, Your Honour. But it happened in Brackenby. And the night was to descend further into the pits of Hell."

Kyle skimmed the pictures surrounding Lucius's account of the death of Grant's maid, Clara. The final picture showed the boy lying limp in Clara's arms. Behind her, Jarvis Rice swung his axe, the blade hurtling towards her neck.

Kyle turned the page, feeling his heart thumping at the base of his throat. Lucius's testimony continued, printed in a neat banner across the top of the newspaper's page.

"John Lincoln ran at the sight of the maid being slaughtered so viciously. He screamed as he made his way to the front door, and turned tail, racing up the stairs, the pattering footsteps of the ghoul Rourke on his heels. Moments later, there came the shattering of glass, and Lincoln's body was seen tumbling from the upper floors, to land dead in the grounds of Brackenby.

"Grant had his hands on the transfixed and stupefied child. The wicked embezzler Pile appeared to him in something akin to priests' robes, arms outstretched. Grant saw the image of the cross around his neck and believed him to have come as a saviour, forgetting the vile spectre that was summoned by his own vision of Deception. He placed the boy in the devil worshipper's arms, paying no heed to my protestations. Within seconds, both the boy and Grant were freed from this life, the boy crushed against the spectre's robes. Grant *followed shortly as another victim of executioner Rice's bloodied axe, his death a mercy after passing his child to his own murderer.*

"Waverley sat incensed in his chair, unable to find the wits to raise his rotund form. The monster Po came up behind, took a hold of him on either side, and in eight quick gouges of obscene hands and one swift pull ripped the man in two from head to heel."

The plane tipped to one side and Kyle scrabbled to catch his drink, slapping his other hand flat against the fold-out table to keep the notebook pages from spilling to the floor. The man beside him let out a snort, shifted in his sleep, and his lolling head followed the plane's trajectory as it righted itself. He snored, blowing stale breath into Kyle's face.

Kyle exhaled slowly and swallowed the last of his Coke, shoving the plastic cup and empty can into the netting on the back of the seat in front of him. He couldn't wait to get off this plane, his nervous agitation beginning to swell into anxiety. He wished he'd ordered some vodka to go with the Coke, but it was too late now. The flight attendants were long gone. Besides, they'd be landing soon.

He was coming to the end of the testimony. The court would eventually decide that Lucius couldn't possibly have inflicted the injuries on the guests at Brackenby. But they would also declare that he was, undoubtably, quite mad. Kyle cringed at the fact that none of their family testified to Lucius's good character at the trial. His father and brothers, including the man who would later become Kyle's great-great-*great* grandfather, abandoned him to his fate.

To take his mind off the turbulence, and to the bleak notion that his grandfather a few times removed might have been a bit of an asshole, he looked down at the papers and willed himself to concentrate.

The engraving to accompany this page was the most brutal. Grant's son lay in a heap on the floor, his nightshirt crumpled around his twisted body. Grant lay beside him in a spreading pool of dark blood. Behind Waverley's chair, the Incan monster that was Po stood towering over the accountant. Again, the Victorian rag had omitted the fact that the beast had three eyes across his forehead, but somehow had no issues showing the two gory halves of Waverley's body held wide in triumphant celebration.

"What the fuck?" came a voice to Kyle's right.

He jumped and glanced to the side. The sleeping man had now woken up and was staring at the engraving on Kyle's table, a horrified expression on his face.

Kyle scrambled to cover the scene with his hands, giving the man an apologetic smile. "It's for work," he managed.

"What kind of weird job have you got, mate?" the man snorted, folding his arms and glaring.

"It's...it's nothing." Kyle quickly folded the newspaper pages and stuffed them into his notebook. One of them crumpled in his haste, and he smoothed it out with his fingers. It showed Lucius on trial, giving his infamous first words to the judge: *"What befell the group that night was an atrocity. It was a suffering like no other. And oh, how they suffered..."*

CHAPTER 3
THE WANDERER RETURNS

Kyle dozed in the back seat of the cab, drowsy from the thirteen-hour flight. He felt a mixture of both relief and trepidation when the taxi crunched to a halt on the gravel driveway of the Victorian townhouse. He absently touched the jasper beads around his wrist and peered up at the windows.

"Thirty-six, mate," the driver called over his shoulder.

Kyle snapped out of his daze and handed the man two twenties. He clambered stiffly from the back of the car and stretched, his calves tight from the combination of his Peruvian trek and being cramped in a plane seat for so long. His boots shed clouds of red dust as he made his way round the back of the cab and retrieved his rucksack. Kyle slung the strap over his aching shoulder, taking solace in the knowledge that this would be the last time he'd need to use it in a while. He clambered up the porch steps and moved to the heavy oak door, slipping his key in the lock, and pushing it open.

Inhaling, Kyle took in the familiar scent of his home. The hallway smelled of a mixture of the shoes that lay scattered beneath the coat rack, and spicy notes that drifted through from the kitchen at the end of the corridor. The remnants of Lance's culinary experiments. Kyle had just missed the weekly feast, arriving home from his two-week trip on the Friday morning.

"Anybody home?" he yelled up the stairs, receiving no response. It was to be expected. His housemates were all at uni. Although it was the middle of the semester, he had permission to take time out for his trip since it was directly linked to his thesis. He'd have to wait for a grand reunion in the evening.

He shrugged off the backpack and dropped it by the pile of shoes, then wandered over to the cellar door, which was situated under the stairs to the left of the kitchen entrance. He frowned, placing his hand on the white-washed wood. He had easily sold the idea of a trip to Peru to his anthropology lecturer, citing the disappearance of the Incans and the remnant ancestry in the local villages as his project. And he had gathered more than enough information to complete his thesis, he knew. But he had also been looking for something else.

The small jasper beads around his wrist stood out in brilliant technicolour against the door. He raised the fingers of his other hand and touched them, rolling them around on the tan cord. It was a protection bracelet, or so Selestino, the village elder, had told him. A scam, Kyle would have assumed, if it hadn't been given to him for free. Selestino had slipped it onto Kyle's arm and peered directly into his eyes, the crags that lined the skin above his cheekbones deepening in silent warning.

Kyle braced himself, muttering, "Let's see how good you are..."

The muscles in his back tightened in instinctive fight or flight defence. He shoved open the cellar door. Dust particles floated into the air, the bare grey brick of the walls making the space around him feel cool and oppressive as he stepped into the dank entranceway. A creaking wooden staircase led down into the depths of the storage room, and his boots left red footprints on the short concrete platform at the top of the stairs.

He held the bracelet against his skin as he made his way down the groaning steps and trod into the dusty grey chalk of the unfinished cellar floor. There was barely any light in the old cellar save for a narrow windowpane at street-level high on the far wall that cast a small sliver of blueish daylight into the space during the day, and the feintest halogen glow of a distant streetlight at night. Apart from that, the cellar was shrouded in darkness. Steeling himself at the sight of the black shadows ahead, he made his way deeper into the room. His eyes darted from the tall shelving ahead to the cardboard storage boxes piled high against the far wall.

To his right, a stack of paintings in ornate frames were propped up against the mottled brick walls. He knew they had been painted by Professor Grant's wife, Lyla, before her death in 1872. The sheet that had been protecting them from the dust had slipped down at one side, revealing a blazing sun casting down onto Brackenby House. Lyla was evidently fond of landscapes, and her own home had been her favourite subject. He stooped to pluck the material back over the frame.

And heard a noise from the depths of the room behind him. A dull scraping.

In the aftermath of their Halloween séance, things had fallen quiet in the house. The housemates had all faced a mutually sleepless week, flinching at each noise, at each drip of the leaky kitchen tap and groans in the rafters. Lance stopped leaving his loose change on the coffee table. Then they began to feel foolish, concluding that the effects of Halloween and alcohol had given them some type of shared delusion. They stopped listening for footsteps along the landing. Slept with their lights off. Managed to stay home alone.

But then, the noises had started up again. Scrapes and scratches in the cellar. Small thuds and clatters like rocks being thrown. At first, they had assumed it was rats. Invisible critters in the walls, going about their business. Then, at night, the noises had begun to grow louder, morphing into violent thuds that shook the walls and sent dust pluming from the cracks in the concrete. It was as if the séance had shifted the house into another gear, and it took a few weeks for it to find its footing.

Kyle stood still and listened.

A grunt.

Always, the distinctive grunt. Coming from right behind his head. "I know your secrets now, you bastard," Kyle muttered.

An exhalation, long and indulgent, ruffled the hair on the nape of his neck. Next to his ear, a low chuckle sent chills scurrying over his arms, the fine hairs standing to attention.

The stair creaked above him.

Gasping, Kyle spun round and saw Lance leaning down,

a beaming smile breaking across his ruddy face. "You're back!"

"Hey." Kyle hurried over to the steps and hopped up to where his friend held out a hand. He clasped it and leaned in for a quick greeting hug. "I thought you were at uni."

"No classes 'til two today," Lance told him, looking uneasily down into the cellar space below. "What the hell are you doing down here, anyway?"

"I thought I heard a noise."

The two housemates stared at each other for a moment before dissolving into laughter. Lance, the level-headed economics student, outwardly put the sounds down to the fact that the house had been around since the Victorian era. Even after what he'd experienced at the séance. Its rooms were nearly two hundred years old. Because of this, the inexplicable noises emanating from the cellar could be nothing more than the result of ancient building techniques and shifting wooden fixtures. That's what Lance usually told anyone who asked, in any case. Kyle knew the truth. That Lance had recently seen more in the house than could ever be explained away by the building's age.

Lance turned and clambered back up the steps. He wore skinny indigo jeans turned up above his ankles and bright white sneakers that matched his white polo shirt. The blond curls piled high on his head bounced like puppy ears as he hopped up the last step. "I can't wait 'til everyone gets home and sees you."

"Me, too," Kyle grinned, following his friend. At the last minute, he turned back and peered down into the shadowy darkness. Out of earshot of Lance, he whispered over the railing, "I'm gonna get you, Po."

He held up his wrist; the turquoise, scarlet, and orange beads looked muddy in the half-light. With his new-found knowledge, he felt a little braver despite the deep chuckle that emanated up from the darkness as he closed the cellar door.

"So, tell me all about it!" Lance called from the kitchen. "Did you see sloths?"

"Oh, yeah. Heaps of sloths."

"I'm jealous."

"You should go there yourself. You'd love it."

"Here." Lance lifted his phone and draped an arm around Kyle's shoulder. Kyle peered up into the camera image of himself, travel-weary and smudged with dirt. But he raised his fingers in a peace sign as his friend took the snap. Lance checked the picture and nodded, typing frantically. "My boy home from Peru, hashtag travel, hashtag no place like home."

"Still influencing?" It was a running joke around the house that Lance was desperate to become a social media influencer to dodge the need to get a 9 to 5 job.

Lance's thumb flew over his screen as he added a few more hashtags to the image. "Travel is key, my friend."

"But you didn't actually go anywhere."

"Not relevant." Finished with his post, Lance pocketed his phone. About to sit at the table, his face fell, and he angrily snatched up a stool that had been placed behind their usual seating. "For fuck's sake! Someone keeps bringing out the spare chair. It's driving me crazy!"

Kyle watched with tired amusement as Lance dragged the stool to the back of the kitchen and set it in its usual spot, out of the way beside the mop and broom. He took the dustpan and set it on top of the seat for good measure, then shook his head and sat next to Kyle at the kitchen table. He grabbed a tangerine from the fruit bowl and began peeling it carefully, keeping the dappled orange rind in one long curling ribbon.

Kyle looked around at the familiar clutter of the country-style kitchen, "So, have I missed anything? What's been happening here?"

Lance let the peel furl on the table and stared down at the fruit in his hand. "I'm not gonna lie, Kyle. Things have been getting worse. Pete thinks I'm overreacting, but Cassie's been sleepwalking. It's not been...normal."

"What do you mean, not normal?"

Lance opened his mouth to respond but froze when a clattering sound came from the hallway. With a burst of chatter, the other housemates tumbled through the front door into the house.

Pete's voice could be heard over them all, which was rare for the usually quiet student. "His rucksack's here. He must be home."

"I'll tell you about it later," Lance whispered, moments before the others appeared in the kitchen.

Kyle stood up to greet his friends, conscious of his sweaty travel clothes as he embraced them one by one. "I thought you had lectures?"

Cassie hopped from foot to foot. "We do, but we had to come home for dinner and see you. We can't stay long, but there's the party tonight."

"Party?" Kyle flinched as Pete shot a party popper over his shoulder, streamers of tissue paper tumbling over his shirt in the wake of a puff of gunpowder.

"Welcome home party!" Lance spoke through a

mouthful of chewed-up fruit. "You didn't think we'd let you get away without one, did you?"

"Oh, God. I'd better have a nap, then. I'll be in no state to party if I don't."

"You can sleep 'til six," Cassie told him, sternly. "But at half-past six the fun begins. Leave it to us."

Pete plucked a segment of orange from Lance's fingers and popped it into his own mouth. "It's going to be epic. We've missed you."

"Missed you, too." Kyle slapped his hand into Pete's and let his friend tug him closer for a shoulder barge. He breathed in the familiarity of Pete's smoky cologne and the padded warmth of his red hoodie.

When Kyle moved to pull away, Pete held tight and mumbled close to his ear, the tang of juice on his breath. "It's been a bit tense."

"Lance said it's been bad...with Cassie."

"It's fine. Lance is overreacting. *She's* fine." He inclined his head toward her.

Nodding, Kyle furrowed his brow and stepped away, hoping that his expression read, *not now*. Cassie was tough and she hated it when anyone fussed over her. She would happily declare that she'd give any ghost the beating of its after-life, if only they were real to start with. Believing that version of the truth was the only way she could sleep at night, Kyle knew, and he was reluctant to take that away from her, no matter what he knew to be fact.

However, he had the ominous feeling that there wouldn't be any hiding it, soon. That the truth about the house would have to come out into the open, and they'd all have to face the facts, whether Pete and Cassie liked it or not.

Kyle sometimes wished he still had a veil of blissful ignorance. He'd originally had the same opinion as the others about the dark history surrounding the property—Victorian spook stories and embellished tales. Nothing to truly be afraid of.

But then he and his friends had moved in, and everything had changed.

THE THUMPING BEAT of the music pulsing up through the floorboards woke Kyle at five-thirty. He lay still for a moment, grateful to be back in his own bed. His duvet felt heavy and soft. He had sofa surfed in Peru, not only stopping at hostels and open houses, but staying with a traditional-living tribe on the outskirts of the jungles. There, his blanket had been a harsh knit that scratched at his shoulders through the night, and he retained more heat from the throbbing bug bites that peppered his skin than from the bedsheets. In the morning, he'd looked quizzically at the soft-looking blankets on his host's bed, at which point the family's son, Alois, had burst into laughter. "Hey, you wanted the traditional experience, right?"

Against his smooth cotton sheets, his legs felt tight and sore from the long trek, and his skin held that oily but gritty sensation that only came from travel.

He swung his feet out from under the covers and stood up.

A shape swung low in the right side of his peripheral vision. He froze, shifting into familiar hyper-awareness, suddenly wide awake. He knew from experience that if he moved his head to try and see whatever it was that was there, it would disappear. Instead, he kept his gaze firmly fixed on the neutral wallpaper in front of him, then softened his line of sight, allowing his vision to blur until his room around him looked like an impressionist painting. The black smudge was still there, crouching near the foot of the bed.

Kyle cleared his throat. "Are you there?" he whispered, his voice rasping over the thundering baseline pulsing through the floor.

The black smudge elongated, as if whatever it was had been crouching and now stood tall.

Fighting the urge to run was torturous, but he was training himself to be bolder. To learn as much as he could to try and help them. If he could send them back to where they were supposed to be, he'd not only free the poor lost souls of the house. He might just save his friends. "Which one are you?" he asked, softening his voice, trying to seem as unthreatening as possible.

A sigh sounded in his room. The black shape remained long and still in the corner of his eye. He could make a guess at who it was, but three of the ghosts were difficult to tell apart until they made their own characteristic move. This black blob could be any of them. Any except the hulking Po, who stayed in the cellar at all times. Or Rourke, the ghost of Stealth, who never stood still.

He decided to make a guess. "Anthony Pile? Is that you?"

The black blob dropped, hunching, and rushed towards him.

All thoughts of standing firm vanished. He couldn't help but duck to the side, holding out his hands in instinctive defence. But, as usual, whichever of the three spirits it was had vanished when he focused on the room. He felt the cold breath of it passing him by.

He shuddered and laughed to himself, the best tool he had for quelling his fear. "I guess it wasn't you, then."

He heard the creak of the floorboards and the light drumming of fingertips knocking against wood. Tad, he knew, even before his best friend opened the door and peered into the room.

"I stink!" Kyle warned as he stepped forward to embrace his housemate.

"Don't worry about it," Tad murmured into his ear, slapping him on the back. "Welcome home."

Kyle untangled himself and grinned. He'd only been gone for three weeks, but he had missed Tad more than anyone. Their friendship had started when they were eight years old, and Kyle had selected Tad's name from a list of pen pal opportunities arranged through his school. Tad was Japanese, and the pair's shared love of manga, Pokémon, and Marvel had grown into a friendship that skipped from laboriously handwritten letters, to emails, to Skype and Facetime calls.

When the boys were fifteen, Tad had come to the UK to stay with Kyle for the summer. They would stroll through the town centre, and people would stop and stare. Initially, Kyle had thought it was because of Tad being Japanese. That people were brazenly gawping at him due to his heritage. Then, it began to dawn on him that Tad was good looking. More than good looking, in fact—his best friend looked like a model. He hadn't even noticed at first, but when a talent scout dashed up to them in the shopping centre and thrust a card into Tad's hand, Kyle couldn't help but feel a burn of shame at his own mediocre looks.

Tad's visit led to a period of deep insecurity for Kyle, at a time where his skin had decided to flare into angry red spots and his voice was unpredictable—squeaking one minute and deep and Dalek-like the next. Meanwhile, across the world, Tad continued to grow taller and more handsome. The modelling offers kept rolling in, and every time Tad screwed up the cards and threw them in the bin.

"Aren't you going to call?" Kyle had asked in astonishment after Tad tore up the first card and tossed the pieces on top of a half-eaten burger.

Tad had looked at him as if he was crazy. "Why would I ever do that?"

The only goal Tad had at that time was to return to England and complete an engineering degree. He'd already won awards for his prototype sewage processing plans and was determined to make his mark in the world of environmentally sound waste removal. He felt as though his looks were holding him back. That nobody took him seriously.

Kyle thought it could be worse. He was average looking at best. Nobody took him seriously, either. He had soon grown used to the difference in their looks, however, and their friendship had gotten even stronger since the pair had moved into Brackenby House together.

Feeling a rush of comfortable warmth toward his best friend, he revelled in the sensation that he was now truly home. "Are you okay? How's things been?" he asked, walking over to his curtains and pulling them open. The room felt stale and unlived-in, and although he knew the light was falling and the moths would come in, he pushed open the window.

Tad sat down on the edge of the bed and hunched over, thoughtful. "Did you speak to Lance?"

"Yeah. He said it's been worse."

Tad nodded, staring down at his hands in his lap. His reluctance was unnerving.

"What is it?" The chill from the window wrapped itself around Kyle's bare arms, and he scraped his palms over the gooseflesh.

"I have a feeling. A hunch. It sounds stupid."

"Try me."

"I think they're latching on to us. One each."

Kyle swallowed, battling against a bone-dry throat.

"It's been happening for a while now. I didn't see the patterns at first. I might be imagining it." Tad raised his almond eyes and fixed them on Kyle, his expression open and vulnerable. "I'm glad you're back. It felt different when you'd gone. More unsettled."

"Who...who do you think has latched on to you?" Kyle asked. But he knew. Even as he asked the question. He could feel the presence of Jarvis Rice lurking behind his friend, a slight scent of mould in the air around them.

"I think mine is the executioner guy." Tad cleared his throat. "Kyle...I'm scared."

Kyle sat down on the other side of the bed, trying to decide whether he should tell Tad what he had discovered. He slipped his hand under the mattress, fingering the pages of the bulging hidden notebook that he had been steadily filling with research. He wanted to reassure his best friend, to tell him that all would be well. In reality, there were no plati-tudes to be made. In reality, he *should* be scared.

He pulled his hands away from the notebook and instead wrapped his fingers around Tad's shoulder. "I'm back now. It'll be okay."

Tad exhaled heavily. "I know. It's just been hard without you here. I guess my imagination's been getting away with me. Right?"

Kyle smiled softly. Tad's English was exceptional, but whenever he felt stressed, his deep voice tripped from conso-nants into vowels, a dead giveaway that betrayed his opti-mistic words. "Right."

"Anyway, we've got a party to get to." Tad stood up, raking his hands through his jaw-length black hair and flip-ping it so that it stood out in spikes at the nape of his neck. He strode onto the landing, his shoulders hunched, looking as though he wanted to do anything other than party.

We'll be drunk, at least, Kyle told himself. Things seemed better when they were drunk.

He thought for a moment about Tad's theory about each ghost choosing a different housemate to latch onto. He sniffed the air.

The mouldering stench had followed Tad from the room.

CHAPTER 4
PARTY ON

Cassie sipped her beer and bobbed along to the music, enjoying people-watching now that Kyle had returned home and the gang was all back together. When he had been gone, the house had felt fractured. It was as though one of the usual residents being in a different country had unsettled the very foundations of their home. There was a blanket-like sensation of calm in the dining room she hadn't felt for the previous three weeks, and it elevated the party atmosphere. She was even comfortable inviting some new friends to the house for the first time in a long while. Now, she beamed as Tara from her swimming relay team approached her, clutching a gin and tonic and wearing an extremely short skirt.

"Who is that?" Tara breathed, nodding her head towards Tad.

Cassie sighed. She hadn't had to go through the *Tad rigmarole* for a while, on account of not having had many female friends to bring to the house. It wasn't that she didn't like hanging out with girls. She just always fit in better with boys. She had a wicked sense of humour and a matter-of-fact demeanour that sometimes came across as callous. Cassie knew she could be a good shoulder to cry on, if only you were prepared to hear both sides of the argument. As a result, she often butted heads with the girls she got close to. Still, she wasn't prepared to change. She was who she was, after all.

She glanced at her best friend, Martin, who pulled a face that showed the whites of his eyes and the dimple in his left cheek. She smiled, and said to Tara, "That's my housemate, Tad. Why don't you go talk to him?"

"He is one of the most beautiful men I've ever seen. He's like a manga character," the girl hissed, reaching out to place her empty glass on the counter. "You really think I should?"

Cassie hitched a shoulder. "Why not? What have you got to lose?"

"He's single?"

"Oh yeah." Cassie nodded encouragement. "Crack on. Go ask him what he does."

She sank back against the wall as Tara sashayed over to Tad and placed a hand on his shirt, flirtatiously leaning into him and asking a coy question.

Martin stood beside Cassie, watching with amusement. "How long?" he asked.

"I'd give him about two minutes."

They stared brazenly while Tad began to animatedly engage with the girl, using his hands to sketch in the air—circles, swirls, and coils that Cassie guessed were detailed descriptions of the inner mechanisms of his latest engineering project.

At around the two-minute mark, Tara made her excuses

and returned, her mouth a tight line. "He was talking about sewage."

"Yep, that sounds like Tad."

Baffled, the girl looked back at him. Unfazed by the abandonment, he had turned back to Kyle to continue their conversation as if nothing had happened. "Why was he talking about...sewage?"

"Oh, you don't like that?" Martin asked with a smirk.

"I need another drink." Tara sauntered over to the drinks table and splashed gin into a glass, chased with a minimal glug of tonic water. She scanned the room and when her gaze fell on Pete, sitting alone on the couch arm, she headed straight for him.

"Interesting choice," Martin muttered, then made an *uh-oh* sound in the back of his throat when Gaia entered the room and made a beeline straight for the girl who was obviously hitting on her man.

The pair observed Gaia making short shrift by wrapping her arm around Pete's shoulder and hopping into his lap, lifting her chin to Tara and throwing her long, dark hair over her shoulder. Backing off, the swim champ spun on her heel and headed straight for Jonah, Lance's cousin.

"Ah," Cassie cried in her best David Attenborough voice. "Finally, the female encounters a suitable mate."

Tara pulled the same move as she had with Tad, leaning in and placing a hand on Jonah's chest. Parting his dyed black hair with her fingertips, she whispered something in his ear. Delighted, Jonah looked her up and down and slipped a tattooed arm around her waist, chewing his lip ring as she murmured against his neck, letting her lips brush his skin.

Moments later, he grabbed her hand and led her from the room, disappearing in the direction of Lance's bedroom.

Cassie wrinkled her nose in distaste. "Eww."

"I'm guessing he didn't talk about sewage," Martin observed, swallowing the last of his beer and setting down the bottle. "I'd better make a move. I'll see you tomorrow."

Cassie squinted at her best friend, already feeling the effects of the drinks she'd had. The night was only just getting started. "Depends how dead I am."

"Don't drink too much," Martin called over his shoulder as he left.

She wandered over to the boys. "Hey, Tad! I see your game hasn't improved any."

He held up his hands in defence. "She asked me what I did! What am I gonna do; lie?"

"You could skirt the truth," Kyle suggested, with a sympathetic grin.

"But then what's the point?"

Lance shook his head. "The point is you get laid."

"If she's not interested in me then I'm not interested in that," Tad mumbled.

"What a waste." Cassie looked her friend up and down and threw an arm across her brow in mock-horror. "The best-looking guy in England and all he wants to do is talk about shit."

Lance laughed. "It's fine. Gives the rest of us half a chance."

"Pete seems to be doing okay," Kyle pointed out, gesturing to the couch where he and Gaia were kissing.

"Women love a shy guy."

Cassie snorted. "Tell that to Jonah!"

"Where is Jonah?"

"I'd change your bedsheets tonight is all I'll say about that one," Cassie advised.

"Oh, for fuck's sake...*Jonah*!" Lance set down his drink and strode from the room, heading down the hall to chase his cousin out of his bedroom.

"Any hotties in Peru, Kyle?"

"Plenty. Selestino's son was pretty cute.".

"But the trip was strictly business," Tad winked.

"*I went all the way to Peru and all I got was this lousy bracelet,*" Cassie said, grabbing his arm, and inspecting the beads. "Strange choice, Birbeck."

Kyle shrugged. "A village wise man gave it to me. It's special."

"Fair enough." Cassie turned as the door was kicked open and Jonah burst in with a face like thunder, one hand shamelessly buttoning his long black cargo shorts. Tara scurried into the drawing room behind him, her cheeks beetroot red. She grabbed her purse and scuttled past Lance, darting for the front door. The other girls from the swim team followed quickly behind.

Cassie opened her mouth to call after them, to ask them to stay a while, then closed it again. She'd tried. If they didn't want to stick around, there was nothing she could do.

"He's such an unbearable asshole!" Lance spat through gritted teeth, retrieving his drink and taking a long slug.

"What did you call me?" Jonah called, squaring his shoulders and lifting his chin.

"He called you an asshole," Kyle told him, helpfully.

"Shut up, *Wankman,*" Jonah sniggered to himself, still

pleased at how his Halloween Ghostbusters prank had played out.

The housemates smirked at each other. Typical cousins, Lance and Jonah bickered like brothers, but their spats never lasted long. Jonah was a handful, but for every drama he brought to the table, he matched it with an easy-going magnetism they couldn't help but love.

"Forget about it, lads. It's beer pong time," Cassie announced, lurching to the table. She shook paper cups from their packaging and started to lay them out in a pool rack formation, with one triangle of ten cups on each end of the table.

"What's in the fuck cups tonight?" Kyle asked, heading for the liquor.

"Tequila!" Cassie trilled.

"Oh, shit," Kyle mumbled, but he reached for the bottle and cracked off the sombrero lid, pouring a good measure into the two centre cups.

Cassie splashed beer into the surrounding containers, emptying six cans with her measures. "Right guys, who's teams? Come on, Gaia! Get up here on my team."

Gaia pushed herself away from Pete and strode over to the table. "Okay, but if I get the tequila, you're drinking it for me."

"Lame," Cassie muttered, raising her eyebrows and drinking straight from the open tequila bottle. After three long gulps she slammed the sombrero back onto the neck and spun it shut.

"Someone's going to have a sore head tomorrow," Kyle grimaced at Tad.

"Ah, leave her to it. She's happy you're home." Tad

smiled at Cassie grimacing as she lapped salt from her hand. "It's been rough for her."

Cassie moved closer to Kyle, heavy footed. She wrapped her arm through Kyle's and squeezed. She was often affectionate when she was drunk. *Never* when she was sober. "Missed you, Birbeck. But you're going down!"

"I'm going to kick your ass," Kyle challenged.

"Not a chance."

They crowded around opposing ends of the table and began to shoot the ping pong ball at their rival team's cups. Cassie was the first to strike, keeping true to her word and forcing Kyle to swallow down the first glug of beer. After a few missed shots back and forth, Gaia scored, sinking her ball into the centre cup for Kyle to drink the tequila. He peered down at the contents of the cup miserably, the slightly dirty ball floating in a sea of fumes.

He groaned. "Why did we go with tequila again?"

"It was you who wanted centre forfeit!" Cassie reminded him with a wink. "Get it down your neck."

The group cheered when Kyle fished out the ball and swallowed the spirit with a shudder. "Your turn to drink the fuck cup!" Kyle pointed at Cassie and sized up the table, taking aim. He made it look as though he was targeting the tequila, but she was pretty sure he was veering wide on purpose. Kyle could be irritatingly protective of them all. He probably knew that downing a triple shot of tequila wasn't in her best interest at that moment. He frowned as though he was in deep concentration and let fly with the ball.

The ball struck the oak with an audible thunk, then spun off to the side.

"I'll find it!" Cassie volunteered, throwing herself down

onto her hands and knees. She crawled around on the carpet for so long the others all began to join her search. "It's not here."

"It has to be here," Kyle told her. "I literally threw it over there."

"Well, do you see it?"

Visibly puzzled, Kyle scoured the carpet, scrutinising any potential hiding place the small white ball may have rolled behind. It was nowhere to be found.

"Damn it!"

"Do you have another ball?" Gaia asked, although she was looking slightly relieved at the prospect of skipping a few beers. She and Pete rarely drank too much, preferring an early night and a clear head in the mornings. They liked to hike at sunup, and a hike and a hangover didn't really mix.

Tad shook his head. "I don't think so. That one was left over from last Christmas."

"Which explains the glitter," Kyle mumbled, holding out his finger to show the piece of red shimmer he'd plucked from his tongue.

"Well, that's that, then." Cassie threw her hands up and moved over to the stereo, deciding that if they couldn't play the game, it was surely time to dance.

KYLE JUMPED on the opportunity to find out more about what had been happening while he was away. When Cassie was fully distracted, dancing with Jonah, Gaia, and a less-than-enthusiastic Pete, he inclined his head to Tad and gestured out toward the kitchen. Tad caught Lance's eye.

The three of them slipped from the room when Bloc Party began to blast out of the speakers.

Kyle scraped one of the large wooden stools from the table in the middle of the kitchen and sat down. "Tell me what's been happening," he prompted, looking at Lance as he pulled up a stool next to him.

Tad moved around the table and went to sit opposite, but he froze, doing a double take when he passed the sink. He looked into the basin, his tawny skin visibly paling.

"What?" Lance asked, craning to see what he was looking at.

Cautiously, Tad reached into the washing up bowl and lifted something out of the water. He turned and held it out between his thumb and forefinger. The ping pong ball.

"So? Someone's fucking with us," Lance said.

"Nobody left the room," Tad told him.

"They must have. What, did you do a head count or something?"

"No, but I was standing nearest the door. We're the only ones who left the room after the ball went missing."

"Maybe there was a second one in the pack after all?" Kyle suggested, although he wasn't at all convinced.

"You think we should tell Cassie we found it?" Lance asked.

Tad tore off two pieces of kitchen paper and wrapped the ball tightly. He strode over to the trash bin and forced it deep inside. "I think we don't say a word about it," he told them, his voice solemn.

CHAPTER 5
HANGOVERS

Pete woke with a start and sat up in bed, the sheet tumbling down his naked torso and lying heavily against his middle. His mouth felt dry, his teeth fuzzy when he ran his tongue over them. He knew he hadn't drunk enough to be hungover, not like the others, but it seemed as though his body had other ideas. A pulsing shock of pain drilled itself into his temple and he grabbed the side of his head. Dizziness washed over him. His mouth soured and saliva gathered at the back of his throat.

"Shit," he said.

Gaia rolled over when he darted for the door. "You okay?"

"Uh-uh."

He stumbled out onto the hallway, flexing the muscles in his throat to keep from throwing up. He fell against the bathroom door, relieved to find the room unoccupied, and knelt in front of the toilet, the tiles cold and hard under his knees. He braced himself against the seat and stared into the still water beneath him, waiting for the jet of vomit to come.

Nothing happened.

He breathed heavily, disturbing the surface of the water, and sending shimmies across the shadowy surface that distorted his reflection. He spat and watched the white curl of bubbles float to the side and cling to the porcelain. What the hell was wrong with him at the moment? He hadn't drunk enough to get even remotely sick. And the bouts of dizziness had been coming more frequently, a disorientating lurch inside him that sent his vision skewed and his stomach leaping up into his throat. Perhaps it was an ear infection, he pondered, peering down at his reflection and trying to work out if he'd had any ear pain lately.

Behind the shadowed image of his face in the water, something large and black dropped down next to his shoulder.

Pete spun to the side, his hand slipping from the seat and sending him sliding down between the wall and the toilet bowl. He landed twisted, his neck turned from trying to see what had fallen behind him, and his cheek crashed against the lumpy old grout.

Gaia dashed into the bathroom. She was wearing Pete's T-shirt from the night before, her hair mussed, her face angered with concern. "What the hell?"

Panting, Pete extracted himself from the space beside the toilet and leaned back against the wall. He watched his girlfriend rush to the sink and soak a washcloth. She knelt beside him and twisted the rag around her fingers, touching the moist material against his cheek.

"Did you pass out?" she asked, staring into his eyes.

"I don't think so." He winced and checked his elbow, aware of a throbbing bruise blooming under the skin. His cheek felt raw and thick and, when Gaia lifted the cloth, he could see his own skin plumping under his eye.

"Then what happened?"

"I slipped. I think I'm hungover."

"From three beers?"

He sighed. "An ear infection, maybe?"

"Did you throw up?"

"Nearly. It's passed now."

Gaia frowned, her concern sharpening her usually soft features. "That's the third time this month."

"Like I say, I think it's an ear infection." He gestured for her to back up and clambered to his feet, freezing for a moment to test his stability.

"Will you go to the doctors?"

"For an ear infection? I don't think they can do anything, can they?" He moved away from the wall, relieved to find that the dizziness had dissipated. He went to the sink and started to wash his hands.

The bathroom door swung open and Lance's cousin regarded them blearily, his dark hair on end and his face ashen. "Christ, I'm hungover," Jonah announced. "Are you two done in here? I am in desperate need of the three S's."

"The three S's?" Gaia asked, passing Pete a hand towel.

"Shit, shower, and shave," Pete explained, balling up the towel and throwing it at Jonah. "The ultimate hangover cure, according to this idiot."

"Although really I prefer shit, shower, and shots." Jonah grinned wickedly.

Gaia laughed and grabbed Pete's wrist, leading him from the room. "Back to bed for you, mister."

"Oh, aye, spare me the filthy details," Jonah called, already dropping his pants and sitting on the toilet.

"He's sick!" Gaia said.

"So am I! Shut the bloody door, will you?"

Gaia slammed the door with a giggle. She and Jonah got on like a house on fire. His brash, crude ways were a perfect complement to Gaia's gentle poise and innocent outlook. Pete was quiet by nature, and sometimes found himself fading from the conversation when his girlfriend and Jonah got chatting. He didn't mind listening rather than speaking —was never too comfortable being the centre of attention after all—but sometimes he wished he could make Gaia laugh the way Jonah could. She had a birthmark on her soft palette, a dark spatter shaped like a continent, and he usually only saw it when she was laughing at one of Jonah's jokes.

He let Gaia guide him to the bed, not usually keen on being fussed over. But the events of the morning had shaken him up a little. He guessed that the shadow falling behind him had been something to do with the dizziness; something ocular and harmless. If only it had been the first time he'd seen it.

Gaia tugged the blanket up to his chest and peered down at him. "Are you sure you're okay? I could ask my cousin..."

"No! For the last time. I'm fine." Pete couldn't think of anything worse than being paraded in front of Gaia's cousin. At just twenty-nine, Arshad was a renowned micro-surgeon. It was impossible not to feel somewhat inadequate in his presence. He really didn't revel in the idea of having the boy-wonder peer into his ears and have to describe for him how he fell down the side of the toilet.

"Okay. But if it happens again, you'll see a doctor?"

Pete rolled onto his side and closed his eyes. "I just need to sleep."

She bent over and kissed his cheek, a frustrated exhalation of breath tickling the throbbing graze. "All right. I'll leave you to it. I could do with getting some sleep in my own bed, anyway. You were lying on my hair again last night."

Pete listened to the sounds of her gathering her things. The sharp squeak of her zipping up her rucksack. He knew she was dressing in her own clothes and heard the soft puff of fabric when she tossed his T-shirt on the bed. He wondered if he should open his eyes and apologise for keeping her awake by laying on her hair again, preventing her from turning. It was a regular bugbear of hers that seemed to be growing in its frequency. Still, she refused to tie it back while she slept, which to him seemed like a simple solution.

He chose to keep his eyes closed and feign sleep. He was cranky and sick, and kind of sore about Jonah crashing into their morning. He knew that if he opened his mouth, he was bound to start something he didn't mean.

IN THE ROOM NEXT DOOR, Cassie listened to Gaia's light footsteps moving down the corridor and Pete's door clunking closed. She had woken with a start when Pete had fallen in the bathroom. She'd sat up in bed, her heart racing, and listened to Gaia dashing to the rescue. She had wondered whether she should get up and check everything was all right, but then Jonah's jovial voice came from the hall, and she figured it must have sounded worse than it was.

It was such a relief for Cassie to wake up in her own bed,

she didn't want to get out of it yet. She stretched out her legs and ignored the tequila headache that rumbled at the base of her skull. It was worth it, she reasoned. Especially if it had stopped her from sleepwalking.

She had no idea why she had begun to roam the house at night. It was Tad who usually found her, himself a light sleeper and general night-owl. She would come to, her eyes already open, as if someone had pulled up a curtain to reveal a new set on a theatre stage.

The rooms of her dreams were dark and confusing, usually involving water. That was no surprise since she spent most of her free time in the pool. She guessed her subconscious was nervous about her upcoming English Channel swim, her dreams full of moonlit seas with endless depths, and unseen creatures moving in the darkness below her legs.

Whenever she woke up, usually downstairs in a random room, Tad's face would drift into view. The first few times it happened his almond eyes had been soft with amusement. Lately, she saw concern etched into his features, and felt tension in the air around them. She had noticed he and Lance talking to Kyle at the party, no doubt filling him in on her exploits over the last couple of weeks. She cringed, embarrassed that her actions were so out-there that the boys had felt the need to bring it up. To *warn* Kyle about what he might expect from her now that he was back home. As the only female resident of the house, she sometimes felt pressure to give a good show of herself. The last few days, she had been failing miserably.

She saw her phone flash out of the corner of her eye and reached out, sliding it from the bedside table to the mattress beside her. She knew it would be Martin, even before she checked the text. *How's the head?* He had written, followed by the bandaged head emoji.

Cassie smiled and swiped the screen, ready to reply. Her fingertip slid along the surface, cutting through a track of condensation. "Damn it," she muttered, and wiped the phone against her pyjama top. She knew the house could be damp, its age leading to more than a few cracks in the foundations. When the cold weather set in it wasn't unusual for the bathroom mirror to steam up or the windowsills to become dappled with black mildew. But her iPhone had recently begun to follow suit, the screen sodden and foggy in the mornings. She had never seen anything like it.

The screen wiped clean, and she fired back a text to her best friend. *I'm okay. Need coffee tho.*

Less than three seconds later, his reply lit up the screen. *I'm on it.*

She didn't want to get up and dressed, but the thought of Martin showing up with a giant cup of hazelnut latte was too tempting to pass up. She glanced at the screen, noticing another drop of water, and clucked her tongue. Scrubbing her shirt over the mark, she peered down and saw the droplet was still on the glass. Frowning, she ran her finger over it. Lifting the phone to her face, she squinted at the small bubble of water.

It was situated on the inside of the screen. "What the hell?"

The thread of texts faded from view and Cassie was left staring at her dark reflection, the water droplet stark on her forehead, her brow furrowed in confusion.

She dressed in sweatpants and an oversized dance sweater, tugging the collar so that it gaped over her left shoulder. She tore a brush through her long brown hair and tied it up in a messy bun on top of her head. Squinting at herself in the mirror, she hissed at her bloodshot eyes and dry, puckered lips. Coffee would definitely help, she reasoned, tugging open her door.

Pete emerged from the room next to hers, his face tight and pensive. A graze puffed his cheek, the skin etched with small red dots.

"Ouch! Are you okay?"

"Fine," he mumbled, cautiously touching his right fingers to his opposite elbow. Cassie noticed a stark blue bruise blossoming on his arm.

"I heard you fall. Did you slip?"

"Something like that." Pete strode past her.

"Hey, have you been having problems with your phone? Like, water damage?"

Pete stopped and turned unsteadily, pressing his hand against the wall. He glared at her with bleary eyes. "What are you on about?"

"My phone...it keeps getting condensation on it. This morning there's a drop of water behind the screen."

"That's impossible."

"Well, it's true." Cassie stuck her hand in her pocket and pulled out the phone for him to see.

Pete shook his head and held up his free hand, dismissing her. He wheeled around and pushed open the bathroom door.

"You know, considering you're the only one of us without a hangover you could try being brighter in the mornings?" Cassie called after him.

He raised his middle finger and disappeared inside.

Cassie puffed air out through her cheeks and shook her head. She had never pegged Pete as the moody type, but in the last few days he'd been acting as though something was bothering him. That wasn't such a huge mystery, she knew. Something had been bothering them all.

She started down the stairs, hearing tap water splashing into the sink and a muffled retch and spit from behind the bathroom door.

Ten minutes later, the doorbell rang. She opened the door to find Martin holding up two huge takeaway coffee cups. His cheeks were pink from the morning cold, and he looked younger than ever in a teal bobble hat and scarf combo, his sheepskin coat just missing a pair of dangling mittens to complete the childlike look. Cassie told him as much, taking her latte and leading him into the kitchen.

"You think I look like a toddler?" he protested, snatching the hat off his head and looking mortified. He tossed it onto the table, his short blond hair sitting askew.

"It's cute! It's a cute look."

"I don't want to look cute," he protested. "I'm twenty-two years old."

"Well, no one would ever know." Cassie teased, sipping at her drink. It was sharp and slightly too hot, but she took three big slugs anyway, ignoring the burning sensation on her tongue.

"Maybe I'll just have to keep your breakfast, then." Martin fake-sulked, holding up his rucksack with a tantalising shake that cast the scent of baked bread into the room.

Cassie rushed for the bag and started wrestling him for it, her headache all but forgotten as she yanked it from side to side, the straps flailing and whipping her arms. "Gimme!" she

yelled, dissolving into laughter as the pair ended up on the
floor, the bag wedged between them, their tug of war
descending into a stalemate.

"All right!" Martin let go and allowed her to reach inside
the zipper of his bag.

"Yes!" She extracted a breakfast muffin wrapped in wax
paper. "You are my hero!"

Martin beamed when she leaned over and planted a kiss
on his cheek, then she jumped to her feet and unwrapped it
with feverish relish. She sat at the table and bit into the flour-
dusted roll, tearing through sausage patty and egg. Her eyes
rolled up to the ceiling as she chewed, and she made happy
little grunting noises when she swallowed.

"I know how to treat my woman." Martin grinned, then
ducked as the rolled-up ball of wax paper hurtled towards his
face.

"Your woman? Get a grip!" Cassie tore off another bite,
ignoring her friend's comment.

The pair had been close for years and had shared
moments where they had almost kissed. Had almost tumbled
into an intimacy that seemed inevitable to those watching on
the outside. But Cassie didn't think of Martin in that way.
He was her best friend. Someone who saw her flaws and
accepted them because there was no come back. She was
frightened that if they took that step in their relationship,
everything would come crashing down. She would never
want to hurt him, and the probability of that happening
seemed tenfold whenever she imagined them as a couple.
Plus, she didn't fancy him. Sometimes, and she wished other
people could see, it was that simple.

He slid onto the tall stool beside her and started on his

own sandwich, smiling to himself, still a little flushed from the play fight.

Tad came into the kitchen and glowered at the thrown paper. He reached down and picked it up, then tossed it at Cassie. It landed on the table in front of her. "You shouldn't get those cups, you know."

"Huh?" Cassie swallowed the last bite and dusted off her hands.

"The takeaway coffee. You should take reusable mugs."

"Oh, uh—that's my fault. It was a spur of the moment thing. I didn't think to bring any with me," Martin explained, withering under Tad's flint-like stare.

Tad went to the fridge, pulling out a jug of orange juice and filling a glass.

Cassie cleared her throat, keen to move on from the subject of the environment on a hangover. "Hey, Tad. I didn't sleepwalk!"

Placing the juice back in the door cubby, Tad's shoulders squared, and he took a moment to answer. He shut the fridge door and turned slowly, his expression one of puzzlement. "Yes, you did."

"No, I didn't. I slept right through. I woke up in my bed."

"Cass, I saw you. You were standing outside Pete's room with your hands on his door."

Cassie laughed incredulously, but doubt flashed through her mind. She vaguely recalled a hazy dream about going to Pete, but she couldn't be sure. "Maybe you dreamed you saw me?"

Tad shook his head. "I was awake. I needed water. I

steered you back to bed. I didn't think you'd woken up, even though you spoke."

A cold knot tightened at the back of Cassie's neck. "What did I say?"

Tad's eyes narrowed, his hair tumbling over his eyes as he glanced down at his feet. After a moment, he looked up and spoke in that gruff, guttural way of his. "I couldn't tell. It was nonsense, I think."

"Okay. Good." She rubbed her flour speckled hands on her pants and scooted out from the stool, not wanting to sit still any longer. She didn't believe Tad when he said her words were nonsense, but she didn't want to hang around to contemplate what they might have been. She recalled a whisper from her own dream—something she felt she desperately needed to relay to one of the housemates. But then, it was gone. "Come on, Marty. Let's go to the park."

Martin jumped down obediently, hurrying to finish his sandwich, and snatched his hat from the table. Under the cool gaze of Tad, he lifted his large coffee cup and held it close to his chest, as though proximity would somehow disguise it. Tad intimidated Marty, which usually entertained Cassie no end. Tad may be beautiful, but he was just a guy to her. A dumb friend with whom she had done crazy dumb shit with. She didn't even notice his looks anymore. In fact, they were usually a source of great amusement to her.

"See you later, Ugly," she called to him, grabbing her own coffee, and raising it in a toast.

Tad drained his juice, watching them leave, trying to ignore the fading waft of sea water, not coffee, that lingered in their wake.

CHAPTER 6
HOUSE MEETING

Kyle wandered into the kitchen, yawning loudly, and headed straight for the coffee maker. "That was some welcome home," he grimaced, opening the bag of grounds. He poured a hefty helping into the filter.

"I think everyone's pretty rough this morning." Tad was rinsing a glass at the sink. He set it on the draining board. "I'll clean up the dining room in a minute."

"I'll help."

"Nah. It was your party."

"Doesn't mean I can't throw away some beer bottles," Kyle offered, following his friend to the room next door. His face fell when Tad pushed the door open and he was confronted with a wall of empty bottles and crushed cans glinting in the morning sunlight. The beer pong cups were strewn everywhere, sticky puddles of spilt beer spread out like a shiny map on the ancient floorboards. "Ah, shit."

"I told you." Tad laughed, then headed for the front door. He appeared a moment later with two recycling boxes and set about filling them.

Kyle moved to the table and started gathering the paper cups. He stacked the empties in an ever-growing tube, leaving the cups that still had beer inside them. He groaned at the stink of the stale alcohol. The taste of it lingered in his mouth, even after three rounds of toothbrushing.

"That game was not worth the clean up since we only got about three shots in," he said, pushing some discarded bottles to the edge of the table for Tad to collect.

"You always were bad at beer pong."

Kyle laughed. "It was a good night, though. I think we needed it."

"Yeah."

"I was thinking about what happened with the ball."

Tad heaved a sigh, lifting the full box of glass. "I'm gonna take this out."

"Wait, man. I really need to talk to you about something."

"I'm just gonna take this out," Tad repeated, his voice soft but laced with warning.

Kyle had never heard Tad shout before. He didn't need to. His steady, calm voice held an edge when he wasn't in the mood to talk that Kyle had never dared push before. But this was different. He followed him out into the hallway, stepping over the drops of beer that tumbled from the box and speckled the floor. He watched Tad place the recycling out by the front steps and come back inside, his mouth a grim line.

Tad froze at the door, looking exasperated, and held his hands out by his sides. "Do I have a choice?"

"I really think we should talk about this."

"Get the mop," Tad ordered, casting his eyes over the droplets on the floor.

"*You* get the damn mop." Kyle countered, folding his arms.

Tad strode past him into the kitchen, letting out a hiss and a Japanese swear word that Kyle didn't recognise. He tugged out the mop bucket and began to fill it at the sink, hunting in the low cupboard for cleaning fluid.

"You're right about them latching on. I feel it, too. I don't know who everyone has, yet, but you're right about Jarvis being with you. And...I think Lisa is with Cassie."

Tad shut off the tap and braced himself against the sink, his shoulders squared with tension. "What makes you say that?"

"Last night. I just felt it. I... It sounds nuts but they all kind of have their own smell, I think. And with Cassie, it's —"

"The sea." Tad turned around and fixed Kyle with an intense stare.

"Right."

"Are we in danger?"

"Yes."

Tad lifted the bucket from the sink and grabbed the mop. He shoved past Kyle and moved into the dining room, scrubbing at the slopped beer on the floorboards.

Kyle stood and watched the steaming water sweep away the sticky puddles. "I mean, I think we are. That's why I went to Peru."

"You went to Peru for uni," Tad corrected.

"No. I went because of the cellar."

Tad froze, the mop handle slipping from his fingers. He grabbed for it, then changed his mind and watched it fall. He looked dazed, the characteristic sharpness gone from his eyes. "We said we wouldn't talk about that again."

"You two got off with each other in the cellar?" A voice sounded behind them.

Kyle whipped round to find Jonah smirking at them from the doorway.

"What happens in the cellar stays in the cellar, am I right?"

"Don't be ridiculous, Jonah," Tad snapped, bending down and snatching up the mop.

Kyle could tell that despite his irritation at Jonah's jokes, Tad was thrilled their chat had been interrupted.

Jonah peered around the room. "Hey, thanks for cleaning up. I was dreading Lance making me stick around to help. I'm hanging as fuck. I've already done three shits this morning."

"Thanks for the update," Tad muttered through gritted teeth.

"I'm still not as bad a Pete, though, poor fucker."

"Pete didn't drink," Kyle corrected.

"Why's he upstairs puking his guts up then?" Jonah folded his arms and slumped against the doorframe. "Says he's got an ear infection, but I call bullshit."

Kyle glanced at Tad whose dazed stare was snatched away by a look of sudden understanding. *Rourke?* Tad mouthed, frowning.

Upstairs, a sudden flurry of footsteps raced along the landing. They weren't heavy enough to be an adult, were too long in stride to be made by a child, too human-like to be a dog or another animal. Kyle's eyes darted towards the ceiling to follow the sound, a pointless, instinctive move.

The three listened for a moment longer, but the house had fallen silent.

"Fucking pigeons," Jonah quipped, but his smirk had slipped. He grabbed the doorframe and swung himself out into the hallway in the direction of the kitchen. "Where's the coffee?"

"You, me, and Lance need a serious chat," Kyle hissed at Tad.

"I think you're right."

Kyle hurried to his bedroom and moved to the mattress, slipping his hands under the heavy weight and tugging out the notebook. He hadn't yet unpacked, but on the plane back home he had painstakingly added the new information he had discovered in Peru. All but the scrap of parchment that he had rolled inside a T-shirt in his rucksack. He considered unwrapping it and taking it down with the notebook, but then changed his mind. The lads might not be ready for the full truth about Po just yet.

He fingered the beads on his wrist, feeling an irrational sensation of calm overtake him. He knew the effect was mostly placebo. He didn't really believe he was immune from harm because he had a few jasper stones strapped to his wrist. But it was something. And right at that moment, it was all he had.

Kyle carried the bulging notebook braced across his chest, both arms wrapped across it like a shield. Stepping back onto the landing, he checked to the right and noticed Pete's door was open. Muffled male voices came from the room. He stepped up to Pete's bedroom, chilled at the thought of the footsteps that had rushed over the landing not ten minutes before and poked his head around the door.

Lance sat swinging in Pete's desk chair, reading aloud from his laptop screen. "...preceded by feelings of vertigo and nausea. Could be that?"

"Labyrinth?" Pete asked, from where he lay prone against his pillows with his arm slung over his eyes. A dark blue bruise crept around the skin under his elbow.

"Labyrinthitis. An inflammation of the inner ear. Could be it, you know." Lance turned and noticed Kyle at the door and gave him a wink. "Of course, if you have it, you have to wear a codpiece and start singing like David Bowie."

"Piss off," Pete mumbled from under his forearm, but his face lifted in a semi-concealed grin.

Lance closed the laptop and turned to Kyle. "Hey, man. What's up?"

"Can we have a word?"

"We?"

"Me and Tad."

Pete groaned. "I'm not up to a house meeting right now, dude. If it's about cleaning up —"

"No, we've done the cleaning. I just need Lance, actually."

"Thank Christ." Pete rolled onto his side and tugged the cover over his head.

Lance left the chair swinging and closed Pete's door gently behind them.

"He okay?" Kyle asked, nodding to the closed door.

"I dunno. I think he's right that it's an ear thing. He fell over a couple of times and had a bit of vertigo while you were away."

"Vertigo?"

"Yeah. It's crazy. We were on the stairs the other day and

I thought he was going to throw himself over the banister."
Lance shrugged. "He said he felt like he was being pulled
over the edge. We cancelled the hike up Helvellyn that
weekend."

Kyle tried to smile, but a cold surge of dread had rushed
down his spine.

"It's not serious, you know. You don't need to look so
worried. What's the book?" Lance asked, glancing back at the
notebook as he starting to trot down the stairs.

"That's what I need to talk to you and Tad about."

"Just us?"

Kyle looked over the handrail and watched Jonah bustle
through the hallway beneath them, a plate full of sandwiches
in one hand, a huge bag of crisps tucked under one arm, and
a family bottle of coke under the other.

"I'm going to watch TV!" Jonah called to nobody in
particular, then disappeared into the living room at the front
of the house.

"Don't you have your own home to go to?" Lance yelled
after his cousin, but the door slammed in response.

"We'll go in the dining room," Kyle said softly, hopping
down the last of the steps and beckoning to Tad who was
watching from the open kitchen door.

Kyle was grateful the old town house had multiple rooms
as he placed the notebook on the newly cleaned but slightly
damp table and sat down at the head. The others slipped into
chairs on either side of him. He knew they wouldn't be
disturbed any time soon. Jonah would be sitting in front of
the TV until he decided he was recovered enough to head
home, and Cassie was out. From the looks of it, Pete
wouldn't feel up to coming downstairs within the next hour

or two, and if he did, he would no doubt head straight for the couch with Jonah.

Kyle opened the book to a random page. Some of the loose papers slipped from their moorings and Lance picked one up, scrutinising the small print.

"Is this from a newspaper?"

Kyle nodded. "I've been doing some research."

"But you've been away," Lance said.

"I've been looking into this for the last two years, guys," Kyle admitted. "You know I've been learning about the history of the house."

"But not to this extent." Tad reached over and grabbed the notebook, leafing through the pages. He pulled out sheaves of highlighted papers with scribbled notes. He dropped the pages and stared at Kyle. "You said you went to Peru because of this. What did you mean?"

"You all know about Professor Grant's séance and the ghosts my great-uncle, Lucius, released."

"Yeah, man. We get it. It's a freaky haunted house." Lance sighed, squeezing his hands between his thighs.

"You said to me yourself that things had been getting worse ever since Halloween. I already knew that. I had to look for the missing piece of the puzzle, and I think I might have found something. Tad helped me to fill in the other gap."

"I did?"

"You spotted that the ghosts are linking to each of us. And that's huge."

"Wait." Lance raked his hand through his blond curls then slapped his palm on the table. "You noticed what?"

Tad folded his fingers and popped his knuckles. "It was

only a hunch before Kyle got home. I kind of had a feeling that Jarvis had been hanging around. I wondered if he'd been coming out for everyone, but then I kind of got the impression it was just me."

"Jarvis?"

"Jarvis Rice," Kyle pressed. "Remember? The over-enthusiastic executioner."

Lance watched Kyle lean over and shuffle through some of the pages, then pass him a handwritten sheet full of bullet points. The executioner's name was written across the top in Kyle's bold capital print. Lance read the first few points, then lowered the page, his expression one of disgust. "This is worse than what they put in the guidebook."

"I know. They were *all* worse than what was printed in the guidebooks. The real truth was pretty much erased. But I've found some answers. I'm learning more about them all the time."

Tad turned the page towards himself and skim-read, his buff complexion paling. "Rice wasn't happy only performing executions when the courts needed him to. He murdered strangers then framed other people just so he could put the axe to them when they were convicted. Well, we knew that..." He read on, learning about how Rice would stalk the nicest, most loving families he could find, until one day he would break into the house and torture and kill the wife and children, making sure to frame the husband for the crime. The devastated men were sent to be executed by the real murderer. Moments before he swung the axe, he would whisper the truth in the husbands' ear. "That's..."

"Genius?" Lance offered with a simper.

"Sick."

"But what do you mean he's latched on to Tad?" Lance turned to Kyle.

"I'm not totally sure. It's just a feeling, really. The same way I think Lisa Vaughan has linked to Cassie somehow."

"Christ, don't let Cassie hear you say that. She'll have a fit."

"It's not just him," Tad spoke up. "I noticed it, too."

"You noticed a ghost hanging around Cass?"

"It's not like that. It's...a feeling. A *smell*." Kyle told him. "Haven't you been smelling the seaside when you're around Cassie?"

"She's training to swim the Channel." Lance sniffed.

"She's still working in the pool, though. It's not chlorine we're smelling. It's salt water. It's stagnant seaweed, for fuck's sake."

Lance sat back. "Are you sure she's not started sea swims yet?"

"Even if she had, she showers! She's not going to stink of the seaside for days after an hour at the beach, is she?"

"It's not only that," Tad interjected. "You know how I mentioned she's been sleepwalking?"

Kyle waited, aware of the tension in the room building.

"Well, she's been saying stuff to me. But it's not her voice. It's just not...Cassie. It's not her at all. It's terrifying."

"Like what?"

"Well, last night I found her outside Pete's door. She was standing there with her hands on the panels. You know how Gaia was in there? When I went over, Cassie said in that creepy sleep voice that Gaia was a useless whore, and that Pete needed a real woman before..."

"Before?"

"She said, *before he's done with him*. She doesn't even remember sleepwalking last night. But her eyes were open, and she was staring right at me."

"That's creepy as fuck." Lance grimaced.

"It's a warning, that's what it is." Kyle looked down at the notebook.

"You think Pete's in trouble?"

"I think we all are."

CHAPTER 7
HELLFIRE AND BRIMSTONE

Jonah finally decided to leave for his own student digs at around dinnertime, much to Lance's relief. Of course, Lance loved his cousin. They were the same age and had grown up like brothers. But he could be a complete pain in the arse.

That evening Kyle and Tad had decided to head to the local pub to watch Jonah's rock band play. Surprising everyone, Pete had chosen to go with them. He'd risen at around four o'clock, still looking a little worse for wear but no longer dizzy, and he'd jumped at the chance to get some fresh air and a change of scenery.

Cassie opted to skip the pub, knowing her willpower would not be strong enough to avoid drinking again for a second night in a row. She was training for the Channel swim, after all, and her liver could certainly do with a breather after the vast amounts of tequila she'd consumed the night before. She had even powered through her hangover and spent the latter part of the afternoon at the university gym, swimming laps.

Making the most of the tranquillity of the rarely quiet house, Lance selected some Kishi Bashi on his phone and laid out the ingredients for a chicken curry. He arranged them on the counter and stepped back to take a few photos from different angles. His cooking shots were always popular, and he sometimes daydreamed about starting up his own YouTube channel to boost his following. He needed to come up with a game plan, he knew, but that was part of the problem.

One of the reasons he wanted to make money online was because he had crippling social anxiety, which made him utterly incompetent when it came to working in an office. He dreamed of finding a business where he could go solo, and the internet might just give him that opportunity. He was looking forward to New Year's Day, when he planned to take advantage of a fresh start and finally get his butt in gear and make a real attempt at setting up a channel.

He shook spatters of turmeric, cumin, and ground coriander onto a wooden chopping board and snapped another pic. "Nice," he whispered, enhancing the colours so the bright orange of the turmeric popped from the picture. He added it to his story with the caption, #feelingspicy, #currynight, and smiled at the screen, pleased with how it came out.

Cooking truly relaxed him. As the orchestra strings played through the speaker and the sauce began to bubble, he leaned back against the counter and closed his eyes a moment, enjoying the peace. In the silence between songs, the pattering sound of dashing footsteps jolted him upright, his eyes snapping open. There was nobody in the kitchen, although he could have sworn someone had just run up to him.

He switched the burner off and cut the music on his phone.

Lance stepped out onto the hallway corridor, listening intently. He could hear faint music coming from one of the rooms upstairs. The driving bass and grunge guitars confirmed that it was Cassie. He imagined her painting her nails on her bed, Alkaline Trio playing through her water-damaged phone. He was happy she was back safe after her swim, and suddenly wished the others were home, too.

He felt an urgent need to keep tabs on everybody. Safety in numbers had never seemed so prevalent.

He froze as the rumble of dashing footsteps tore across the landing above him. The footsteps were hurried, soft and fluttering like a bird's heartbeat. There were never any creaks when the dashing ghostly feet crossed from one side to the other and vanished. Never any suggestion that whatever caused the noise placed any weight on the ground at all. Lance listened as they crossed from the far right-hand side of the landing, from the direction of Tad's room, all the way over to Pete's. Usually, they vanished there.

They pattered back towards him.

Still above him on the landing, the footsteps dashed away from Pete's door and stopped halfway across, at what would be the entrance to Lance's room. Lance stepped forward and peered up at the banister.

The stairwell was silent, the shadows behind the wooden ballasts still.

He held his breath, his heart thumping in his ears. He

stared up at the spot where the footsteps had halted. There was no sound.

The hair on the back of his neck stood at attention and a creeping chill like a whispered breath lapped at his bare skin. He cringed and whipped round, expecting to see someone standing behind him.

As he turned, a shape dropped from the middle of the balcony. It plummeted straight down as though a heavy sack had been thrown over the banister. Lance cried out and staggered to the side, falling into the wall between the living room and dining room doors. His eyes whipped across the terrain of the stairs, darting from side to side.

Nothing.

He could have sworn something had fallen from the landing.

Then again, he could have sworn someone had been standing right behind him. But there was nobody there.

He looked back in the direction of the frozen breeze and felt his cheeks tingle with sudden fear.

To his right, the cellar door was open.

It was just a crack, the black line of the interior showing a centimetre against the stark white gloss of the doorframe. But it had been shut when he walked by to check the landing. He was certain of it.

Standing straight, his back flat against the wall, Lance sidestepped to the cellar. His senses were on fire, his nervous system urging him to head straight to the front of the house, into the living room and turn up the TV. To hide under the blanket and wait for the others to return home. Or, better yet, dash outside and keep running to the pub.

He stepped forward and reached out his hand.

He was just about to touch the handle when a shape caught his attention out of the corner of his eye. Lance glanced up at the entrance to the house. The old wooden door was large, wider than average by modern standards. Tall and slender windows stood on either side of the oak, designed to flood the large hallway with natural light. The panes were swathed in gauzy white drapes to prevent prying eyes. To the right of the door, back-lit by the streetlights, a human-like shadow stood on the porch beyond the glass.

Lance held his breath, his fear of the open cellar door directly beside him overridden by the shadow up ahead. It looked as though someone was standing staring through the translucent curtain, a hood pulled up over their head.

Wait a minute, Lance reasoned. Had Cassie ordered take-out? Had he mistaken an innocent knock at the door for the rumbling footsteps coming from the landing? He pictured the delivery boy standing out in the cold, his hood yanked up against the wind, peering in and wondering why nobody was answering the door.

He let out a shuddered breath, embarrassed at himself, and took a step.

The shadow turned. Slowly pivoting, almost gliding.

Lance watched, trying to fight the irrational sensation that something wasn't right. The point of the shadow's hood moved to the side, hanging down over the nose and framing a strong chin tucked down above a barrel chest swathed in robes. The shadow moved forward, and a small glowing light bloomed at chest-height behind the gauze of the draping curtain. It passed behind the solid space of the door, the shadow disappearing. Lance waited for the odd delivery man —if that's what he was—to knock again.

Instead, moments passed with no sound.

He was about to move to the entrance, or to shout to Cassie and discover whether he had just screwed up her dinner, when the small yellow glow appeared on the left-hand side of the door, closely followed by the human shadow that hovered into view in the other window. The person stepped to the centre of the pane and gradually turned again, staring straight forward. He *was* wearing a hood, but it stuck out on either side of his temple in two triangles, as if the figure was wearing horns underneath it. The light glowed at the centre of his chest and Lance realised he was carrying a candle. The hefty jumper, or robes, as they appeared to Lance through the gauzy fabric of the curtain, draped down on either side of the man's bulky frame, leaving only an inch of streetlight visible beside each of his arms.

A heavy knock thundered against the front door.

Lance gasped and staggered backwards, the breath knocked from his lungs. It didn't sound like the knocking was actually coming from the door in front of him. The hammering shook the house, like someone were throwing their full weight against the very timbers of the framework. But the door didn't move against its hinges, not even a fragment. And neither did the figure. His arms hadn't budged from their place at his chest, holding the candle. The sliver of streetlight at either side of his bulk proved it.

The knocking sound came again. It was like premium fireworks being set off in the next garden. Like a heavy-goods vehicle shuddering over a pothole in the road. But it pelted through the hallway, icing Lance's blood. The sound reverberated within his core.

Outside, cats began to yowl, overlapping screams from two of the neighbourhood toms that sounded otherworldly.

He stared at the shape in the porchway, feeling his knees trembling. He couldn't move, even if he'd wanted to. His legs were rooted to the spot. The shadow remained staring straight down, but the candle's glow began to rise. It was gradually brought to the point where the man's mouth would be. With a violent gust of air that Lance swore he could hear, the candle went out.

And so did all the lights in the house.

Dull terror quickly escalated to utter panic. The room plunging into pitch black had come as such a shock that his brain was momentarily a step behind his body's fear reaction. Then he felt the cold breeze coming from the open cellar door beside his right arm, and a flurry of disembodied ghostly footsteps above reminded him that he was certainly not alone in the darkness.

He pressed his palms back against the wall, as if the solid stability of it could somehow make him less exposed. Less vulnerable. He thought he'd blinked when it first went dark, but now he stood with his eyes wide open, willing them to see. They watered, and he wasn't sure if it was because of the need to blink or through sheer fear.

Above him, he heard someone walking—real, human footsteps. Cassie, heading for her bedroom door. It creaked open, and he heard her tentative, strained voice, her doorway closest to the top of the stairs. "Lads?"

He tried to answer her, but his throat was constricted. Still, having another human engage with him was enough to drag him from his terror-induced paralysis. He coughed sharply and tried again. "Cass— I'm here."

"Why have the lights gone out?"

Because of Anthony Pile, Lance heard himself think and the moment the name forced itself into his mind, the lights came back on. He looked back to the front porch, but the shadow had gone.

Cassie crept forward and leaned over the banister, peering down at him with her hair tumbling forward like arms reaching out to him. "Lance?"

He knew he looked like a coward, crouched with his body pressed against the wall, but the terror of the last few minutes had shaken him to his core. His limbs still trembled, and his joints ached with tension.

There was a sudden rattling at the front door, and he cried out and stumbled to the side, hitting the ground when it flew open.

Kyle led the housemates into the hall, their post-pub chatter falling to silence as they took in the sight of Lance sprawled at the end of the hallway and Cassie peering down uncertainly.

"What happened?" Kyle asked, his eyes instinctively scanning for signs of the ghosts.

"The lights went out," Cassie told him, heading down the stairs.

Tad moved past Kyle and held out a hand to Lance. Lance wrapped trembling fingers around his wrist and allowed him to haul him to his feet. "Was it the executioner?" Tad asked, skipping over his consonants. His accent was always stronger when he was stressed.

"No. I don't know. Rourke was running around like a madman." Lance said with a shudder.

"He's getting worse," Kyle pointed out.

Cassie shook her head. "I never hear him. I didn't notice anything until the lights went out."

Jonah had evidently tagged along with the group after performing with his band. He swaggered past the house-mates into the kitchen, shaking his head. "I love how you talk about them as though they're people. So, you had a power cut and there's some pigeons in the attic, and Lance had a hissy fit. I don't understand why you guys have to obsess over this ghost crap."

Lance turned on him, smacking a palm into the cellar door so that it closed on his way to the kitchen. "It isn't crap, Jonah! You're just lucky you don't live here, and you've never had them come at you. We all have, and it's no joke, let me tell you."

Jonah opened the fridge and took out a beer, twisting off the cap and chugging from the neck. He swallowed and burped. "Did you ever think that maybe I don't have any experiences because I keep a level head? When you guys first moved in here you thought it was bullshit, Lance. And so did you, Tad!"

"But now I've seen them. And one day, so will you." Tad's voice was an octave lower even than usual.

"Is that supposed to be some kind of threat?"

"No!" Tad threw up his hands in frustration. "How can I threaten you with ghosts? You're crazy."

"I'm crazy? I'm the only sane one here." He finished the beer and slammed it down on the side, voicing what the others were thinking. "And that's saying something! Anyway, thanks for coming to see the band tonight. I'm going to leave you to your paranoid ghoul talk. I'm going to watch TV."

"You know, you have your own home to go to!" Lance called after him, a common sentiment between the cousins.

Jonah pushed past the housemates and disappeared down the hall, slamming the living room door behind him. The group knew Jonah well enough to guess why he was choosing to stay. He was proving that there was nothing to be afraid of.

Kyle moved to the kettle and took it to the sink, filling it almost to the brim. "I think we could all use a tea or something."

They sat round the kitchen table and watched Kyle make the tea, each of them on edge with a million things to say. Instead, they remained silent until Kyle had presented them with their drinks.

He sat back against the counter and folded his arms. "So, you think it was Rourke who put out the lights? That's new."

Pete rubbed his upper arms. "I'm hearing Rourke all the time. He's a fucking pain in the ass."

"But he's gaining power if he's messing with the electrics. Footsteps is one thing. Power outages is something else entirely."

"It wasn't Rourke," Lance mumbled, miserably.

"You said Rourke was going crazy."

"He was. But it wasn't him. There were...a few, I think. I don't know. The cellar door opened."

Kyle fixed him with a sharp look, but Lance went on, knowing that if he didn't blurt it all out then he might be reluctant to say it later.

"And I went to see what it was. There was a cold breeze.

Then Rourke started running around. He didn't do his usual thing... He didn't stop at Pete's door."

Pete shuffled in his chair, looking uncomfortable, and grabbed for his mug.

"He ran the length of the hallway, but at Pete's door he stopped and came back halfway. It was like he was looking over the banister at me."

"Did you see him?" Kyle questioned.

"No, but I swear I could feel him looking down at me."

"Jesus," Cassie whispered. "With the cellar door open, too? Jesus."

"Then there was someone at the front door."

"Us? Is that when you freaked out?" Tad asked.

"No, I don't mean when you guys came home. It was before the lights went out. I thought maybe Cassie had ordered take-out or something. It was like someone was standing on the porch with a candle."

"Right, I usually order my food from Medieval Deliveries R Us," Cassie quipped.

Although he was still shaken, Lance huffed a laugh. "I know, it sounds crazy. The person passed by the other window. Then he lifted the candle and blew it out. That's when the lights went out."

Collectively, the group reacted with terror. Pete clutched the back of his neck and Tad visibly shivered. Cassie held up her arm, showing that the hairs were standing on end.

Kyle furrowed his brow. "Lance, who do you think it was?"

But Tad answered for him. "The Hellfire guy, of course."

"What do you mean, of course?" Pete looked perplexed. "I've never seen him before."

Tad sighed and looked at Kyle for guidance. Kyle jumped up to sit on the countertop next to Lance's discarded curry paraphernalia. He dusted spices from his hands. Tad raked his fingers through his hair, leaning back in his chair and frowning as though he was carefully considering how to put what he was going to say next into words.

"Guys, you're scaring me." Cassie wrapped her palms around her mug to warm her shaking hands. "What's going on?"

"I have a hunch." Tad said. "It's just a hunch. I don't want to scare any of you. When Kyle was away, I noticed something. Certain sounds and smells that we'd associated with the ghosts before. But following each of us."

"You think I smell?" Cassie laughed, using humour again to try and mask the panic growing in her eyes.

"Of seawater. Yes."

Pete turned sharply, recognition in his eyes. "Oh, my God. I've smelled that in your room. I thought it was something to do with your swimming gear. I didn't want to say anything."

She scowled. "Maybe it *is* to do with my swimming!"

"Have you swam in the sea yet?" Tad pressed.

"No...sea training starts in a week."

"Well, it certainly doesn't smell of chlorine." Tad looked to Pete, who nodded confirmation.

"It's Lisa Vaughan," Kyle said, gently.

Tad reached out and cupped Cassie's hand with his own. "With me, it's mould. I kept smelling it around myself whenever I felt someone was in the room with me. It's Jarvis Rice."

Cassie just stared blankly.

Lance raked his hands through his unruly curls and

clasped his fingers around the back of his neck. "I've been smelling smoke. I didn't even think of it until you just said that. And I hear cats screaming, as if they're fighting. But the Hellfire Club were known to sacrifice cats. I heard it tonight when Pile came to the door."

Kyle rested his elbows against his knees, hunching forwards. "We think one of the spirits is linking to each one of us in the house. Perhaps that's how they gain power. I don't know. It looks like Anthony Pile has taken a shine to Lance, no light pun intended."

Pete looked at Kyle. "So, who's latching on to me?"

"Isn't it obvious? You're getting vertigo all the time, feeling like you're falling. The footsteps run around then stop outside your room. It's Rourke, man. You're linked to Rourke."

Pete swayed on the stool, paling. He gripped the table and Lance reached out a hand to steady him in case he should fall. "But it's just an ear infection. That's all."

"Is it?"

Pete looked down at the table and shook his head.

Cassie peered curiously at Kyle. "So, who's linking to you?"

"To be honest, I'm not sure, yet. I think I'd know if it was Po. I see a shadow sometimes, but it isn't big enough to be him. Plus, Po doesn't seem to ever leave the cellar." He rubbed his thumb over the smooth stones at his wrist. "And from what I learned in Peru, we're lucky he doesn't."

"Wait, you learned about our ghosts in Peru?" Cassie snorted, incredulous.

"It's why I went there in the first place." Kyle grimaced as Pete and Cassie raised their heads as one and gawped at him. "I know some stuff. I didn't want to get you all alarmed."

"Alarmed? You're telling us we have ghosts attached to us and you don't think we're already alarmed?" Pete snapped, leaning his forearms heavily on the tabletop.

"I know, I know. Just...hear me out." Kyle held up his hands in defence and was about to explain, when Jonah burst from the living room and stumbled into the kitchen, a furious expression on his face.

"Will you guys quit it already! It's not funny, God damnit!"

They blinked up at him in confusion, his outburst completely counter to the numb, stunned energy of the room. Kyle eventually answered. "What are you talking about?"

"Oh, good one, Wankman. You don't think I can tell when you're pranking me. I'm absolutely sick of it! I've let it ride for the last two weeks thinking you'd get tired of it if I didn't react. But you've gone too far tonight!"

Kyle hopped down from the counter. "We've been sitting here the whole time."

"And nobody's been pranking you, Jonah." Pete shrugged. "Why would we?"

Jonah stood, heaving deep breaths, his face slowly contorting from anger to confusion. "Then what the hell just happened in the living room?"

The housemates clambered from their stools and followed Jonah to the door of the room he had been in. He opened it and backed away. "No, this isn't right."

Kyle peered into the room. Everything looked the same as it usually did. "What's wrong, Jonah?"

Jonah pointed, breathing heavily, looking like a kid about to break into a tantrum. "All the stuff had moved. I woke up and the TV was over there... The couch was turned toward the fucking wall! The bookshelf was up against the other wall. I swear it!"

Tad walked into the middle of the room. "Everything looks normal now." He froze. Sniffed at the air.

"What is it?" Kyle asked, stepping forward.

"I smell smoke."

"I do, too. I didn't smell it on you in the kitchen."

"Looks like you had a visit from Anthony Pile," Tad told Jonah, ruefully.

"Fuck this." Jonah snatched up his leather jacket and marched from the room, throwing a middle finger back at them as he left. "You're all full of shit!"

"He said we'd been pranking him for two weeks," Cassie pointed out.

"I haven't done anything to him," Lance mumbled.

"Me either," Pete confirmed, resting his elbow against the couch top. Lance could tell he was trying to make it look as though he was casually leaning, but it had become obvious to the housemates when he was struggling to hold himself upright. Cassie stepped closer to him, ready to catch him if he fell.

"None of us has been pranking him," Kyle said, firmly. "But now we know who has."

CHAPTER 8
DISBELIEF

If Kyle had thought for a moment that Jonah's experience with the living room furniture might have finally made him a believer, he soon realised that notion was a foolhardy one. The next day, Jonah dropped by unexpectedly in the early evening, determined to prove that he still wasn't afraid of the Victorian ghost house. The group had just finished eating Lance's abandoned curry, and while the housemates set about cleaning up, Jonah lay into them all for believing in spirits. The more Kyle tried to explain, the more Jonah's expression twisted into a sneer. The shaken confusion of the night before was long gone.

Jonah had always been a bit of a loose cannon, but he usually had a relaxed, playful side they all adored. This confrontational, aggressive Jonah was completely new, and the housemates watched him warily as he paced the room.

"So, you're expecting me to believe that some ancient Hellfire Club wanker is whiling away his afterlife by moving your furniture around? Come off it, lads."

Tad looked over his shoulder at Jonah from where he was

washing the dishes, visibly frustrated. "You saw it, last night! There was no explanation for that. We were all here in the kitchen when you came out of the room. We couldn't have switched the furniture back."

"I must have dreamed it. That's all."

"Well, how likely does that sound?"

"About as likely as Cassie roaming around every night, but she still does it. Or are you guys going to put that down to ghosts, too?"

Cassie blushed, scalded. She stopped wiping the table and stared down at her hands. Pete slid his arm around her shoulder and gave it a squeeze. She leaned into him, her face showing relief. Pete had been acting so distant with her lately, Kyle could tell it was bothering her. As she rested her face into Pete's shirt, the scent of dusty timbers, like an old museum storage space, wafted out of the fabric. Cassie pulled back her head in surprise.

Pete glanced down at her, looking a little hurt. He tugged his arm away.

Cassie opened her mouth as though she wanted to explain, but Jonah started to shout, his voice swamping the room. He was the loudest person Kyle had ever met, especially when he was being challenged.

"You've got into my head with all this haunted house shit and now I'm having fucked up dreams because of you guys. Thanks a bunch!"

Lance rounded on his cousin. "If you're that sick of it, why don't you stop coming round for a while?"

Jonah squared up to him, his cheeks turning puce. "Fine, then!"

For the third time in as many days, Jonah stormed from the house, slamming the front door.

Kyle pinched the crooked bridge of his nose. He felt torn —relieved that Jonah's dramatics the previous night had interrupted him just when he'd been about to tell the others what he knew. But equally, he longed to tell them everything. His notebook still rested on the kitchen counter, waiting for him to reveal its secrets. Instead, he kept his mouth shut, scooping the book towards him. Now wasn't the time.

"Do you think his mood swings are to do with the ghosts?" Lance suggested. "He always used to be so chilled out."

Tad sighed. "He's scared. Not that he'd admit it."

"He's not the only one around here who's had mood swings." Cassie looked under her lashes at Pete, who tutted and turned to the wall.

"No, she's right. You've all seemed kind of off since I got back," Kyle admitted. He was treading carefully, trying to show his friends concern rather than judgement. But emotions were high, and no matter how cautiously he trod around the subject, it was never going to land the way he'd intended.

"I've not been moody!" Cassie protested.

"No, but you've been... I dunno. Bolder. It's like you're getting more outgoing."

"I'm training to swim the Channel! Excuse me if I need to get a bit pumped up to do it. You want me to stay a quiet little mouse and drown halfway across?"

"No, of course not! If that's what it is, then good for you. I just thought it might be Lisa's influence."

"Well, it's not!" Cassie's cheeks and lips pinkened. "Coach is teaching me some assertiveness techniques, that's all. Heaven forbid a girl should grow a pair of fucking balls around here!"

The boys flinched as she pelted the sponge she'd been cleaning with against the wall and fled the room, taking the stairs two at a time. Upstairs, her bedroom door slammed.

Lance placed his head in his hands and rubbed his eyes. "Well, guys, as fun as this last couple of days has been, I think I'm gonna head out for a while."

They watched Lance stoop to grab the sponge on his way out. He tossed it to Tad, who set it in the soapy water to soak and snapped off his rubber gloves.

Kyle listened to the sounds of Lance tugging on his shoes and coat in the hallway. He carried the notebook to the kitchen table and dropped it onto one of the stools. Pete had been leaning against the seat next to it, but as Kyle sat, he shakily stood up. Tucking his hands inside his sleeves he raised his shoulders up toward his ears, shivering.

"I'm going to check on Cassie," Pete said.

Kyle flinched under the steely glare Pete threw his way. He hadn't meant to upset Cassie. Or any of them. He had so much he wanted to say. But how could he ever make them understand? He covered his weary eyes, still dry from lingering jetlag, and groaned into the flesh of his palms.

"Here," Tad's deep voice sounded over him, and he slid a glass between his elbows.

"What is it?" Kyle peered down at the huge measure of amber liquid.

"Whiskey," Tad told him.

The word was pretty similar in both languages, so Tad had used his home tongue. It sounded like hooeeski. Like most Japanese words he had learned from his best friend, Kyle much preferred it to English.

He wrapped his hand around the heavy crystal glass. "Isn't it a little early to start on this?"

"It's after midnight in Japan," Tad replied with a shrug. He tapped his glass against Kyle's, then sat opposite him and sipped at the biting liquid. "What time is it in Peru?"

Kyle thought. "Umm, like, just before midday?"

"Ah. Glad I didn't use that as the excuse." Tad smiled and tilted the glass to his lips.

Kyle did the same and watched his friend swirl his glass and stare pointedly at the notebook. Between them, a black Zippo lighter with a daubed cannabis leaf lay on the table. Jonah's, naturally. Kyle reached for it and stuffed it into his hoodie pocket, making a mental note to pass it back to him at uni the next day.

Tad locked eyes with Kyle. After a moment of what appeared to be deep thought, he said, "Speaking of Peru, though...you had something you wanted to tell us?"

Trust Tad, Kyle thought. No matter what hysterical interruption Jonah could throw at them. No matter the arguments and tensions. Even hours later, he still remembered the matter at hand. Tad was a good man to have in a storm, his mother always said. He was inclined to agree with her, more so now than ever.

Kyle took another swig of whiskey, draining the glass. "I had to find out about Po. Properly. The guidebooks hardly said anything about his origins. Only that he was some incredibly strong man who lived in Incan times. But there was a post put on one of the history forums that said he wasn't just a big guy; he was a giant. An actual fucking giant. With three eyes on his forehead and nothing here." Kyle poked his fingers at his own eye sockets in demonstration.

Tad listened, only moving to refill their glasses. He added triple measures to his own and swallowed one as Kyle spoke. Tad wore a heavy silver ring on the middle finger of his left hand, and it clinked against the glass whenever he took a sip.

Kyle continued. "The other people on the forum trolled him like crazy. Told him he was nuts. But the guy insisted his great grandma had lived around here all her life, and she said it was common knowledge. I chose to do my anthropology thesis on Incan descendants because it was one way of getting closer to the truth about him. The *only* way. I didn't really think I'd get anywhere. But I was right. I met with an indigenous Quechua community and the elder knew all about him. Po was *pre*-Incan, Tad. He was an abomination. He was kept like a slave by the Killke people, used as some kind of bodyguard and builder. There's a fortification called Sacsayhuaman. Nobody knows *how* they managed to build it. The bricks are huge...but it was Po! They had a fucking giant build it for them."

"And now he's in our cellar," Tad mumbled.

Kyle laughed, but it was a wet kind of laugh, covering sudden brimming tears that threatened to spill. He turned the protection beads around his wrist, then flicked through the notebook, pulling out a piece of parchment. He shoved it across the table to Tad and watched him study the sketches that were more than a hundred years old. After a while, Tad looked up at him, his eyes bloodshot.

Kyle reached over and pointed to each sketch. "This is Po

as a child. He was already as tall as the biggest villager at three, so they kept him chained up. This is him as a teenager, taking care of business."

Tad grimaced at the gruesome image that showed the monster tearing an attacking warrior limb from limb. Chains hung from his bloodied arms. Tad took another large swallow, suddenly looking quite drunk.

"This one...this is him building Sacsayhuaman. You see, even though he's so much bigger than his captors, they're whipping him. He was like a pet to them."

Tad stared at the final two drawings and looked up at Kyle. "When was this drawn?"

"In the 1880s. Nearly three hundred years after all this happened," Kyle told him, draining his second glass and stabbing his finger onto the fourth picture. "This is Po's death. He's covered in pox, see? So, he must have lived until the Spanish invaded. Selestino said he was the reason they had to resort to germ warfare. Those assholes would never have succeeded otherwise. God knows how old Po was by then, though. We could be talking hundreds of years. And then this."

Tad gasped and swivelled his chair to turn away from the image drawn by a woman over a hundred years before. The sketch accurately pictured *their* dining room. The monster tore his hands into a rotund man sitting at their dining table, cascades of gore spilling in all directions. The woman had drawn the original Suffering séance, and the gruesome death of Cillian Waverley.

Tad went to reach for more whiskey, then thought better of it, sucking in his cheeks as he gathered his thoughts. Eventually, he asked, "Who drew these? How did they even know?"

"Selestino—the wise man—told me it was his mother. That she had visions." He held out the beads on his wrist. "He gave me these. They were hers. She had them made to protect her from Po coming to get her during her visions. That's all I know."

"Is that everything?" Tad narrowed his eyes in drunken scrutiny.

Kyle hesitated. He thought of the parchment he hadn't yet unpacked. After hesitating, so slightly his tipsy friend didn't pick up on it, he ducked his head. "That's it."

Tad pursed his lips and hauled himself to his feet, the alcohol apparently making him as wobbly as Pete had become. "I'm going for a lie down."

Kyle sipped at his remaining whiskey and listened to Tad carefully ascending the stairs. Now wasn't the time to tell him about the other drawing. The sketch that had been painted much later, in the shaking hand of a dying old woman.

KYLE ABSENTMINDEDLY PLAYED with Jonah's lighter in his hoodie pocket while the lecturer wrapped up his talk on the psychology of religion in ancient tribes. He prised open the top and began to flick at the spark wheel, then jerked his thumb away. Lighting a flame against the material of his hoodie was probably a dumb idea.

"Okay, that's it for today. I'd like you to submit the first five hundred words of your dissertations to me by next

Friday. Don't forget!" the teacher called as the class bolted for the door.

Kyle turned against the flow of the crowd and moved towards the room where Jonah was taking his criminology lecture. He glanced at his watch, curling the Zippo into his fist. His own lecturer had wrapped up a couple of minutes early. He pressed his back against the wall and waited. Down the corridor, another class erupted from one of the rooms. Kyle sucked in his breath and shrank back as the students milled by, smiling at those that he knew, ducking his head at those that he didn't. He didn't know why he always felt so self-conscious when he was waiting for people. He wished Jonah would hurry the fuck up.

A student he recognised left the class and gave him a nod as he passed. With a jolt of realisation, Kyle called after him, "Hey, Eldon! Wait up!"

The kid pivoted, tall and thin and turning like a stiff plank of MDF. Eldon was a foot taller than the rest of them, with a sharp, triangular Adam's apple that bobbed and twitched almost constantly. "Kyle, what's up?"

"Are you still running the paranormal club?"

Eldon's thin mouth flickered. He frowned, his throat spasming. "It's not a club. It's investigative research."

"Okay, sorry. I know it's serious stuff. You have the gadgets and everything, don't you?"

"I have an EMF detector and a spirit box, if that's what you mean?"

"Spirit box? Is that like one of those Ghostbusters traps?" Kyle asked, suddenly hopeful despite the irrationality of the idea.

Eldon snorted. "I wish. You can't catch ghosts, Kyle. But

you can hear them sometimes, through the spirit box. It helps them to communicate."

"What, they talk to you?"

"Indubitably." Eldon's interest was piqued, and he stood even straighter, if that were possible. "Why are you asking me? Are you experiencing activity?"

Kyle hesitated. Eldon used to approach him all the time for permission to run an investigation at Brackenby. He had always declined, not because he wanted to be unkind, but because he had thought it was a load of rubbish. He also didn't think Cassie would take kindly to Eldon traipsing through her room. She used to laugh at the paranormal group when they tried to conduct investigations outside, shouting out of the living room window for them to get a life and leave them alone.

"Did you ever get anything?" Kyle asked. "When you were outside the house, I mean?"

"Once or twice. Things started to get quite good, but Cassie pinned Albert against the wall, so we stopped coming. We got energy spikes and a couple of messages. I can't remember what they said. I'll have to check my notes."

"Great. Hey, let me know, okay?"

Eldon gave him a funny look. "Has something happened?"

Shrugging, Kyle fiddled with the Zippo, glancing back to Jonah's classroom, the door of which was now standing wide open. "Oh, shit! When did they leave?"

"Just now, while we were talking. Kyle, is everything all right?"

Kyle stuffed Jonah's lost lighter back in his pocket and

rubbed his hands over his face. "Look, if we ever did want you to come to the house...?"

"Just hit my DMs!" Eldon grinned, delighted. "I've upgraded my spirit box. Last week at the cemetery I heard a man say, 'you're standing on my feet', as clear as day!"

"That's great, man," Kyle mumbled, feeling tired.

"Well, let me know. Just say the word and I'll be there!"

CHAPTER 9

RECREATION

Cassie had woken up that morning still annoyed at Kyle, determined to avoid her housemates until she'd shaken off the lingering cloud of outrage from their altercation at the dinner table. After the argument, she had stayed holed up in her room, watching old swim competitions on her phone and brooding. Pete had tried to cheer her up but had soon realised she needed her own company. After lying on the bed with her for twenty minutes, tickling her feet and trying to elicit a smile, he gave up. He'd stood up and turned to leave and had almost hit the deck, his body slamming heavily against the doorframe. *I'm worried about you*, Cassie had wanted to say, but the words had stuck in her throat. Instead, she had done her usual goofy laugh, praising him for cheering her up with a bit of slapstick.

Her irritation was aimed at herself as much as at Kyle, and she had spent the day distracted in class, writing notes that didn't make much sense upon a second reading. Her mind wandered, returning to Pete and his recent illness. It bothered her, but it wasn't her place to do anything. Pete had

Gaia to fuss over him, and Gaia had made it clear that Pete was her territory, eyeing Cassie warily whenever she and Pete fooled around in front of her. Still, Cassie didn't have to be completely distant with him. She *could* tell him she cared, at least, if she wasn't such an emotional vacuum sometimes.

Not wanting to go back to the house, Cassie stayed at the library until late. At eight, she'd headed to the gym, determined to swim her way to a better disposition.

She loved being the first or last person in the pool. With either the peachy light of dawn or the navy shadow of night at the large picture windows, she felt as though she was the only person on the planet. She had always been at home in the water—had gained her 1500 metres badge at five, progressing in the school's swim team over the years and making nationals. Her physique was big and broad, and her powerful stroke meant that she could often match the boys. That's the thing she loved most about swimming; she was an equal. Physicality didn't mean a damn thing in the water. It was all down to her technique and power, and she knew exactly what she was doing. She stepped up to the edge of the water and curled her toes, loving the gritty sensation of the tiles digging into the undersides of her feet. The chlorine smell lifted her senses, ejecting any residual fog from her brain, clearing her mind and her lungs as she huffed a deep breath. Bending her knees, she forced her body forward into a swan dive, loving the rushing sensation of falling through space, before her arms disappeared into the water. She always tried to feel the exact moment her fingertips touched the surface, but never quite managed, her brain unable to process the change in sensation before the water was consuming her head and shoulders and her whole body submerged.

She somersaulted, planted her feet against the wall, then pushed off, torpedoing through the blue.

Cassie worked through fifty lengths of crawl before stopping, hooking her elbow over the side, and pushing her goggles up onto the brim of her swim cap. She snaked her fingertips around the edge, checking the seal and making sure her hair was still safely tucked away. There was nothing she hated more than getting her hair wet, her naturally dry curls prone to frizzing and breakage at the best of times.

Deciding to switch up her stroke, she reset her goggles and launched herself backwards into a brisk backstroke. Droplets of water pattered down onto the plastic lenses. She'd travelled no more than three quarters of the length of the pool when she felt another swimmer's hand connect with her thigh, a brushing grab that meant they had come too close to her lane. Irritated, she reached the wall and turned around, eager to see the idiot who had managed to come into her pathway in an otherwise empty pool.

The water was calm and even, reflecting the strip lighting on its surface in jittery rectangles. There was nobody else in the pool.

Frowning, she tugged off the goggles and checked again, wondering if the interloper was swimming underwater and would pop up in a far corner at any moment.

Nope. Other than her the room was empty.

She must have imagined it, she reasoned, although how she could have dreamt the sensation of someone else's hand sliding down her leg, she didn't know. She had been swimming since she was a toddler. She knew every sensation, every stroke of water against her skin. It hadn't been the current, she knew. Although, at the same time, she told herself firmly, that was all it possibly could have been. Right?

Taking a few deep breaths, more to settle her nerves than to engage her lungs for the swim, she dropped her goggles on the edge of the tiles and began to leisurely breaststroke for the opposite side. The Channel swim would be a brutal run of exhausting conditions, and she had been advised by her coach to mix up her strokes whenever she felt as though she was tiring. Cassie could speed crawl with ease any day. Forcing herself to turn down both her speed and power and tug herself through the water like a frog was the toughest challenge for her so far. She grew impatient with light swimming but had been warned that the breaststroke was as important as the crawl when you were in the middle of the sea.

Swimming with her head above the water made her feel like a dog. So, although she wasn't wearing her goggles, she began to turn up her energy as she neared the side, ducking her head deep under and popping up with a breath as she forced her arms wide. She did this three times, then felt the side of the pool graze her fingertips. She floated up through the blue lit water and felt a hand clasp her scalp, preventing her head from breaking the surface.

Alarmed, Cassie's body curved underneath her, and she treaded water, flailing her arms. She smacked her wrist against the wall, then raised her hand up out of the water to feel for the person who was pushing her down. Her hand waved through the air above her head, touching nothing but dead space. But she could *feel* the person pressing on her scalp, their palm a hot weight in the tepid water.

She was usually adept at holding her breath, but the

stunt had taken her by surprise, and she wasn't ready. Her lungs began to burn, a plug of chlorine water caught at the back of her tongue that she needed to cough away before she could take in any oxygen. Her throat constricted painfully, the muscles spasming.

The hand went away.

Cassie burst to the surface, clawing for the side, choking. She grabbed the edge of the tiles and hauled herself up onto solid ground, expecting to fall at the feet of the person who had held her under. But there was nobody there.

Chilled to the core, Cassie stumbled to her feet and rushed for the changing area, heart in her mouth, anticipating that whoever had grabbed her might make ready to attack her again. The room was empty and stale. It didn't *feel* as though anyone had been in there for a while. She grabbed her towel from her hook and hurriedly dressed, too afraid to risk a shower.

She felt a little calmer once she was in her clothes, the heavy jeans and sweater making her feel less vulnerable than the skimpy Lycra swimsuit. She rooted in her purse and pulled out her small spray deodorant, popping off the lid and holding it out in front of her like Mace. She knew it wouldn't be quite as effective should she have to use it, but it might hurt if it was sprayed in someone's eyes. That followed by a swift kick in the balls, in any case. She figured it could give her a few extra seconds to escape.

She opened the door to the corridor and stepped out, her body tense, finger poised on the deodorant can's nozzle. The corridor was empty, but a smell caused her to wrinkle up her nose. It took her back to summer days spent strolling the promenade, the occasional wind bringing with it the deeper smells of the sea—the rotten, decaying sewage smell of things long since dead in the saltwater.

Lowering the can, Cassie ran for the car park. She sprinted for her hatchback, keys clasped in her hand, but the fear of being grabbed by an attacker had lessened. She was thinking of what Tad had said about smelling seawater in her room. About the droplets that miraculously formed inside the screen of her phone. She was thinking she wasn't necessarily at risk of a human causing her harm.

She ducked into the car and slammed the door, sweeping her gaze over the back seat before locking the doors and leaning back against the headrest, panting. She scrabbled for her phone and fired Martin a text: *Are you home? I need you.*

Cassie waited for his reply, holding the phone cradled in her lap, too shaken to drive. Minutes passed. She wondered whether she should call home and ask one of the lads to come meet her when there was a sharp rapping on the window beside her.

Yelping, she threw her hands up in shock. The phone spun down into the footwell. She jerked her head to the side and saw Martin peering in the window, a beaming smile on his face. Relief and exhaustion tore through her. Cassie turned the key in the ignition and pressed the button to lower the window.

"What the fuck, man? You scared me half to death."

"I got your text but then I saw your car and came over. Thought that made more sense than texting back that I could see you." Martin was still smiling, but his eyes were narrowing in growing concern. "What's up?"

"I don't know. I think someone was fucking with me in the pool."

"Like how?"

"Holding me under."

"Are you kidding? Who was it?"

"I didn't see them. I don't know... It was like I could tell someone was there, but every time I looked around for them, they were gone."

A twist of doubt flashed across Martin's expression. Only for a second. But Cassie caught it.

"You don't believe me."

"No, it's not that. I just think since Kyle got back the guys have been getting all pumped up about this ghost stuff. I think you're all on edge."

"I didn't imagine being held underwater, Martin. I couldn't *breathe*."

"Shit. I don't know what to say, Cass. Do you think we should report it?"

Cassie snorted. "To who? The police? Hi, Officer. An invisible man tried to drown me. Do I have a description? Well, he smelled like the sea, if that narrows it down at all."

Martin peered at her through the window, his expression helpless.

Suddenly irritated by him, Cassie twisted in her seat and stared up at him. "What are you doing here, anyway? You don't go to the gym."

Martin looked around as though he was newly aware of his surroundings. "I don't know. I was out for a walk and I kind of wandered over this way."

"Did *you* go into the pool?"

Martin blinked at her. "No, of course I didn't. You know I hate water."

"Is it you who's fucking with me?"

"What?" Martin sputtered, his eyes springing open.

"Did you think you'd play a stupid prank on me, but you realised you took it too far?"

His face hardened. "I can't believe you would even think that of me for a second. Night, Cassie."

"Oh, shit." Cassie hissed, slamming her palm against the wheel. *Of course* Martin hadn't held her under. He would never do anything to harm her, and she knew it. That coupled with the fact that he was petrified of water made the idea it could have been him fooling around seem even more ridiculous.

But she didn't chase after him. She watched him walking away in the side mirror, his back hunched, his hands pushed deep into his coat pockets. He was upset, and she knew it. She'd have to make it up to him. But not today. She couldn't face stepping out of the safety of the car.

Instead, she rolled up the window and found her phone under the brake pedal. She sent a message to Pete: *You home?*

His answer pinged a moment later. A thumbs-up emoji.

Immediately feeling calmer, she released the handbrake and drove away.

LANCE DICED ONIONS and red peppers and threw them into a sizzling pan of oil. Pete watched from the table, chatting about a hiking trail he'd been reading about. Lance didn't mind cooking for the guys. None of his housemates had a culinary bone in their body, and he enjoyed the fact that a couple of nights a week he could gather them all together and create something good for them to eat. Tad was busy hunting in the storage cupboard, and he eventually ducked his head out triumphantly, tins of tomatoes and kidney beans in each hand. He set them on the counter next to the cooker.

Pete's phone vibrated against the table, and he bent forward to read the screen. "Cassie's on her way," he told the others, his slender fingers quickly tapping a reply.

"Perfect." Lance shook seasoning into the pan.

"Do you think Jonah will come round?"

"I think he's still sulking, but who knows." Lance added the tomatoes to the mixture and lowered the heat.

"Do you think he *was* dreaming when he said the furniture had changed?" Pete asked, thoughtfully.

"Maybe."

"Kyle's sure that it was Rice, though. I agree with him," Tad admitted, grabbing knives and forks from the drawer. "He thinks it will happen again."

"It's some brave dumb-ass ghost who'll keep messing with Jonah," Pete grinned.

Tad pulled an expression that read, *tell me about it*, and began to set the table.

Kyle came into the kitchen, zipping up his jacket. "Oh, shit! I forgot."

Lance turned to him, a steaming jug of stock in hand, and pulled a face. "You're going out?"

"I said I'd meet someone. I'm sorry, man. I totally forgot."

Lance sighed. "This was supposed to be a proper catch up night."

"I know. I should have remembered."

Pete turned in his chair, looking at Kyle over the shoulder of his red hoodie. "Do you have to go?"

Kyle smiled, regretfully. "I have to. I'm sorry."

"Okay, well... We'll save you some."

Kyle muttered his thanks and hurried down the hall. He rushed back a moment later, holding a package in his hand. "This was on the porch."

He tossed it to Tad and watched his friend slice open the sides with a knife.

Tad pulled out a folded letter displaying neat rows of carefully written kanji and a ball of tissue paper. "It's from my grandparents." Tad scanned the kanji, frowning. He'd admitted his Japanese reading was getting rusty since he'd moved to the UK, but after a few moments of quiet contemplation he evidently got the gist. "My grandfather had a bad dream about me. They've sent me a yakuyoke to protect me."

"A what?" Kyle asked, checking his watch. Lance could tell he was worried about missing the bus but was too intrigued about Tad's delivery to leave.

Tad's slender fingers unravelled the paper and he held up a small red pouch. "It's an omamori. Like a talisman. It keeps you safe from spirits. Every time the thread gets frayed you know it's done its job and kept something from harming you."

"That's pretty cool." Pete eyed the pouch with interest. "Can I share?"

Lance held up his pointer finger. "Yeah, I think I want in on that, too."

Tad shrugged, tucking it into his back pocket. "It's superstition. It doesn't really mean anything."

"I wonder what your grandad dreamed?" Kyle asked. Tad

cast him a narrow look and he decided not to push the issue. Whatever was in the letter, Tad obviously didn't want to share it. "Ah, shit. Anyway, I have to dash, or I'll miss the bus."

He waved and hurried away again. A moment later, the front door slammed shut.

"You think he's got a date?" Pete asked.

Tad shook his head. "Nope. No aftershave cloud."

Pete laughed and stretched, his long arms reaching up toward the ceiling. "You're not wrong. But in that case, who's he meeting at this time of night?"

"Fuck knows," Lance muttered, stirring the stock into the mixture. "But I guess it must be important."

Chapter 10
Caleb

Kyle hurried up the street, anxiety causing him to duck his head into the collar of his jacket. He shouldn't be experiencing nerves. He'd just come back from travelling on his own, from staying in strangers' homes who he could barely even communicate with. But this felt different somehow. He'd received the email the previous night after drinking the whiskey with Tad and had nearly fallen off his chair when he read the opening line: *They're getting stronger, aren't they?*

Now, he waited at the bus stop and wondered exactly what he was letting himself in for.

The bus arrived a minute after he'd reached the stop. On board, a woman was trying to shush a noisy toddler. A wizened looking old man slept stretched across the back seat, an empty bottle of cider rolling around the floor beneath him, and a young couple bickered tersely in the middle seats, their staccato voices hushed but urgent as they attempted to fight their corners without drawing any attention to the fact that they were having an argument. Kyle chose a seat two rows in front of the sleeping man and tried to drown out the sound of the screeching child.

He whipped out his phone and read the email again, his hands trembling a little with the motion of the bus.

Kyle, They're getting stronger, aren't they? I can feel it. When I lived in the house, I knew I wasn't enough for them. They messed with me, but I couldn't give them what they needed. Since Halloween, something has changed. You are all in danger. Meet me tomorrow night at the library. We need to talk. Regards, Caleb.

Kyle's uncle, Caleb, had been a distant figure in his life until the Halloween phone call. He had met him at a few family gatherings, but the man kept to himself, watching the parties from the shadows and sipping bourbon. That was how Kyle remembered him, anyway, a man in his forties, slightly chubby and dishevelled. He always seemed pleasant enough but was hardly the life and soul of the party. It unnerved Kyle that Caleb had an intuition about the house, and that fact alone made him even more certain that something was going terribly wrong for them.

By the time the bus reached the town centre, the old man was snoring fitfully, and the child had calmed down, its attention now focused on a cardboard book in its hands. The couple were no longer talking, and the girl was scrolling angrily through her Facebook feed while the boy stared out of the window, music from his earphones making tinny noises that floated down the aisle.

Kyle thanked the driver and hopped off one stop before the station, a few doors down from the library. The red-bricked building was open late for chess club on Mondays, so when he shoved at the double doors, they opened and enveloped him in a warm cushion of coffee-scented air. He moved through the brightly lit lobby area. The walls were adorned with pinboards covered in leaflets detailing local clubs and events, missing cat posters, and self-care awareness flyers.

Stuffing his hands in his pockets, Kyle entered the main area of the library. It was a huge building, split into sections of tall shelving marked with various categories. Downstairs was fiction, with signs in place for romance, crime, thriller, and horror. The children's section nestled at the back of the room, the far wall painted in garish colours. A square of soft blue carpeting lay in place for toddler readings on Monday mornings. The nonfiction section was on the first floor, up a set of wide pine stairs that joined an attractive picture balcony. Kyle climbed the steps, breathing in the dusty scent of the old paper.

Caleb was leaning against the landing rail, watching the comings and goings of the library's patrons. He didn't look up as Kyle approached.

"I knew you'd come." His voice was gravelly, as though he had just woken up.

"Your email intrigued me."

"So, I'm right, then."

Kyle looked at his relative's broad back, his shaggy salt-and-pepper hair hanging in tangles past the collar of his faded khaki jacket. He had no reason to lie or to try and sugar-coat the truth. Caleb probably knew more about what they were experiencing than anyone, and suddenly Kyle was relieved to see him. "You're right. It's getting much worse."

Caleb turned then, his hangdog eyes locking onto Kyle's with grim ferocity. "Come with me."

He led Kyle to the back of the true crime section, stopping at the vending machines to buy coffee. "We'll need it," he insisted when Kyle initially refused.

Kyle took the small plastic cup, then waited while his uncle made his own. It felt like hospital coffee, the cup a strange sickly shade of yellow, the coffee a peculiar balance of being both watery and mind-blowingly strong at the same time.

They moved to sit at a deserted set of tables at the back of the reference area. Kyle knew it well. In his research of the house's history, he had pored over reels of microfiche in a small darkroom to the left.

Caleb sat opposite Kyle and looked him over as though he was seeing him for the first time. "You've grown up."

"I'm twenty-two."

"Fuck. I don't know where the time's gone. I was that age when you were born."

"We never saw you."

Caleb looked at his hands. "I'm not so much of a people person."

"Okay."

"Still. It's good to see you."

Kyle gave a half-smile and sipped his coffee.

Caleb's eyes followed a young woman walking past their table, her perfume wafting candy-sweetness that for a moment masked the dusty old books. He inclined his head towards her. "She was a bit all right."

Kyle shrugged. "I'm gay."

He hadn't meant it to sound as hostile as it did, the underlying tone one of, *if you'd bothered with our family more, you'd have known*. But Caleb didn't rise to it. "Calm down! Bloody hell, how was I supposed to know? Your mum didn't put that in the Christmas newsletter, did she?"

Kyle blinked at his uncle, feeling the irritation ebb away. "You're right. Sorry. I'm just tired and fucking freaked out."

"What do you know about the house?" Caleb asked, lifting his satchel onto the chair beside him and tugging out a bulging notebook. It looked so much like the one Kyle had compiled himself, he couldn't help but laugh. Caleb glared. "Something funny?"

"No, it's... I have something similar."

"This is everything I have about the history of the house."

Kyle reached down to his rucksack and tugged out his own notebook, placing it down beside Caleb's. They looked so alike that even Caleb snorted.

"Oh. I see what you mean." He reached out a tobacco-stained finger and nudged Kyle's book. It fell open to a newspaper clipping about Lucius Holgrove. Caleb glowered. "I guess you know more than I anticipated, then."

"I should think so. I've just come back from Peru."

"Peru? What the fuck did you go there for?"

"Po. I wanted to find out why Grant chose him. I've been researching the ghosts. Isn't that what you wanted to talk to me about?"

Caleb raked his hands through his straggly hair. "No! It's not about the ghosts."

Kyle stared at him, incredulous. "You've lived in that house. You know what they're doing to us. *Of course*, it's about the ghosts! I need to find the answers—"

"All right, Zak Bagans, shut the fuck up for one second

and listen," Caleb hissed. "It's not about the ghosts. It's about Lucius. Lucius is the key to the house."

"Lucius escaped."

"He went back."

"To the house? What do you mean?"

Caleb reached for his own notebook and riffled the pages at the back. He tugged out a photocopy of an old ink-blotted letter and slid it across the table. "Look. This was written by a friend of his. I found this letter in a box of her things after a liquidation sale. It says that he went back to the house and never came out again."

"I thought he jumped off a cliff." Kyle pointed to the newspaper article that stated as much.

"That's what they wanted everyone to think. His friend says he was obsessed with the house, that he went back and never came out again."

"Why would he go back to the house he was so scared of?"

"*Exactly*. Shit. I thought you had some answers." Caleb sat back, deflated.

"I do have some answers. Like I told you, in Peru I found out that—"

"You might as well have gone to Ireland, instead," Caleb interjected, his hands twitching in irritation.

"Why?"

"Grant's tome, that's why. The book that had the spells. I think it's still in your house. I reckon that's what Lucius went back for. I think he wanted to lock it up again."

"Back up. Lock it up?"

Caleb let out a grunt of frustration. "Grant gathered the group for his night of divination, right? The reason he did that was because he'd come across a tome at his museum and deciphered the spells inside. The book came from an Irish monastery. It was found by builders, wrapped in locked chains, and bricked into a secret chamber underground. Why had someone gone to those measures to hide it forever? Well, we fucking know why, don't we?"

"The ghosts."

"The *spells*. It doesn't matter who the ghosts were. It was always going to end badly. Lucius had powers. We know the deaths weighed on his mind. Maybe he wanted to go back and get rid of the spirits once and for all."

"You think Lucius died in the house?"

"I do now."

Kyle frowned, thinking of the dark shape he often saw in his bedroom. What if it was Lucius, trying to reach out to him? "Well, at least *one* of the spirits might be on our side in that house."

"He spent the final months of his life trying to make amends for what happened. It's probably fair to think he might want to help you guys now that the spirits have been released again."

At the mention of his séance, Kyle groaned. "I really fucked up, didn't I?"

Caleb nodded. "I'm guessing they're latching on to you and your friends."

"How did you know?"

"Just guess work. When I was on my own in the house, they never seemed to do much. I kind of knew they were there, but they didn't have the power to do anything. When I had friends around the energy got...playful, I guess. I didn't realise for a long time. It's people that feed them. I begged your mother not to rent the house to you kids. I want you to know that."

"Thanks for trying."

"Fat lot of good it did you."

Kyle groaned. "Nobody tells Mum what to do."

Caleb grinned and rolled his eyes. "You're right there."

Kyle looked down at his notebook. He had been so excited at the idea of talking to someone about The Suffering ghosts he was a little disappointed to find that his uncle thought they were irrelevant. He flipped through the pages until he came to a drawing he'd cut from a local history magazine. It showed Lisa Vaughan as she was often pictured, standing on the dock, waving to a boat full of doomed sailors. The artist had pencilled the crew part skeletal already, staring back at the fortune teller with eyeless sockets and waving bony fingers. "She was some piece of work."

Caleb puffed out his cheeks and blew the air through pursed lips. "Yeah, she was the one who always freaked me out the most."

"Really? How come?" Next to the Incan monster that was Po, or the axe-wielding executioner, Jarvis Rice, Kyle had never considered Lisa as being the most threatening of the ghosts.

"It's what she did to those sailors in their palm readings. She was a teenager, but she had the power to take someone's hand and turn them into a suicidal zombie. Then she packed them off to sea, which was tough enough in those days, let's face it. Two or three days out on the open water, she snapped her fingers back home and the sailors climbed overboard and jumped into oblivion. It creeps me out. How could she have that power over them, from so far away?"

"Do you think she really started wrecking whole ships? Like the rumours said?"

Caleb rummaged through his notes. "I think anything's possible. She told them to jump overboard, so she could just as easily have told them to smash a hole in the hull and take everybody else on board down with them. Here, this is the statement that led to her execution. Captain Leonard Rose. Three of his men went to visit a palm reader while the ship was docked at Lancaster quay. Captain Rose said there were multiple witnesses, but the crew were too afraid to testify against Vaughan at trial. That all three of the men who had their palms read were working on deck when they suddenly stopped and stood up. Then, at the exact same time, they marched to the edge and jumped overboard. You can't square that away with an explanation of someone going mad at sea. Three guys don't drop what they're doing and run off the edge of a ship. The other sailors were right not to piss her off."

"The captain's testimony was enough to convict her, though."

"And you know what the bloody snowflakes say about it now? That the three men died because Rose's ship was a death trap, and he used the rumours about Lisa Vaughan to cover it up." Caleb snorted. "But we all know what happened to Rose after the trial."

"An accident on his own ship, which kind of backs up what people say."

"An accidental *hanging* on his own ship. From the fucking mast. It's the weirdest accident I've ever heard about." Caleb slugged his coffee, spilling down his beard and onto his T-shirt. He swiped the back of his hand over his mouth, then wiped his hand on his jeans.

"He wasn't the only captain to testify." Kyle flicked through his notes and tugged out a copy of a newspaper report. The caption read: *Capt. Fairbrother's testimony final nail in Vaughan's coffin. Execution set for 29th Feb.* "This Captain Fairbrother guy didn't die, after all."

Sneering, Caleb waved his hand, dismissively. "You know fuck all about Jonathan Fairbrother. He was into all sorts of creepy shit. Ship's captain turned demonologist—he was probably as bad as she was."

Kyle skim-read the newspaper account which detailed Fairbrother's suspicions of the fortune-teller after hearing rumours about her. He tied the sailors who had visited her to their bunks so they couldn't throw themselves overboard. They returned home from the voyage alive but driven insane by the fact they couldn't fulfil the paranormal urge to join Lisa's horde, and spent the rest of their lives in incarceration. "Well, maybe Rose's crew had a bit of a mutiny. It happens. This is how rumours about witches start, isn't it? A series of coincidences or someone trying to cover up their own negligence?"

Caleb hiked a bushy, white-flecked eyebrow. "You don't think the ghost in your house was really all that bad of a gal?"

Kyle smiled, knowing it sounded ridiculous to defend her. "No, I know. I'm just playing devil's advocate."

"Well, I'm sure she's well acquainted with him." Caleb smirked and drained his coffee, crushing the empty cup. "Look, all I'm saying is, she freaks me out the most because she gets people to do things. It's not her killing them. It's *them*. All on their own, without her having to be anywhere near them. It's like possession, isn't it, before she was even a ghost to begin with."

Kyle felt a chill scurry over his neck. "Well, when you put it like that."

"Just don't underestimate her. Or any of them, for that matter. There *is* a reason Professor Grant picked them for Lucius to bring through at the séance. They're all fucking dangerous, and we need to work out how to get rid of them for you."

"So, what do you want to do?"

"There's a bunch of old history books up here. I thought we could start by looking through them. See if there's anything new about the house or the rumours about the original séance. Little details get lost over time, especially when people start to forget the truth. Take Rourke, for example. Do you know why he was chosen by Grant?"

"He was a thief? Died running through the rafters. Seems a good match to take the role of Stealth."

"Just a thief? Don't you think Grant wanted the ghosts to be a bit worse than someone pinching a few pennies from their bosses?"

Kyle narrowed his eyes. "That's all the history books say about him."

"That as may be." Caleb whipped a photocopy from the back of his notebook and pushed it toward Kyle. It was a copy of a letter, the bottom of the original torn away and leaving a wavy black line halfway down the stark white of the A4 sheet of paper.

"This is Lucius's handwriting."

"It's a letter he wrote to one of his friends while he was in prison. He tells them some of what he saw that night. But look here... See what he says about Rourke?" Caleb leaned forward and jabbed a chewed fingernail toward the bottom sentence.

To see Lincoln stumbling up the stairs, chased by the child-killing monstrosity that was Rourke—

Kyle flipped the paper over, hoping to see more, but the page was blank.

"That's all I have. But you see what I mean? There's always more to the story than what we already know. There's more to each one of them."

Rourke wasn't just a thief. He had killed children, as well. Instantly, the light footsteps pattering across the stairs seemed all the more chilling. "That's definitely worse than stealing from his boss."

"I think they're all that bit worse. There's always more to unpack with the ghosts."

Kyle whipped his hand up and pointed, triumphantly. "Ah! So, you *are* interested in the histories of the ghosts, too."

He immediately dropped his arm, withering under his uncle's glare. "Fine, Kyle. You carry on doing your Sherlock Holmes bit and find out what each of the ghosts liked on their crumpets while I work on finding out a way to save your fucking lives."

Growing more used to his uncle's biting wit, Kyle smirked down at his hands and shut his mouth.

Caleb hauled himself up and went to the far shelving, coming back with three large leather-bound books. He tossed them on the centre of the table, the scent of dust and damp filling the space between them.

Kyle pulled the top book close, anticipation growing. He

felt like they were on the verge of discovering something, and he tore through the first few pages with eager expectation.

Two hours later, his optimism had waned. They had come across three references to the house itself, and one to Lucius's death. None of the entries were of any use or told them anything they didn't already know.

Caleb yawned loudly and slammed his book closed. "Well, that was a waste of time."

"Do you want to carry on?"

His uncle tilted his wrist and checked his watch, then shook his head. "Nah, it's late. Don't worry about it. I've still got a bunch of Hestor Morello's things to go over."

"Hestor Morello?"

"Lucius's mate." Caleb tossed their cups in the bin but left the books on the tabletop. "I've managed to get a folder of documents, but the real money shot is the leftover belongings in the family attic. I keep trying. They're cagey about it, though."

Kyle hesitated, not wanting to be rude and leave the books for the library staff to have to put away. But Caleb was already heading for the staircase, talking about Hestor's belongings. He quickly stacked the books in a neat pile and rushed after him.

"So far there's only been a few letters back and forth. A couple of diaries. Not much about anything useful. I can't really get a read on their relationship yet, but there's plenty more in the boxes to go at," Caleb said as he plodded down the stairs, oblivious to the fact that Kyle hadn't been beside him the whole time.

"I could help you look through the boxes, if you like."

"Yeah, I could use an extra pair of hands. We'll sort something out." Caleb waved his hand around, vaguely indicating a date in the future. "Listen, can I come see the house some time?"

"Of course." It would be interesting to see if Caleb could feel the change in the house since he lived there. Since they had conducted the second séance.

They left the library together, Kyle smiling bashfully at the young man at the reception desk, knowing he'd be cursing them later when he had to put their books away. Maybe when he knew his uncle better, he'd be bolder about telling him to clean up after himself.

Outside, Caleb drew a cigarette from his pocket and patted his jeans, letting out a frustrated grunt. "Got a light?"

Kyle went to answer with his usual negative reply, then remembered Jonah's discarded Zippo still sitting in his front pocket. He handed it to Caleb who looked at the cannabis symbol and spiked an eyebrow.

"It's not mine," Kyle told him.

"Can I keep it?" Caleb sucked on the cigarette, a full centimetre of the white tip spiralling into ash.

"Sorry, I'm supposed to give it back to my friend."

Caleb tossed the lighter back, laughing when Kyle fumbled to catch it. "Good to see you, nephew."

Stuffing Jonah's Zippo back into his pocket, Kyle nodded, meaning it when he said, "I hope we can meet up again soon."

"Kid, something tells me we don't have much of a choice."

. . .

BACK AT BRACKENBY, Kyle stepped into the quiet hallway and listened for signs of life from his friends. The gentle strains of chatter from the TV came from the living room, and pipes clattered upstairs from what he guessed must be a shower in progress. He hooked his jacket on the rack and climbed the stairs, going to his room and sitting on the edge of the bed.

In the quiet, he closed his eyes and began to speak out loud. "Lucius? Is it you that I'm seeing in here?"

He let his eyelids flutter open and saw the telltale smudge of a shadow to the right side of his outer vision. His heart juddered in excitement. Had he really called Lucius and the spirit responded to him? If so, didn't that validate the fact that it could be his distant relative, after all?

"Lucius, if that's you, give me a sign."

The black shadow expanded a little, elongating along the wall.

Kyle held his breath and tried to sit as still as possible, watching. "That's great. Thank you. Can you make a noise?"

At that moment the bedroom door flew open.

Kyle jumped, instinctively tumbling back on the mattress, his heart in his mouth.

Lance crashed into the room. "Hey, man. Who you talking to?"

"Oh my God, mate. You almost gave me a heart attack!"

"Sorry. I heard voices in here. I thought you'd brought your friend home."

Kyle sat up and crossed his legs, his hand on his chest. He felt the ramming beat of his heart under his skin. "No. I'm alone. And it was my uncle. That's who I went to see."

"Caleb? The one who used to live here?"

"Yeah." Kyle watched Lance close the door and pull out his desk chair, sitting forward on the seat intently. He wore a thick-weave fisherman's jumper, and that coupled with his wild blond curls and ruddy cheeks made him look as though he'd just come back from a trawl in the Irish sea.

"Did you talk to him about the house?"

"He thinks Lucius is here."

"Lucius went off a cliff."

"Caleb doesn't think so. He thinks he came back here to get rid of the spell book but died in the process."

"Oh, mate. That's heavy."

"That's not all. I think he's in this room."

"Lucius?" Lance looked around, as if expecting the young psychic to suddenly materialise in front of him.

"I've been seeing a shadow. I thought it was one of the ghosts from the séance, but now I'm wondering if it might be Lucius instead. It doesn't feel bad. It just kind of hangs around."

"Oh, that's great. I get the demon worshipping Hellfire guy and you get your charming great-uncle."

Kyle gave a half-smile and scratched an itching bite on his ankle. "Sorry."

"Do you think he can help us?"

"That's exactly what Caleb was wondering."

"What do you want to do, set up a ouija board or something?" Lance beamed at the prospect of a spooky Instagram shot.

"There's no way Tad will go for that."

"Well, who says we have to include the others? Why don't we sort it out ourselves?"

"I guess. But a ouija board is off the table. After last time, there's no way I'm doing another. But we could try something else. When do you want to do it?"

"As soon as possible."

"All right. I'll call Eldon. See if he can bring over his ghost hunting equipment."

"Okay. You're on," Lance said. "I'm kind of excited."

"It feels good knowing one of them might be on our side, doesn't it?"

"That's exactly it. We might actually be getting somewhere."

Kyle grinned and grabbed his phone. Eldon answered on the third ring.

"Kyle! You got my message?"

Pausing for a moment, Kyle guiltily remembered a Messenger notification had popped up from Eldon during the day, but he had ignored it. "Uh, yeah. Sure."

"So, what did you think?"

"About...?"

"About the EVP! I can't believe I'd forgotten. I tried to tell Cassie about it the night it happened, but she told me to... Anyway, I'm glad you're interested now. It's the clearest voice I've ever gotten."

Electronic Voice Phenomenon, Kyle's brain sluggishly translated. Supposed ghostly voices captured on electronic devices. The main reason Eldon and his paranormal group used to spend hours hanging around outside Brackenby House. Until Cassie told them in no uncertain terms to get lost.

"It's also the nastiest, mind you," Eldon continued, breathily. "The hairs on the back of my neck stood up when I heard it again."

"Yeah, okay. That's great. Listen, would you be able to come over with some of your tech stuff? We've been having some activity and we thought now might be a good time for you to see if you can get anything else."

"Yes!" Eldon yelled, then pulled himself together. "I mean, sure, whatever you need. Just let me know when you want me."

"We will. Thanks, Eldon."

"Does Cassie know you're asking me over?"

Kyle smiled at the anxiety in the chastised ghost hunter's voice. "Don't worry about Cassie. She'll be fine."

"Right. Well, how have you all been? Any problems?"

Kyle hesitated. "How do you mean?"

"Well, you said you're having activity. You need to be on the lookout for signs of oppression."

"You mean possession?"

"Oppression. It's what comes before possession. When there's a lot of paranormal activity happening in a living space, you need to watch out for changes in personality. Depression. Anger. Irrational thoughts or actions. Troubles in relationships. That kind of thing."

Kyle thought of Jonah's recent outbursts, of the growing tensions between the housemates and the people around them, and he shifted uncomfortably. "No. Nothing like that."

"Well, good. Just be on the lookout. And don't show them you're afraid. If they see a weakness, they'll thrive on it. I'm here to help, Kyle. Remember that."

Lance looked up from his own phone as Kyle hung up and swiped straight to his messages with a frown. "What did he say?"

"He said he sent us an EVP. Wait, here it is." Kyle thumbed the message and read Eldon's excited text: *You're not gonna believe this voice we got outside your house last year.* There was a short sound bite pasted below the text, a twenty second clip. Kyle turned his volume up and pressed play.

The sound of traffic passing by poured from the speaker, followed by the shuffling of feet.

"*That was Albert moving, contamination sounds,*" Eldon's voice sternly told the recording.

Lance glanced at Kyle and smirked. "Oh Albert." He sighed, shaking his head.

He froze, his eyes widening as a strange, scratchy voice came through the speaker. It was unclear if it was male or female—the voice sounded like three or four people speaking at once.

"What the fuck?" Kyle whispered, thumbing the recording and toggling back a few seconds.

The nightmarish voice spoke again, and the words were unmistakable. "*Pape Satan. Pape Satan aleppe.*"

"What the hell does that mean?" Lance asked.

From behind them on the bed came a low chuckle.

Kyle spun around, his nerves flaming, to find the bed empty.

Lance stared at him and, even though his eyes were wide and glassy with sudden terror, he said in a cheerful voice, "You wanna go downstairs?"

"Yeah, that sounds good." They both stood up and dashed for the door.

CHAPTER 11
WALKING NIGHTMARE

Cassie was dreaming of a dirt road. She felt the sun baking her shoulders and heard whispers coming from the rustling trees that surrounded the dusty pathway. Her feet were bare, and red sandy granules scratched between her toes as she trod closer to the forest. She felt a firm shove in her back and her feet clipped together, sending her tumbling to the ground, faceplanting the chalky red earth.

She woke in the darkness of Brackenby's cellar with a shock, the tops of her ankles slamming the wooden lip of the bottom step. For a moment, she lay in the black, the ringing echo of her fall reverberating back at her from the stone walls. Disoriented, she let out a whimper. Her ankles throbbed where they had clipped the step, and her chin had smacked against the dusty floor, causing her teeth to clash together. An ache ran up her jawline to her ear and dust caked her nostrils.

She shivered in the cold room, blinking rapidly but finding no light whatsoever. She hauled herself up to a sitting position and tried to get her bearings.

Someone let out a heavy breath behind her.

She froze, liquid ice shooting down her back.

Someone groaned.

In the pitch blackness, Cassie heard footsteps sliding along the ground towards her.

She screamed.

Kyle jolted awake. He didn't know what had woken him, but moments later, a door down the hall flung open. Someone dashed from their room, thundering down the staircase.

It had taken him hours to drift off to sleep. He'd sat up stiffly in bed, thinking about the creepy laugh that sounded as though it had come from his pillow area. Torturously, he hadn't been able to stop imagining what it would be like to hear it again. He couldn't help but replay the hypothetical scenario on a loop—a chuckle right next to his sleeping head, ghostly lips tickling his ear. It was a miracle he'd managed to doze at all, although it felt as though he'd only been asleep for a couple of minutes. He kicked off his bedcovers, grabbed his phone, and headed out onto the landing, seeing Tad running, almost at the bottom step.

A faint scream coiled up from below them. "What's going on?"

"It's Cassie!" Tad yelled, dashing along the hall. "Shit!"

Kyle rushed for the stairs and followed his friend down, finding him tugging on the cellar door.

"It won't open!" Tad cried, exertion straining his voice. He wore only black pyjama bottoms, and the muscles in his back flexed when he tugged against the handle.

"There's no lock in there." Kyle pointed out.

"I know! This keeps happening." Tad grunted, then paused as another scream wailed from down in the cellar. "We're coming, Cassie!"

Pete padded down the stairs, confused and dishevelled. "What the hell's going on?"

"The door's stuck." Kyle told him.

Pete moved cautiously over to Tad's side and held out his hand. His fingertips barely grazed the handle and the door sprang open, as if it had been kicked from the inside. Pete staggered back, stunned, expecting Cassie to burst from the room.

Instead, she cried out from down in the darkness below them.

Tad sprinted down the wooden steps into the black. Kyle followed, thumbing the flashlight on his phone. The white glow lit the grim cellar. Cassie lay crumpled in the corner opposite them, frozen and trembling, her eyes wide with terror. Two lines in the dust led from the bottom of the steps to the corner, and the heels of her feet were caked in thick muck. Tad bent down and scooped her up, whispering soothing words into her hair as he carried her to the steps, his expression grim.

Pete watched from the top of the stairs with one arm braced against the open door. If it had locked on them once, who could say it wouldn't happen again. Kyle grimaced as he passed him, shining the light back on Tad and Cassie until they were all out in the safety of the hallway.

Kyle opened the living room door and snapped on the light. Tad carried Cassie to the couch, laying her gently on the cushions. She hauled her legs up, covered her face with her hands, and sobbed, shivering all over. Pete moved to sit beside her, and she flung her arms around him, crying into his grey pyjama shirt.

Kyle looked at Tad, who watched her with concern. Cassie never cried. Not in front of the guys, at least. "How many times has this happened?"

"This is the fifth."

"What if you hadn't heard her?"

"I always do."

"But what if you didn't?"

Tad ducked his head, refusing to answer. He was right. It didn't bear thinking about.

When she could speak, Cassie lifted her head and took a few deep breaths. Pete's shirt was soaked through, and dusty smudges from Cassie's arms and chin peppered the material. "Thanks, Ugly," she gasped, reaching out a hand to Tad.

He squeezed her fingers. "Don't mention it."

"What happened down there?" Pete asked, smoothing down her wild hair.

"Did you get dragged?" Kyle asked, pointing to her grubby feet.

She bobbed her head in confirmation. "I'd been dreaming. I was in a hot country, on a long dusty pathway. There were trees all around."

Kyle tensed and an instinctive, familiar picture formed in his mind.

"I felt as though something had rushed out of the forest and tackled me. That's when I must have fallen down the last step. I woke up lying at the bottom of the stairs. Then something groaned." She shuddered.

Kyle thought of the breathy groan he had experienced in the cellar upon his return from Peru. He touched the bracelet and exhaled through pursed lips. "Then what happened?"

"It felt as though someone picked me up and pulled me back to the corner of the room. My ass actually came up off the ground."

Kyle pictured the two steady trails in the dirt, corroborating his friend's allegation.

"Did it hurt you?" Tad asked, his accent pronounced, his voice solemn.

Cassie felt her shoulders and under her armpits, searching for bruising where the creature had handled her. "I...I don't think so."

Pete reached down and touched his fingertips to her ankles. "You're bruised."

"That's from falling off the steps," Cassie told him, wincing at the raised purple welts.

"Jesus, Cass. This is getting out of control."

"I can't help it." Tears filled her lower lids then spilled onto her cheeks. "The dreams just feel so real. One minute, I'm in a forest. The next, I'm in the cellar."

"What colour is the dirt on the path in your dream?" Kyle asked.

Cassie looked up at him, then narrowed her bloodshot eyes. "What colour do you think it was?"

"You tell me..."

They both spoke at the same time. "Red."

"What the hell, man?" Pete asked. "Are you having the same dream?"

Kyle reached for his phone, scrolling through his picture library until he found a specific day of his trek. There, amidst the greenery of the Peruvian jungles and images of local children carrying sloths, he found what he was looking for.

He held out the phone to Cassie. "Is this the path?"

Cassie just gawped. She didn't even need to confirm it. "What is this place?"

"It's where Po comes from. Where he used to live. Hundreds of years ago."

"How could you even know that?" Pete asked.

"I told you, I went to Peru for a reason."

"Is Po your connection?" Pete frowned. "Like, Rourke is mine?"

"I don't think so," Kyle said. "That's another thing I found out. I think my connection is Lucius."

"Lucius Holgrove?" Cassie asked, her teeth chattering.

Pete reached for the throw blanket on the back of the couch and draped it over her shoulders.

"I think he's in my room," Kyle said. "I keep seeing a shadow. I don't identify it as being one of the five ghosts. I think we have a sixth. I think it's him."

Tad shook his head. "Impossible. He didn't die in the house."

"My Uncle Caleb thinks that he did."

Cassie swaddled herself in the blanket and leant heavily against Pete. "This is getting to be too much."

Pete gave her a squeeze. "Isn't it more likely to be another of Grant's guests rather than Lucius? We know the people who attended the séance were killed here. Isn't it more likely to be Grant over Holgrove?"

"I don't know. Caleb found a bunch of letters from a

friend of Lucius. In one of the letters, they wrote that he'd decided to go to the house and destroy the spell book."

"Makes sense," Tad muttered.

"The spell book isn't here, though. Your family would know about it, wouldn't they?" Pete asked.

"I guess." Kyle shrugged.

"Well, probably Lucius managed to destroy it after all." Pete guessed. "Then he left and ended it all."

"Maybe he took it with him when he jumped off the cliff?" Cassie suggested.

"He could have. That doesn't explain why he'd come back here in the afterlife, though." Pete pointed out.

Cassie gave him a sharp look and rebutted, "If he even did."

Kyle heaved a sigh. "I feel like it's him in my room. I can't explain it."

"Because you're blood relatives?" Tad asked.

"I dunno. Is that so crazy?"

Tad offered his friend a weak smile. "No, I suppose not."

Cassie looked at him, wide-eyed. "So, one of the spirits is a good guy. That can only be a positive, right?"

"Fat lot of help he's being." Pete glanced pointedly at her ankles.

"We don't know that," Kyle countered. "What if Lucius being here is the only thing stopping them from doing to us what they did at Grant's séance?"

Cassie grimaced. "I can't imagine it getting any worse than tonight. And Po's not even my ghost."

"She's right." Pete wrapped his arm around her shoulders and tugged her closer. "What if Tad hadn't heard her scream? Anything could have happened down there."

"Pete!"

"I'm sorry, but it's true. I don't like thinking of it any more than you do, but we have to face facts. It's getting worse. I don't think you should sleep here anymore."

"I agree." Tad folded his arms.

"Well, if I'm not sleeping here anymore, neither should Pete." Cassie looked up at him. "My ghost isn't making me sick."

"She has a point." Kyle sighed. "You're the ones who are most affected. Maybe the two of you should stay away for a couple of nights. Let us see what we can do to get rid of the ghosts in the meantime."

"Like what?" Cassie scoffed.

"I called Eldon. Me and Lance are going to see if we can use his gadgets to contact the ghosts and try and get rid of them."

Tad steepled his fingers and pressed his nails to the soft flesh under his chin. "Look, I don't think I want to stay here, either. Not if you and Lance are going to try something."

Kyle stared at his friend. "Are you sure?"

"Call me a wuss or whatever, but I've got a bad feeling about it all right now. I'm going to go to a hotel. Just for a couple of nights."

Cassie shot him a serious look. "Has something else happened to you, too, Tad?"

Pete patted her arm. "If he wants to get out of here, he wants to get out. I don't blame him. I'll call Gaia and see if I can crash at her place for a couple of nights. You'll head to Martin's?"

Cassie gave a nod.

"And you call in your ghost hunters," Pete said.

"I'm surprised you're happy to miss the ghost gadgets," Kyle told Tad, who pulled a face.

"Can their gadgets turn sewage into renewable energy?"

"Umm...no."

"Well then, I'm not interested." Tad gave a wry smile, and even Cassie crumpled into laughter.

They stayed in the living room until sunup. When light spilled in through the picture windows of the Victorian house, Tad, Pete, and Cassie went to their rooms to pack their bags.

Kyle slipped into his bedroom and stood at the foot of his bed. He lifted the mattress and tugged out the piece of parchment Selestino had given him.

In the dark shadows of his hut, the old man had held the parchment out in a shaking hand and pointed to the shadowy figure sketched into the background. "I believe this is you," the man had told him.

Kyle had looked down at the picture and recoiled, throwing a hand over his mouth. The figure that Selestino's mother had drawn in the background did look somewhat like him, with wide features, deep-set eyes, and dark hair tumbling forward over his forehead. The sketch showed Brackenby's cellar, the stairs leading up from the chalky floor, the grey and red brick walls, and open rafters overhead. But it was the image in the foreground that shook him to the core. That had made the wise old man slip a band of jasper protection beads onto his wrist.

Like the woman's sketch of Cillian Waverley's death at the original Suffering séance, Po stood towering and bloodied over a torn apart body. Only this time, the victim wasn't an overweight man. It was a slim woman in a baggy sweatshirt.

Her hair was short, but there was no denying the face. It was Cassie, lying twisted on the cellar floor.

Kyle shuddered and folded the parchment, shoving it back under the mattress.

When Cassie trundled her suitcase out of the front door, he breathed a sigh of relief.

CHAPTER 12

SLEEPOVERS

"Thanks for letting me stay over." Pete tossed his rucksack on the bed and looked around the room. His girlfriend's bedroom was the sunniest in the house, its pale-yellow walls and lace furnishings only adding to the ambience of rustic cosiness. He used to love escaping from the stale, shadowy white walls of the old townhouse. But today Gaia's room felt alien to him. The cold oppression he had come here to escape had beaten him to it.

Gaia went to her wardrobe and tugged a woollen cardigan from a hanger, wrapping it tightly around her shoulders. "I'm glad you're here to keep me warm. There's a cold snap tonight."

"I can definitely do that," Pete told her.

He slipped his arms around her and pulled her against him, the cardigan scratchy under his palms. He kissed her eagerly, needing to feel close to her again. What with everything that had been going on at the house, he knew he had grown distant from her. Perhaps this visit was just what they needed to get back on track.

They tumbled onto the bed, and he nudged his bag away with his foot, making room for their limbs. Conscious that Gaia was cold, he slipped his hands under her clothing, pushing his fingers under the wiring on her bra until the tips brushed her nipple. She shuddered beneath him, her breath gushing out and warming the underside of his chin. He felt his cock spring to attention, straining against his jeans.

Slipping his hands free, he braced his left palm against the mattress and put the other hand to his mouth, wetting his fingers. He pushed it under Gaia's skirt, using his dry pinkie finger to hook the waistband of her leggings and her underwear. He plunged his wet fingers into her, feeling her lips part and swallow up to his knuckles, the flesh changing from soft and yielding to springy and damp. He turned his hand and bent his fingers, finding the spot that made her arch her hips and moan.

Gaia scratched her fingernails down his back. Slightly too rough, maybe. *God, it stung!* But his cock was fighting to be freed from his pants, the blood pulsing a steady beat inside the fabric. He slipped his hand out of his girlfriend and tore at his zipper, pulling his jeans down to his ass and allowing his hard length to find its mark, the wet opening tightening around his flesh when he thrust, the scratches down his back burning like fire as he pumped into her.

He came a moment before her, his climax tipping her over the edge into her own. Pete could feel her trembling under him, heat now coming off her in waves as she twitched. He collapsed on top of her and gave a breathy laugh. "Are you a little warmer, now?"

"You could say that." She gasped, exhaling with satisfaction.

Pete rolled away and winced when his back touched the bedding. "Jeez, you really did a number on my back. Maybe trim your nails next time, babe."

"What are you talking about?"

"The scratches. I mean, it's hot, but I think you took about ten layers of skin off me."

"I didn't scratch you." Gaia turned to him, puzzled.

"I felt it! I can still feel it now. It kills."

"Pete, look at my nails. Even if I'd tried to scratch you, I couldn't." Gaia held her fingers out close to his eyes. They were trimmed down so close that the pads of her fingertips bulged over the top. "We went rock climbing this week. I had to take off my gels and cut them down."

Pete felt ice rocket down his spine, the heat of the tear down his back a contrasting sensation that only made it more painful. He sat up, fear causing his cock to lose the last of the blood that remained. It shrivelled against his upper thigh, leaving a wet trail.

"I'm going to use the bathroom," he mumbled, unzipping his rucksack and pulling out his toothbrush.

Within the privacy of the Hassans' bathroom, he stood in front of the standing mirror and lifted his shirt, twisting so he could see his back. Three deep red welts stood up on his skin, as though he had been lashed. After seeing Gaia's fingers, he knew there was no way she could have done that to him. He scowled and mouthed, *what the fuck* to his reflection. The middle scratch was so deep that small dots of blood were forming in the centre of the gouge.

IN THE BEDROOM, Gaia mopped herself up with a tissue and tossed it into the bin, before quickly changing into her pyjamas. Although she'd love to wear something silky and sheer for Pete's visit, it was way too cold to consider wearing anything other than thick flannels. She snuggled under the duvet and leaned her head back against the pillows, smelling the lingering tang of sex mixed with Pete's earthy cologne, and feeling the warm throb at the front of her pubic mound.

Pete stopping over was a reassurance that couldn't have come soon enough for her. She thought he had been pulling away from the relationship and she'd been secretly waiting for the inevitable, trying to pluck up the courage to make the call herself before he did it for them. But this changed everything. Perhaps she'd been too hasty. Maybe his recent illness had been the cause of his withdrawal, after all. Maybe he did still love her.

She moved to turn and reach for her phone, only to find her hair caught. She glanced to the side in shock and felt a sudden release as whatever it was let her go.

On high alert, she sat up, palming the side of her head where her scalp had been tugged.

Pete opened the bedroom door and returned his toothbrush to his rucksack, then looked at her with concern. "You okay?"

Gaia felt her head and stared back at the empty mattress. "I guess. It was the strangest thing. It felt like when you lie on my hair, but there was nothing there."

"Did it get caught under the pillow?" Pete suggested.

"Maybe..." but she wasn't convinced. She remained propped up on her elbows until Pete had clambered under the covers beside her. Only then could she relax, pressing herself into his side. She coiled her hair around her fingers and tugged it so that it rested over her chest. No chance of it being snagged by anything.

As Pete texted on his phone beside her, Gaia shook off the creeped-out feeling that she usually only experienced within the walls of Brackenby, and drifted off to sleep.

KYLE WAITED while Lance took the perfect paranormal selfie, used to his housemate's antics. The same couldn't be said for Eldon, and Kyle was enjoying watching the ghost hunter getting more and more annoyed.

"Are you done?" Eldon snapped, impatiently.

"Just a second!" Lance held a ghost-hunting gadget in one hand and his phone at arm's length in the other, his camera flipped towards himself. He adjusted the angle of his hand so the spirit box was clearly in frame, widened his eyes, raised a brow, and snapped a few shots in quick succession.

"Gimme that!" Eldon snatched the spirit box from his hand. "This isn't a toy, you know? This is serious."

"Well, I'm documenting it, aren't I? Isn't that what ghost hunters are supposed to do?" Lance selected his favourite shot and set it to his story with a flurry of ghost-related hashtags.

"Can we get started, now?" Eldon asked, exasperated.

Lance slipped his phone away and held up his hands in defence. "Ready."

Eldon switched on the machine. Bursts of static filled the downstairs hallway. It was unnerving, far louder than either of the housemates had anticipated.

Kyle winced and pressed a finger to his ear, slowly becoming acclimatised to the noise. "Is it always this loud?"

"Yep," Eldon called over the repetitive swish of white noise. "Is there anyone in this house who wants to talk to us?"

Kyle's phone buzzed in his pocket, making him jump out of his skin. What with the various noises coming out of the spirit box, the sudden vibration in his pants did nothing for his jangling nerves. He snagged the phone from his pocket and stared down at Pete's message. *I think it's come with me.*

It took him a moment to realise what his friend was talking about. He wrote, *Rourke?*

When Pete texted back the affirmative, mentioning scratches on his back, Kyle held the phone out to Lance.

Eldon spoke to the spirit box, his voice loud enough to be heard over the crackling waves of static. "I want to speak to one of the spirits who was present on the night of Professor Grant's séance. Can anyone tell me who is still residing in this house."

Lance passed the phone back to Kyle with wide eyes. He looked toward Eldon and the contraption, then called, "Can we speak to Connor Rourke?"

As deep male voice rattled through the machine, causing a clean break in the static. "He's not here."

"Holy shit!" Eldon grinned.

Lance spoke again. "Where is he? Where's Connor?"

The static continued to blast in juddering bursts.

Kyle tried. "Is he with Pete?"

There was a fizzing pop of electricity from the machine, then another voice hissed through the speaker.

"Did you hear that?" Kyle asked.

"I couldn't make it out," Eldon frowned. "I think it was just static interference."

"No, it said *Always*. I heard it. Didn't you?" he turned to Lance.

"I dunno, man. I heard the machine fizzing."

"Damn it." Kyle sent a text back to Pete: *You might be right*.

"We haven't heard any footsteps tonight, that's for sure," Lance pointed out.

"Footsteps?" Eldon switched off the spirit box.

The sudden silence was a welcome relief after the droning bursts of static.

Lance pointed toward the ceiling. "One of the ghosts always makes running noises upstairs. We haven't heard anything since Pete left today."

"You don't hear it every day, surely?" Eldon asked, incredulous.

The boys looked at each other, realisation dawning on them.

"Since I got back from Peru it has been every day," Kyle admitted.

"You know what? I think Pete's got the right idea. I'd be getting the fuck out of here if I was you." Eldon looked around nervously.

"What? I thought it was your big dream to live in a haunted house."

"Dude, this place is fucked up. I'm interested in the paranormal, but I don't want to fucking die because of it."

"Nobody's going to die," Lance said, although he didn't sound one hundred percent convinced, himself.

"Besides, it sounds as though Connor Rourke's gone with Pete, after all." Kyle pointed out.

"I wonder how Cassie's getting on?"

"I'll text her and find out."

Kyle fired off a text to Cassie, a heavy feeling of dread settling in his stomach. If Lisa had also followed Cassie to Martin's, that meant the house wasn't haunted anymore. *They* were.

A few moments later his phone buzzed with Cassie's reply. *I'm fine, we're watching Mean Girls.*

Relief flooded through him. "Okay, Cassie's good."

Lance gave a tight smile, but Kyle could tell he was still worrying about Pete. Although Connor Rourke at face value appeared to be the ghost with the tamest history, the effect he seemed to have on Pete was getting more and more physical. It was one thing to give him vertigo. It was another to cut his skin. Lance's smile morphed into a grimace. "Do you think we should tell Pete to come home?"

"I don't know." Kyle was torn between taking care of his friends and trying to find answers. "What if he just caught himself on a thorn or something? Maybe Connor's still here after all. I say we carry on investigating but try and get Connor, Jarvis, and Lisa to make contact. That way we'll know they're still here."

Lance wrinkled up his nose and looked to the front door, expecting to see Pile's shadow at the window. "Anyone else smell smoke?"

"I guess someone else wants to talk," Kyle told him, hearing the cats begin to yowl and fight outside.

"Why?" Eldon asked, sniffing the air. "What does the smoke mean?"

Lance leaned toward the spirit box and said firmly, "Anthony Pile? You have something you want to say?"

They listened pensively for a moment, straining to hear through the sweeping static. A deep voice suddenly overlapped the swishes with clear intonation. "Pluto, I am thine."

Lance whipped his phone out, searching for the phrase. "It says here 'Pluto, I am thine' is a Hellfire Club toast."

"Definitely Pile, then."

Eldon looked elated. He held the box up higher, staring at it with watery eyes.

The voice spoke again. "Why do you —?"

Kyle furrowed his brow. "Did he just say *whore*? Why do you whore?"

Lance shook his head. "Why do you hoard."

The boys shrugged at each other.

Kyle turned back to the spirit box, hoping for another EVP from the ghost from the Hellfire Club, but the box spat nothing but static.

After fifteen minutes, Eldon turned it off and passed the machine to Kyle. "You want to try upstairs? If that's where Connor runs around, that's going to be our best bet to find out if he's here or not."

"Good call." Kyle took the gadget and led them up the stairs. When they were on the landing, he pressed his back against the wall. "El, don't go too near the banister."

"Why?" Eldon swerved away from the stairs and stood beside him.

"Connor makes Pete feel like he's going to fall. He's nearly thrown him downstairs a few times. If Pete's not here, he might try it with someone else."

Eldon sank back, flattening his palms against the wallpaper.

Kyle flicked the spirit box's on switch, the dreadful hissing noise filling the landing. "Connor? Are you up here?"

No reply.

"Connor, can you come close to us and speak into this box I'm holding?"

They strained, listening closely, but neither voices nor footsteps sounded through the device.

A loud thud came from the right of the landing.

Kyle snapped off the box. "I think that was my room."

They hurried across the corridor and Kyle opened his door.

Eldon held out the EMF detector, waving it around in the dark of Kyle's room.

"What does this one do, again?" Lance asked, watching from the doorway.

"It measures spikes in electromagnetic energy and temperature fluctuations. Basically, it lets you know if there's a ghost standing there." Eldon walked into the far corner and the device burst into life, the alarm sounding a steady chime. "Whoa. Something's here, all right."

Kyle stepped up to him and turned on the spirit box. "Lucius? Is that you?"

A throaty laugh came over the radio waves. It sounded just like the chuckle he and Lance had heard by the bed.

Lance pulled a face. "Dude, I don't think that's Lucius."

"Who was that we heard laughing?" Kyle asked the box.

"Me!" Came a sudden burst lunging through the machine. At that moment, Kyle felt a sharp shove in his back, and he stumbled forward, the gadget spilling from his hands and clattering to the floor. The static ceased, plastic shards broken and scattered on the floorboards.

"Shit!" Eldon hollered, scrambling on the ground, collecting the pieces.

"Dude, I'm sorry." Kyle rubbed where he'd felt the shove in his back as Lance snapped on the light. "Is it broken?"

"I think it's just the casing," Eldon muttered, trying to slot the pieces back in place.

"Was it expensive?"

"Seventy quid." Eldon looked at the machine sadly, then flicked the switch. The static bursts sounded again. "Phew. Okay, who is in this room?"

"It's me... Luuuuuucius!" came a sing-song voice that sent chills scurrying over Kyle's forearms. There was no way that was Lucius Holgrove, a thirty-year old Victorian male. This voice, although playful, sounded like a sinister old hag.

Eldon held the gadget out in front of him, holding the broken casing in place with his long fingers. "We don't believe that's you, Lucius."

"Then *fuck you!*" screamed the box in three different voices ranging from low and male to squeaky and feminine. The spirit box flew out of Eldon's hands and hit the door with such force that not only did the static bursts cease, the machine fractured into multiple pieces.

"Well, that's done it," Lance cried, leaping over the broken machine, and disappearing through the bedroom doorway.

Eldon followed.

Kyle stood his ground. It was his bedroom, after all. There was something futile about escaping to the landing.

The ghosts could move, in any case. And this room belonged to him.

He took a deep breath, fighting the urge to run, and spoke aloud. "You're not Lucius. I understand that. So, who are you?"

He listened, knowing the chance of hearing a ghostly voice with his own ears was unlikely. They needed energy to make sounds. Eldon had explained how the ghosts that came through the spirit box could very well be screaming at the top of their lungs to make the smallest whisper. Still, he knew they weren't talking to just *any* ghosts. Its last outburst had proved it was stronger than anything Eldon had ever encountered before.

"Is it you, Lisa?" Kyle almost hoped it was. At least then they knew they wouldn't have to worry about Cassie and Martin.

A cold breath whispered against his neck, sending the hairs shooting up like needles. The faint voice carried a word; *die*, although he couldn't swear to it.

"You need to get out of my room. I want you out." He turned in a slow circle, his eyes darting from corner to corner, searching.

He heard nothing.

"You have to get out of here. No more shadows. No more voices. I want you out!"

Silence.

After a few moments, he went to the doorway, finding Eldon and Lance on the landing, looking tense.

"Did it work?" Lance asked.

"I don't know. It didn't make any more noises. I can't tell

if it's gone, though. This fucking house always feels like something's there."

"That's because there is," Lance pointed out, with a grin that didn't reach his nervous eyes.

"Do you have any other gadgets to try?" Kyle asked, hopefully.

The shattered spirit box lay in pieces on the floor by Kyle's feet.

CHAPTER 13
HOTEL

Tad sat at the bar and gently turned the glass of whiskey between his palms. The glass chimed against his silver ring. He tapped it a few times, enjoying the gentle clink that only he could hear over the chintzy pop of the bar's music.

Beside him, the bartender busied herself cleaning the pumps, casting nervous glances toward him under her lids. He caught her eye, and she blushed and turned quickly back to her task. He stared down at the dense liquid in the glass, peering at his own eye in his reflection. The girl was cute, but he felt wary at the notion of starting up a conversation with her. He'd long since learned the futility of trying to talk to girls about his true interests.

People saw his exterior and assumed he'd want to talk about...well, all the things that so-called handsome men are supposed to talk about. He wasn't a movie star. He was an engineer. An expert in sewage, for Christ's sake. He sometimes reasoned that if he looked a little different, more 'normal', he might not feel so lonely. It was something he couldn't confide in his friends about. He'd tried it a couple of times but being "too handsome" wasn't really something his friends felt the need to offer much sympathy over. He understood but wished sometimes they could see it from his perspective.

A young couple approached the bar and ordered drinks. The man glanced at Tad and physically body-checked his girlfriend's view of him.

Boxed out and thoroughly fed up, Tad grabbed the whiskey and headed for the elevator. He slipped his room key card from his back pocket and pressed it against the scanner on the door, then stepped inside when the doors slid open.

The lift moved at a snail's pace, inching up through the floors. Tad swirled his drink and inhaled the bitter fumes of the spirit, breathing deeply.

And got a face full of mould.

It was the type of mould written about in poems by Seamus Heaney. Earthen and born of rotten vegetation and decay from the ground.

Tad turned around and looked at himself in the full-length mirror. In the four-foot box of the elevator cab, Tad was no longer alone. A man stood behind him in the small space, shirtless but wearing torn cotton pants held up with a rope. He was covered in what looked like a fine coating of dried mud, and specks fluttered from his arms. His face was almost skeletal but a thin sheet of yellowed flesh draped the bones and puckered around a lipless mouth. His shaggy brown hair hung down to muscular-looking shoulders. In his gloved hands, he held a long-handled axe. The blade was square and daubed with gore, the few clean sections of metal glinting in the strip lighting. The back of his head was reflected in the full-length mirror behind him. His skull was missing a fist-sized hole that revealed putrid green brain matter.

Jarvis Rice's mouth twisted into a leer and, without warning, he swung the axe.

Tad threw the whiskey glass, droplets of the spirit raining down on his clothes. He dropped to all fours, cowering under the metal rail of the armrest, and the whiskey glass rolled to a stop next to his knee. He waited for the smack of the axe against the side of his head, the scent of mould in the tiny room overwhelming. A moment later, along with the sensation of there being another person in the space with him, the smell vanished.

Gingerly raising his head, Tad looked around at the four corners of the elevator and blinked in stunned silence. It was empty.

Tad rose to his feet on quivering legs and dared to glance over his shoulder at the mirror, expecting the figure to make its return. Instead, all he saw was himself, dejected and panting, his almond-shaped eyes sunken and smudged with dark circles. Frowning, he pressed his fingers to the mirror and touched a dint in the reflective surface that he was certain hadn't been there when he'd first walked into the lift. The glass splintered under his touch, cracking into fine tendrils that spread over the reflection of his face. When he pulled his finger away, fresh dirt stuck to the pad, the same red gore that coated the axe head. Sickened, he realised it was highly likely that there was more than just mud coating the blade of the executioner's axe.

The pinging noise of the lift reaching his floor made him flinch and he hurried backwards when the door slid open. He stumbled out into the corridor and rushed for his room.

He rubbed the muck from his trembling fingertip against his pants, wishing he hadn't thrown the whiskey in his panic. He could use it to calm his nerves.

Wait, he reasoned. The crack in the glass could have come from the thrown glass. It didn't explain the dirt, but the reddish substance could have come from behind the mirror, after all. If he'd thrown the glass with enough force, it made sense that some of the plaster or brick had been disturbed behind the glass.

He slowed his footsteps, his anxiety waning with the introduction of some scientific reasoning. He exhaled, feeling foolish, and turned the corner onto the stretch of corridor that led to his room. Directly opposite him at the far end of the long corridor, standing tall with legs spread wide, Jarvis Rice held out his axe in both palms and stared right at him.

Tad's lungs shrivelled. He clenched his groin muscles to keep from ejecting a squirt of piss.

The executioner lifted the axe with his left hand, raising it at an angle, then let it fall so that the handle close to the blade slapped down into his gloved right hand. The sound reverberated toward Tad, a noise he had been hearing in his bedroom at Brackenby but had optimistically dismissed as being the old pipes clunking. Rice hoisted his chin, dropped his head to one side, and broke into a wide leer that tore into the sinews of his cheeks.

Tad's mind raced. He took in the executioner's yellow complexion, his cheek dappled with what looked like spattered blood. His trousers, Tad realised, had once been tan linen, not dark brown, but were coated in a mixture of earth, blood, and shit that daubed him like clay. He scattered the carpet with rancid dust when he took a step forward. Not just one step, Tad realised.

The executioner began to run full pelt down the corridor towards him.

He was fast, far faster than Tad. Every fibre of his being wanted to turn tail and run for the staircase next to the lifts. But logic convinced him to stick with his plan, that he couldn't hope to outrun the monster. In the split second it took to make a fight or flight decision, Tad chose neither. He lunged for his room three doors away, situated directly between himself and the advancing ghost. He slapped his palms against his door and dared to look up.

Rice was halfway down the corridor, gleeful malice in his sunken eyes.

Scrabbling with his key card, Tad jabbed it into the slot at the top of the door handle and tugged it out again.

The lock status light flashed red. Denied.

"Come on!" Tad yelled, slamming the card back into the hole and whipping it out.

Red again.

He swore, glancing to the side.

Rice was just metres away now. The axe was suspended high above his head as he ran. Though the spectral being's boots should have been thundering against the floor, his large frame enough to quake the floorboards, he was deathly silent.

In the blink of an eye, he was less than three feet away and Tad would have to make this fucking key card activate one last time or he would have to turn around and run, and he knew that would be the death of him.

He jabbed the card in and out and turned the handle the

split second the light mercifully flickered green. Tumbling into the hotel room, he slammed the door as the axe plunged down, inches from him.

The stench of mould wafted into the room.

Tad staggered backwards and fell onto the bed, chest heaving. He was too shocked to sob although his eyes had flooded with panicked tears. His nerves on fire, he expected the ghost to appear beside him at any moment. After all, walls couldn't stop them. The ghosts of Brackenby House could apparently find their housemates anywhere.

Unless... Tad fell on the travel bag at the foot of the bed and rummaged in the pockets until his fingers grazed silk. He snatched up the yakuyoke amulet his grandparents had sent him and held it tightly.

Outside the room, visible in the crack under the door, a shadow stood, legs spread wide, the rectangular axe resting on the ground between his feet. Tad heard a huffing sound, like a dog sniffing for its owner.

Knowing that the ghost was about to step through the door, Tad impulsively threw the silk pouch. It landed with a soft thud next to the door.

Rice lifted the axe, the light spilling through the gap under the door. He slammed it down in fury, the flint-like reverberations on the floorboards rocking Tad's bed.

Then the shadows were gone.

Tad scrambled back until his body was flat against the wall and he could see the whole room. He snatched his phone from his pocket and called Kyle. After two rings, his friend spoke.

"Lemme guess," Kyle said. "He followed you."

"It's worse... They're worse away from the house!"

"Pete had it, too."

"Come get me...please! Please come get me before he comes back."

Kyle's startled breathing fizzed against the receiver for a few seconds. Since Tad was usually the calm and collected one out of the five housemates, his outburst had stunned his friend.

"All right," Kyle said after a beat. "We'll come. Be outside in fifteen minutes."

ELDON'S CAR crept up to the front doors of the hotel exactly thirteen minutes later. Kyle had begged him to give them a ride since neither he or Lance had a car. After what Eldon had experienced at the Victorian house, Kyle knew there was no way he could really refuse to offer Brackenby's residents a helping hand. The paranormal enthusiast had seen more in that one night than most ghost hunters saw in a lifetime, and although his expensive tech lay in bits in the boot of the car, he had excitedly told Kyle that it had been one of the greatest nights of his life.

Tad sprinted from the lobby. He dashed to the car and threw himself into the back with Lance. Kyle turned around in the passenger seat and gawped, astonished at seeing him so unravelled.

"Drive!" Tad yelled. "Just drive, whoever you are!"

Eldon stepped on the gas and headed back toward the house.

"Maybe we should get Cassie and Pete, too?" Lance suggested.

Tad nodded, furiously, sweat glistening on his cheeks as they passed by streetlights. "Get them. They're coming for us."

Lance patted his shoulder, looking as bewildered as Kyle was at seeing Tad hunched and shaking, sweat and tears dampening his face. Whatever had happened at the hotel, it was obvious the ghosts now had the strength to step up their game.

"Look..." Tad opened his trembling palm and showed them the small charm his grandparents had sent him from Japan. "See how it's started to fray all along the side?"

Kyle craned his neck from the front seat and paled at the sight of the silken bag. The talisman looked about twenty years older than it had when Tad had first pulled it from the tissue paper.

"That's what he did to it. That's what he would have done...to me. We have to go get the others."

"Marty only lives around the corner. Maybe we should swing by," Kyle agreed, giving directions to Eldon, who silently took on chauffeur duty.

They turned onto Martin's drive and found both him and Cassie standing outside Martin's house, screaming at each other in the road.

"What the fuck?" Lance opened the car door and jumped out.

Tad remained hunched in a ball, trembling. He looked like he was going through a bad trip, his eyes wide and glassy, flicking and darting, searching for an unseen threat. Tears streaked his cheeks.

Kyle leaned back and touched two fingers to Tad's knee. It was bouncing furiously up and down. "Hey, it's okay."

Tad shook his head, tightly, and screamed, "It's not okay. It's not okay, Kyle!"

"All right!" Kyle pulled his hand away. Steeling himself, he pushed open the car door. The sound of Cassie and Martin's argument assaulted his ears. Curtains were twitching in the neighbours' houses as they slyly watched the spectacle unfold. He shut the door and walked up to the rowing friends.

"You're acting crazy!" Martin yelled. He was only wearing knee length flannel shorts, shivering in the cold street.

"*I'm* acting crazy? You're the one who's full of shit!"

Lance stood to the side, watching, his palms extended in a helpless effort to calm them down. They hadn't even noticed him.

Kyle moved forward and stepped between them. "What the hell's going on?"

Cassie was furious, her hair tangling in front of her pinked cheeks, her whole body raising up and down as she breathed through gritted teeth. "This creep came on to me when I was asleep!"

"You weren't asleep!" Martin spun around on the spot and raked his hands through his hair in frustration. "You climbed on top of me, you psycho! Your eyes were open, and you were talking to me... What the hell was I supposed to think?"

"Convenient story, asshole!" Cassie screamed, but her anger gave way to sudden doubt, and she hitched a jolting breath.

Kyle looked at Cassie and spoke with wary softness. "You have been sleepwalking, Cass."

"You're calling me a liar?" she spat, scraping her sleeve over her mouth and returning to her angry stand-off.

"Fuck, no! I don't know what to think. But how long have you known Marty? He's never pulled shit like this before." Behind him, he heard Martin shuffle from one foot to the other.

"He's been following me to the pool!" Cassie suddenly accused, pointing her fist at him, her jumper hooked over her clenched fingers.

"I have not!" Martin hollered.

"Well, you keep turning up! What, have you been sleep-walking, too?"

Kyle turned to Martin, who blinked back at him in bemusement. He shrugged with exasperation. "I have no idea what's going on. Did she call you to come get her?"

"No. Something...happened to Tad."

"What happened to Tad?" Cassie stepped forward, worry overriding her fury.

"He's okay. He's in the car." Kyle gestured over his shoulder to Eldon's red Fiat. "Will you come home?"

"Gladly. Fuck you, Martin," Cassie spat, striding for the car with her arms swinging, her back ramrod straight.

As Kyle moved to follow her, Martin reached out and grabbed his elbow, a pained look on his face. "I honestly don't know what happened, Kyle. She was awake...but it wasn't *her*."

Kyle patted his arm. "I know. Don't worry. We'll sort it."

Lance gave Martin a sympathetic smile, then walked with Kyle back to the car. Kyle hopped in the front seat once more while Lance squeezed his broad frame into the back. Cassie was in the middle, her arm wrapped around a still trembling

Tad. He was refusing to respond to her probing questions, staring at his hands clenched in his lap. His shudders rocked the whole car.

"What about Pete?" Lance asked.

"Hey, I can't fit anyone else," Eldon protested.

Kyle looked at his phone. "He texted a while back saying he was going to sleep. I haven't heard from him since."

"He's got his own car with him, anyway. If he needs to come home, he will," Lance reasoned.

"Is anyone going to tell me exactly what the fuck is going on?" Cassie barked.

"We don't think it's safe to leave the house at night anymore," Kyle explained as Eldon drove out onto the main road. "Tad and Pete got attacked tonight. It got...physical. For them both."

"Jesus. But, even so, it's a stretch to think the ghosts are gonna attack us whenever we leave. Let's be sensible. After all, Lisa Vaughan didn't come to Martin's house."

Kyle said nothing, staring at the road markings as they sped back to Brackenby. He wasn't too sure if Cassie was right on that one. Not sure at all.

Chapter 14

Sometimes, people are worse

Cassie had few energy reserves for relay swim training that morning. Like her relationship with Martin, her already tenuous kinship with her team was growing more fractured. She had thought she'd built some bridges by inviting them to Kyle's welcome home party, but as usual she'd been too optimistic. Jonah had screwed the chance of her building any friendship with Tara, and the girl's misplaced hostility towards her was rubbing off on the rest of the relay team. A small part of her wanted to skip the group training altogether. Sometimes it didn't seem worth the hassle.

She steeled herself in front of her bedroom mirror, knowing that swimming usually took her to a place where she didn't have to think about personal problems. There was no way she would miss the chance to ditch the stress of her argument with Martin in a cloud of chlorine.

The household had been subdued after the events of the night before. She'd expected Tad to sleep in, but when she walked into the kitchen, he sat bolt upright at the table, his

159

long fingers wrapped around a mug of black coffee. "You feeling better, Ugly?"

"I'm waiting for Pete," Tad told her, anxiously checking his phone.

"He'll be all right."

Tad glanced up at her and shot a look that was so unlike him it startled her. It was a look she'd have expected from Lance. Even from herself. A churlish arch of an eyebrow that dared her to repeat what she'd said. It was a look that said, *Really? You really think he's okay?*

Instead of rising to it, she walked up behind him and wrapped him in a bearhug. His skin was cold to the touch and his clothes smelt like a book that had been left festering at the back of a damp old cupboard. "It's gonna be okay," she whispered into his back.

Tad just stared down at his coffee, saying nothing.

Cassie arrived at training wearing her swimsuit under her clothes. She tore off her sweater and jogging bottoms in the communal changing area, slinging them into her drawstring swim bag. She hooked her goggles strap over her wrist before tugging the swim hat over her head and securing it in place, tucking her hair into the rubber rim at the back.

"What reeks?" she heard a voice behind her hiss.

She turned, her heart plummeting. Three of the girls from her swim team were huddled in the corner, turned into each other conspiratorially, their noses wrinkled in distaste.

Cassie breathed in, instantaneously aware of the sour salt stench of the seaside that surrounded her.

Coach Morris yelled from the corridor, "Coming in in ten seconds! Make yourselves decent, ladies."

He appeared approximately three seconds later, striding

through the changing rooms with his clipboard propped against his forearm.

The girls snickered at something one of them had said, their narrowed eyes cutting in Cassie's direction, their lips turning down in sneers of disgust.

She blushed and ducked her head, wrapping her hands around her upper arms and hoping the smell would fade before Coach got a whiff of it.

"Right, guys, relay is going well. Smythe, we are so close to shaving that handover time down to perfection. Robinson, work on your crawl today. I need you strong for the night swim. Tara, for fuck's sake wake up on your push-off. The hippos in the tank at the zoo get away faster than you do."

"Hippos are one of the fastest predators in the wild, Coach," Tara pointed out, arching a perfectly tattooed brow.

"Not in the water they're not, smart arse," Morris shot back. "All right, get in the bloody pool and give me fifty lengths. That's your warm-up, so make it quick and don't get too comfy, ladies."

Cassie let the other girls file past her, trying to ignore the glances they shot in her direction. She was about to follow them when Coach stuck out his clipboard, blocking her path.

He gave two loud sniffs and wrinkled up his pitted nose. "Look, Thompson, I know you always like to be the best, but you're not supposed to have started the sea training yet."

"I haven't, sir."

"Bollocks. I can smell you a mile off. And a word to the wise, Cassandra. If you're going to try and pull the wool over the team's eyes, at least wash your fucking swimsuit before you come to the pool."

Cassie felt her cheeks burning, humiliated. "Coach, this costume's fresh out of the wash today. I haven't done a sea swim yet. I don't know what that smell is, but it isn't me."

Morris sighed through his nostrils, letting out a whistle from somewhere deep in his sinus. "You'll do what it takes to get ahead. But I didn't have you pegged as a liar."

Cassie winced, feeling a sick bubble of indignant humiliation burning in her chest. "Maybe the girls are pulling a prank. I swear, I've not been to the sea."

"You're not a team player. I know that, and it's fine. I let you train before and after hours because I know that's how you work best. But the Channel swim is a different kettle of fish. You all need to pull together. That means you need to start behaving like a member of this team. Otherwise, I'll have no choice but to pull you. Understand?"

Battling the sting of tears, Cassie chewed her inner lip and nodded, passing the coach and heading for the pool.

"Oh, Cassie?" he called.

She turned, hopeful for a reprieve.

"You're about ten laps behind the girls now. Don't think you're shirking out of it. You can give me fifty-five."

"Yes, Coach," Cassie grunted, pulling her goggles over her eyes and striding to the water's edge. The other girls were darting through the middle section of the pool, already in their stride. She sprang from the edge and felt the air blast from her lungs, the cold shock of the water magnified by her upset. She came to the surface and kicked, willing herself to become lost in the motion. Swimming always soothed her in the past, no matter what was going wrong. She couldn't let Lisa Vaughan ruin it for her now.

By the time she'd completed her fifty-five reps, the other girls were well on their way into relay manoeuvres. Cassie swam up to Jen Robinson and gave her the nod. "Count me in on this exchange," she smiled, treading water.

But when Jen received the baton, she turned and cut straight for Tara, letting out a whoop as she shoved the rod into Tara's hand and ducked out of the splash-back of her teammate launching herself forward.

Cassie swam to the side of the pool, her eyes stinging from chlorine. At least that was what she told herself.

She looked up at the row of glass windows, at the slowly rising sun that shone orange light over the car park. She couldn't wait to get in her car and head for home. Even if her home *was* haunted by malevolent spirits, it couldn't be any worse than this, she reasoned. Chilled and miserable from the lack of exertion in the cooled water, she stared longingly at her car. She blinked and squinted.

A figure stood by the front of the car, peering back at her.

Martin.

Angry, she pulled herself up and planted her ankle on the edge, hauling herself onto the rough tiles.

Coach blew his whistle. "Hey! We're not done here!"

"I have to go," Cassie called, hooking her fingers under the base of her suit and covering her ass as the team turned to watch her leave.

"I want to see you tomorrow at eight sharp, Cassie!"

Ignoring him, Cassie dashed to the changing rooms and gave herself a brisk towel rub, peeling off her swimsuit and getting into her clothes before she was completely dry. She stuffed her suit into her bag and plunged her wet feet into her trainers. The material felt tight and pinched her skin, but she wanted to catch Martin before he slinked away.

She didn't need to worry. She rushed out into the car park and saw him standing there, his hands stuffed deep in his pockets, his expression blank and his gaze fixed on the tarmac in front of his feet. A flare of anger snagged her throat, and she marched over to him. "What are you doing?"

He didn't answer for a moment, then sluggishly lifted his chin, and gave her a blank look. "Huh?"

"Drop the act! Why do you keep following me here?"

"I...I don't."

"You're standing by my car, Martin!"

He turned and regarded the vehicle as if he had only just noticed it. "I think I'm out on a walk."

"An early morning wander that happens to bring you two miles from your house?"

He blinked rapid lids over glassy eyes. "Yeah, I guess so."

Cassie stared back at him, suddenly sympathetic. "Look, I know I could have handled things better last night. You just took me by surprise, that's all. I love you, but not in a romantic way. I would never break the bond of our friendship or put it at risk. Hooking up would probably end in disaster. And I don't want to lose you."

"Okay." Martin gazed at her, slack jawed. The lights were on, but Martin certainly didn't seem to be at home.

"Well, I'm going home now. I had a shitty practice, and I don't have classes 'til later. You want a lift?"

"No, I'm good." Martin said in a breathy, dazed voice.

"Okay." Cassie moved to the car and tossed her bag into

the passenger footwell. She slid behind the wheel and was about to shut the door when Martin spoke again, still standing facing away from the car. "What did you say?"

"Give my regards to Pete," Martin said again, his words no longer breathy, but cold and void of timbre. He had turned his head a little, as though he were speaking to his shoulder, but all the same it felt as though he was glaring right at her.

"What the hell's that supposed to mean?" Cassie snapped.

But Martin was already walking away.

LANCE TUGGED open the heavy front door and blinked in surprise.

Jonah was leaning against the porch, looking apprehensive. He wore a studded leather jacket and torn grey jeans, a check shirt tied around his hips. He peered through his fringe, the tips of his hair now dyed lilac, and grinned, his shoulders dropping with evident relief when he saw it was Lance who had opened the door. "Hey, Cuz."

"What are you doing?"

Jonah sighed and tongued his lip-ring. Lance had never seen him looking so bashful. "Look, I know I've been a dick and I might not be welcome and all—"

"Don't be an idiot. I meant, why haven't you just let yourself in as usual?"

Jonah's eyes widened and reassurance showed in his expression. "Are we cool?"

"Of course we are. Are you coming in?"

Eyeing the hallway, Jonah hesitated. "Who's home?"

"I'm not sure. Cassie and Kyle are out. I think Tad's upstairs. Maybe a few ghosts knocking about." Lance pushed the door wide and stepped back to make room for his cousin.

"Very funny." Jonah ambled down the hallway and went into the kitchen. "Expecting me?"

"What?" Lance asked, then his eyes fell where Jonah was pointing, to the spare stool that seemed to have a mind of its own. It had been positioned directly behind Lance's chair. "Shit. Don't sit in it."

Jonah froze, arching an eyebrow. "What?"

"Just, sit in one of the others." Lance hurried to the rogue stool and picked it up by the seat. It felt ice cold, as if it had been pulled out of a freezer. He tried to ignore the tingling, chilled sensation in his fingertips and carried the chair to the far side of the kitchen. He was in half a mind to throw it out into the back yard. It was the sixth time that week the stool had appeared at the table. He now knew it definitely wasn't one of the housemates messing with him.

It was Anthony Pile. And, worst of all, Lance knew why he was doing it.

"Did I leave a lighter here the other night?" Jonah asked, helping himself to grapes from the fruit bowl.

"Yeah. Uh...Kyle has it, I think. He meant to catch you at uni and give it back."

"Where is he?"

"At his uncle, Caleb's. We've both got classes this afternoon, so I don't think he'll be back today. Sorry." Lance rubbed his hands together and sat down opposite his cousin, pushing his chilled fingers between his thighs to warm them up.

"It's okay. I have a spare, anyway. Hey, listen. I came over to say I'm sorry about everything."

Lance widened his eyes in surprise. Jonah didn't say sorry. That's not to say that he was a total ass. If he screwed up, he'd make it up to you in other ways. But an actual apology coming out of his mouth was something completely alien to him. "That's all right, bro."

Jonah held up his hands, his fingers heavy with silver rings. "No, I need to say this. I've been a dickhead to you and the guys. I don't know what it is. It's like, I spend any time in the house and I just get carried away. The whole ghost thing makes me angry sometimes, then I end up losing it. It's like a red mist coming down. I can't explain it, but I'm going to try and be better from now on. Okay?"

Lance smiled, nodding enthusiastically. "Thanks, man. I mean, you're fine. We've all been on edge lately. Whatever's happened, people will get over it. Don't worry."

"Well, so long as we're cool." Jonah held out his fist, and Lance bumped it with his own.

"We're cool. I like your hair, by the way."

Jonah snatched at a few strands, twisting them in front of his eye and peering at the colour. "It's not bad, is it? It's for the big gig on Saturday. You're still coming, aren't you?"

Lance opened his mouth to answer then turned as the floorboards creaked behind him. Pete came into the kitchen, wearing his red hoodie with the hood up, his face pale against the bright scarlet.

Pete gave Jonah a steely glare.

Jonah made a show of trying to peek into the hallway behind him. "Is Gaia with you?"

"No, she's not," Pete gritted out.

Lance caught his cousin's eye and held up his hands as if to say, *What the hell happened to you not being a dick anymore?*

Jonah visibly struggled to bite back a smirk and cleared his throat as Pete moved to the sink and poured himself a glass of water. "Anyway, Pete. I'm glad you're here, actually. I was saying to Lance I feel pretty crappy about being a dick lately. I just wanted to tell you all I'm really sorry."

Pete stared at him over the rim of the glass and took three long swallows. Then he set the glass down and swiped his hand over his mouth. Ignoring Jonah, he looked to Lance. "Is this a possession?"

Lance shrugged his shoulders. "I think he means it."

"I do!" Jonah cried. "Look, I hope we're cool. I am truly sorry I've been an asshole. That's all I wanted to say."

"All right." Pete blinked slowly, suddenly looking exhausted. "I'm going for a lie down."

Jonah watched him trudge for the stairs then frowned at Lance. "Well, it wasn't quite the show of forgiveness I was hoping for."

"He's not feeling good. Leave him alone," Lance warned. He reached out and took one of the grapes. "Thanks though, for apologising. I know he didn't say it, but I think you'll be good now."

"If I can refrain from being a douche for five minutes."

"Well, there is that."

"Did you say Tad's home?"

"He is, but he's upstairs working on his big pitch."

"Big pitch?"

"You know. He's got his interview with the grant people

for his sewage machine in a couple of days. I don't think he wants to be disturbed. Sorry."

Jonah rapped his knuckles on the table and stood up. "Can't say I didn't try. I'll let you get ready for class. Hey, tell the others I was here and wanted to apologise, will you? If you all come to the gig on Saturday, I'll say it in person."

"We'll be there." Lance followed him down the hall, gave his cousin a hug at the door, and closed it behind him.

Lance moved back to the kitchen and froze in the doorway. The spare stool was back at the table, placed next to where Jonah had just been sitting.

Lance backed away and grabbed his rucksack. He'd been idly reading about the Hellfire Club that morning, trying to gain a better understanding of his ghost and its motives. One of the sentences he'd read about them had sent chills down his spine. The members of the club always added an extra seat to their table. Knowing this was a Hellfire Club custom made Lance certain it was Anthony Pile who was messing with their kitchen furniture. But the reason why he was doing it shook him to the core.

In the club, they always set out an extra seat for the Devil.

And, if the rumours were true, sometimes he accepted the invitation.

CHAPTER 15
GHOSTS

Kyle watched as Caleb picked up a box and dropped it in the middle of the floor, a plume of dust wafting up into his face. Caleb spluttered and wiped his hands on his jeans before pinching his irritated eyes.

Getting down onto his knees beside his uncle, Kyle peered into the cardboard box. It looked as though someone had run through a thrift store, scooping items from the shelves at random. Trinkets, fabric, crockery, and notebooks were stacked higgledy-piggledy in the box. "What is all this?"

With his hangdog eyes growing red and weepy from the dust, Caleb turned to his nephew and held out a palm to the box in proud presentation. "This, my intrepid, haunted, little sidekick, is a box full of possessions which belonged to one Hestor Morello."

"Lucius's friend, right? Do you really think any of this will be useful?"

Caleb exhaled, his shoulders hunching. "Just when I think you've got it all in hand, you go and surprise me by being dumb as a pile of elephant shit. Hestor Morello was *close* to Lucius Holgrove. In fact, if you'd bothered to read any of the newspaper reports properly, you'd know that she was the person who provided a statement to the press after his death. A statement informing them that he'd taken the long hop to sea."

Kyle thought back to the death announcement. "It's ringing a bell, now."

"Well, why would Hestor write in her own diary that Lucius went back to the house and never came out, if she knew he'd jumped off a cliff?"

Kyle stared at his uncle, baffled. "That...makes no sense."

Caleb nodded. "She's the key to learning more about what really happened in that house. Like I told you, I've had my eye on Hestor's house for a while now. All of Hestor's remaining belongings have been in storage in the attic. The last remaining family member is no longer with us, and the guys clearing the house let me swing by to take it off their hands."

"You're a genius."

"I am. This box might contain the secrets of exactly what happened before Lucius decided to get fitted for his wooden onesie."

"You really think they knew each other that well?"

"It was scandalous for the time, but widow Morello was getting more than psychic readings from our favourite distant relative. Check this." Caleb snatched an envelope from the top of the box and passed it to Kyle. "I didn't have time to go through much in the attic, but this letter showed me that the crap in here is exactly what we might need."

Kyle thumbed back the lip of the envelope and slipped the folded paper from inside. The writing was scrawled in dense black ink, familiar to him from seeing Lucius's signature in the guidebooks. He read out loud. "*My dearest Hestor, I fear that running from the house was a testament to a true weakness deep inside me. I long to return to put right the wrongs I caused but know in my heart that there should be only one path for me. Without your strength and guidance, I fear I would go mad. I grow tired of the sea, which does nothing more than bring me closer to Lisa Vaughan and her dreaded pirates, and further from you, my dear. I shall return to you Tuesday next. Keep me in your thoughts, as I do you in mine. Always, Lucius.*"

"See? They were banging." Caleb sniffed and rummaged in the box. He plucked out a black and white photo with bent, yellowed edges, pushing it along the floor towards Kyle. It showed a serious-looking woman in a black button-front dress and feather-plumed hat. She was gazing into the distance, past the photographer, but her small eyes looked shrewd. She had a sculpted face, with two dark hollows showing under her prominent cheekbones and lips that arched up into a steep cupid's bow. Caleb pulled a stack of papers from the box. "I've not looked at any of the rest of it yet. Thought I'd wait for you. Two heads better than one, and all that."

"This is awesome," Kyle said, excitedly leaning forward to snatch at another letter. "Shit, wait! I can't stay long. I have a lecture at three."

"Bunk off."

"I can't. It'll go on my record."

"Get a friend to sign you in." Caleb glared.

"It's not like that anymore. It's an automated system. I have to swipe my student card... I really can't miss this one. It relates directly to my thesis. If I miss it my tutor will ask questions."

"All right, don't cry about it. Go on then. Fuck off and leave me to it."

"I'm sorry! If I could stay and help, I would."

Caleb sighed, staring at the mis-matched objects in the box, relenting. "It's okay. It'll take me a while to sort the crap from the chaff anyway."

Kyle smiled, gratefully, then hesitated. "Wait. Isn't it the chaff that's the crap and the wheat that's—"

"Piss off, Kyle. I'll call you if I find anything."

LANCE SAT IN ECONOMICS CLASS, waiting for his lecturer to begin. The professor was busy setting something up on the table at the front, his back to the class. Lance was eager for the lesson to start, his last one of the day. After the crazy night they'd had, first with Eldon and the spirit voices and then with Tad and Cassie, he really needed to distract himself. Even if it was with some boring information about economics. His mind was overloaded with facts from his research of The Hellfire Club, and he was almost looking forward to losing himself in his study notes. Since Professor Hedges was still busying himself with the props on the table, Lance figured he had enough time to check how his latest social media post was performing. He snuck his phone up onto the desktop and laid it flat. The screen lit up, showing reams of messages, the tiny pink Insta icon beside each one.

It's obviously fake.

Why waste your time with such a shit scare post.

My little sister can make scarier graphics than that.

Puzzled, he swiped his thumb and opened his Insta feed, tapping the picture that was gaining all the traction. It was innocuous enough. He had taken it the previous night before Eldon had arrived, sitting at his desk with his back to the mirror. His hair had been sitting well for once, a cool kiss-curl hanging down into his eye. He'd taken advantage and snapped a couple of shots, not thinking too much of it. Selfies were fillers, after all. Useful for when he couldn't think of anything to post about.

He frowned and moved to the comments, elated to see how many there were.

Dude, sick mask.

Why are people so obsessed with faking hauntings nowadays?

Someone's desperate to get on Slapped Ham.

Is that your girlfriend? I'd bone her.

Lance felt heat rising up his cheeks. Were they talking about him? About the way he looked? He felt sudden hot shame and swallowed. His thumb hovered, ready to delete the selfie that had backfired so badly.

But that's when he saw it.

Just above his shoulder was what looked like a smudge on the mirror at first glance. He pinched at the screen and flicked his fingers apart, zooming in on the image. He almost dropped the phone. In his bedroom mirror, in front of the reflection of his blue bedding, a human face leered out of the shot. It was smeared, surrounded by glowing yellow lines streaked with red. But in the centre of the smudge was a clear feminine face. Its eyes and mouth were wide open in what looked like a cry of anguish.

Another comment popped up as he stared.

Don't you all see the little boy, too? Standing by the bedside table.

Holding his breath, he swiped across the image and found the reflection of his nightstand. The boy had his back to the camera, his dark hair and the curve of his right ear visible in the shadows. He wore a long white nightshirt.

"Right, eyes on me, everyone!" Professor Hedges called.

Lance flinched, relieved to be pulled away from the image of the ghosts in his own bedroom. Just as he knew when Anthony Pile was around, an insistent voice spoke to him, telling him who he had been looking at; Grant's young son and their maid—the innocent bystanders who'd been slaughtered at the original séance. It always angered Lance that they'd died, too. That neither the boy nor the maid had known what was going on in the dining room until it was too late. He supposed it was one of the reasons why he made sure to be in the heart of the action when it came to Kyle's investigations. He'd sooner get hurt because of something he'd chosen to do, rather than being a victim of circumstance.

He slipped the phone into his bag, sick anxiety rolling through him in increasing waves.

His forehead itched under the rolled-up brim of his beanie hat, but he didn't want to take it off. His unruly hair embarrassed him at the best of times. But today Abina Khumalo had chosen to sit at the desk right next to him. No matter how shaken he was, he'd never be too distracted not to notice Abina. She was the most exotic person he'd ever seen.

The exchange student stretched her long limbs, the scent of jasmine drifting by his desk. The band that held her bleached dreadlocks rested on her shoulder and sent the long, stiff tendrils of hair stretching towards him like fingers. He glanced at them when she flipped them back over her shoulder, shooting him a warm smile. Heat scorched his cheeks, and the scratching sensation of sweat broke out under the brim of his hat. He pushed his fingertip under the woollen band and dug his nail into the skin, wishing he didn't have such dumb, ugly hair and that he could take the damn thing off and be done with it.

Hedges was in the middle of a rant about the dollar and the pound and the historical events that had caused the most impact in the last century. He'd painstakingly stacked about forty pound coins in three teetering towers beside a stack of dollar notes. Abina picked up her pen as if she were about to take notes, but instead, she slotted the barrel between her index and middle finger and began to tap the nib against her pad. Lance knew she smoked—had often seen her leaning against the large oak tree near the IT centre. She'd close her eyes as she drew from the butt and inhaled, holding the smoke for a long time before she gently released it through her nostrils. He guessed she was daydreaming about getting out of class to have a smoke. In answer to his theory, she brought the pen to her mouth and tapped it against her lips. Again, she caught him watching.

He quickly looked to the front of the room.

And nearly fell off his chair.

The lecturer was still ranting about the pound, using the

pile of coins to emphasise his points. He pinched one of the discs between his thumb and forefinger, waving it around for emphasis.

Pile stood in the corner, watching. Or, at least, that's what Lance thought it was. There was a grey shadow hovering, like a smudge on a negative, like the smoke that plumed at the sides of the oak tree when Abina smoked. The shadow became solid in the middle, expanding. The smell of burning began to fill the room. In the centre of the shadow, a small spark of yellow flame began to glow.

"I just want to show you a couple of slides a second..." Hedges stepped to the whiteboard and reached up, stretching for the toggle to pull down the projector screen. He stood inches from where Pile had now almost fully materialised, the white smoke darkening and thickening into hanging black robes. "Damn it, I need someone tall. Lance? Would you mind pulling this down for me?"

Lance hesitated. He did not want to go anywhere near to the mass standing next to where the projection screen was rolled up a fraction too high for his lecturer to reach. Attracted to the coins, Pile slid closer to the desk between the teacher and the class.

"Lance?"

He realised he had been holding his breath. He began to clamber to his feet. Abina watched him curiously, then looked pointedly in the direction he had been staring, right at the ghost, not that she could see him. He felt sweat bloom around his collar, the heat of his forehead tickling every hair follicle under the heavy hat. Concentrating on his legs, he made his way to the front of the room, to where Hedges waited with an expectant expression on his face. The lecturer tossed the coin straight up and caught it with his other hand.

Pile jerked towards Hedges, lurching for the currency. Lance felt the cold chill of his ghostly presence as it slid through the space between him and the whiteboard. The smoky scent of struck matches grew stronger.

"Is someone burning something out there?" Hedges asked. He strode over to the windows a moment before the moving mass of Pile's ghost touched him. He peered out, then closed the ventilation grate.

Lance hurried forward, reaching up to snag the projector screen toggle in his fingers and giving it a firm yank. Pile was now on his left-hand side. The spirit turned and began to flow closer to him.

The screen didn't budge.

Lance tugged the thin coil of rope again, panic rising inside him. He could feel the eyes of the class on him, knew he must look a little odd, hot and bothered and tugging frantically at the screen. Exposed.

Pile edged ever closer.

The rope made a small sizzling sound, and on his next tug, snapped off in Lance's fist. A few of his classmates stifled laughter. He turned his hand over, the white cord draped across his palm, the two singed edges still faintly smoking.

Hedges looked at Lance, unimpressed.

Pile gave a pompous laugh.

Unbalanced, Lance staggered forward, his thighs ramming into the lecturer's table. The three piles of coins teetered, tumbling onto the desktop.

Directly opposite him, on the other side of the table, Pile materialised.

Lance let out an audible gasp of fear. Although the hood hung down over most of the ghoul's face, Lance could see Pile's broad chin and the curve of a sneer on his lips. The top of the hood stuck out in points, and Lance could see silhouetted horns beneath the material of the cape. The candle had vanished, and Pile lifted his arms to hover momentarily over the coins. Then, he swiped his hands down and back, scattering the pounds behind him.

They shot out into the room of students like shrapnel. Dollars fluttered around the desk like confetti.

"Lance!" Hedges protested. "What the hell?"

Shaken, Lance tripped over his own feet as the room erupted into shouts and swearing from classmates who had been hit by the flying coins.

Sweat now pouring down his face, he grabbed his bag, snatched off his hat, and ran for the door.

"Lance! Get back here right now and explain yourself!" Hedges yelled.

But Lance had already fallen on the door handle, his sweaty palms sliding over the smooth metal nob. He struggled to open it, eventually hoisting his shirt over his hand and twisting with full force. The door shot open, and he stumbled out into the corridor. He made a dash for the bathroom at the end of the hall.

Hunching over the sink, he ran the cold water at full blast and stuck his wrists under the flow, breathing heavily. His sodden hat and the coil of burnt rope rested on the porcelain. He splashed his face, keeping his eyes clear of water so he could see if Pile had decided to follow him. But the bathroom was empty. The "Hellfire wanker", as Jonah had once called him, must have decided his little stunt was enough of a kick for one afternoon.

He hid in one of the stalls and waited out the class, not wanting to see any of his classmates. Truth be told, he didn't want to see any of them ever again. He was humiliated. Pile had made him look like a maniac. He'd hurt some of them. Not enough to need medical attention, he didn't think, but he'd bet there would be a few bruises on his classmates' cheeks and arms. Enough damage for him to find himself in serious trouble.

And there was nothing he could do about it.

The class had seen him ram into the table, placing his hands down by the coins the split-second before Pile sent them flying. They had been looking at his face when he gasped. Nobody would have been watching his hands. None of them would have seen that he didn't actually move. That the coins flew of their own accord.

What would they think of him?

Sitting on the closed toilet seat, his chin in his palm, Lance ran through a few viable explanations. He could tell Hedges that he guessed someone could have slipped something into his drink. Or that he'd accidentally taken something. Perhaps he could claim a reaction to a prescription drug? But no, the university would want proof from his doctor, and Lance hadn't even had a reason to visit his GP in a good few years. A running joke between his housemates was to blame every injury on a skateboarding incident, after a series of scrapes and cuts that had occurred when the group as schoolkids had been up to no good. But that wouldn't work here, Lance knew. There was no bump on the head that could explain away the strange scene in class.

He waited until doors slammed behind the next set of classes and the corridor outside fell silent. Nobody entered the bathroom while he was in it, but he was glad he'd hidden, in any case.

When he was certain the coast was clear, he headed outside. The air was crisp and wintery, the pavement damp from an earlier burst of rain. Behind the oak tree, a plume of white billowed.

Shit. He hunched his shoulders and ducked his head, hoping she wouldn't notice him.

"I guess you saw a ghost, my friend," came her voice, deep and playful.

Lance froze, then turned. Abina was leaning against the wet bark, her smooth skin glossy in the glow of the streetlights that had just sparked to life. She lifted her cigarette and took a drag, lip gloss pinkening the tip.

"It's okay. Your secret is safe with me." She grinned and tapped the side of her nose, the cigarette tip looming dangerously close to her eye.

He swallowed, struck dumb. He wanted to blurt out, *You saw it, too?*

But then she laughed, a deep, belly laugh that in normal circumstances would have thrilled him. She shook her head. "That was some crazy shit right there. Best thing I seen since I came here. You want my advice? Where I'm from, we don't sit around and wait for a ghost to mess with us. We call it out. Never give it the upper hand and you'll stay one step ahead."

Still struggling to respond, Lance stood in silence as she tossed the butt under her shoe and twisted her toes to grind out the flame. Without another word, she slung her backpack over her shoulder and strode away.

Something prodded his back.

Lance yelped and twisted round in fright.

Kyle held up his hands in defence, then reached out to steady him. "Whoa, it's just me. You okay?"

Lance opened his mouth to speak, but relief at seeing someone who knew what was really going on overwhelmed him. He felt his lip tremble and he closed his mouth, shaking his head.

"All right, it's fine. Let's just go home," Kyle suggested, stepping to his side and keeping pace.

They walked in silence for a while, Kyle allowing Lance to pull himself together without pushing him. When they were halfway home, Lance managed to explain what had happened in the class. First, the terrifying photo of the ghosts in his room, then Pile's scene. Kyle listened, a grim expression on his face.

Lance was finally glad of his hat. He felt as though everyone was staring at him, although he knew it was a ridiculous assumption. But the idea of having a public outburst, of standing up in front of his class and having a tantrum out of nowhere, was so unlike him that he found the shame overwhelming. It might have been better if it really *was* him who had done it. But somehow the outrage of knowing Pile had set him up to look stupid made it worse. It was one thing to be haunted, to be made to feel afraid. It was another to be made a fool of. He pulled the collar of his coat up to meet his ears and walked looking down at the pavement.

"I'm going to ask Caleb over tonight. Hopefully, he'll have found some more answers today," Kyle said, chewing on the side of a hangnail, his words muffled.

"Do you think he can really help us?"

Kyle shrugged. "It's better than nothing. He's got letters written by Lucius. If anyone knows how to defeat the ghosts, it's the guy who put them in the house in the first place."

"I'm sad for the maid and the kid. Do you think they've always been there? Or do you think we brought them back at Halloween, too?"

Kyle winced. "Christ, I hope not. It makes sense, though. If Lucius is here, then it's not just the bad ones who came back."

Lance stared at the damp, leaf-strewn ground, feeling dejected and hopeless. Causing a scene in class wasn't everybody's idea of a worst nightmare. In fact, there were plenty of kids he'd known throughout his education who'd thrived on it. But he wasn't one of them. Embarrassment had completely knocked his confidence. Perhaps that's what Pile had wanted all along. He looked at Kyle, an idea suddenly dawning on him. "They're haunting us using our fears."

Kyle peered at him strangely. "Yeah."

"No. I mean, they're ghosts and it's scary and all, but they're attacking us where we're most vulnerable. Take Pile embarrassing me today. Someone like Jonah wouldn't give a shit about it. But for me, it's giving me crippling anxiety now, just thinking about going back to class."

"Okay."

"Pete can't go walking anymore. He can't get out and about, where he used to clear his head and feel free. Again, none of us would really care if we couldn't hike. But Pete? You've seen how dejected he's getting. He hates being stuck on the ground."

Kyle furrowed his brow. "Maybe."

Lance snapped his fingers. "Cassie! What ghost has she got? The one who fucks about with water. Where does Cassie feel safest of all?"

"Water."

"It's a fucking onslaught, man. A mental and emotional onslaught. They haven't hurt us physically because they don't have to. This is so much worse." Lance's attention was drawn to the local shop, where three of his earlier classmates were huddled outside. "Oh, shit."

Kyle followed his gaze. He watched the students' reactions at seeing Lance, the group gawping and whispering. "Just keep walking," Kyle instructed, protectively switching sides on the pavement, creating a buffer between them.

"I feel like I'm back at school. Like I'm thirteen again."

"It'll be all right. It'll blow over. Someone else will do something stupid in no time. Jonah, probably." Kyle smiled at his own joke. He peered over his shoulder at the shop.

"Are they following?" Lance asked, his heart pounding.

"Nah. They're not even looking this way."

Lance knew Kyle sometimes wondered if social media was the best choice of potential career for him. As nervous as Lance got around people in a work environment, Kyle often pointed out that there was nowhere on earth more savage than the comments section of an online post. On days like this, Lance thought he might be right.

THEY TRUDGED up the driveway of Brackenby house. Kyle raised his eyes to the windows. Tad's bedroom and the bathroom window were positioned at the front of the house. He kind of expected to see Rice or one of the other ghosts staring down at them, but Tad's curtains were drawn, and the bathroom window was empty.

In the hallway, Lance took off his hat and tossed it amongst the shoes at the foot of the coat rack. His hair looked insane, flat on top but corkscrewing out in all directions around the nape of his neck. He raked his fingers through it, fluffing up the unusually greasy-looking curls. He looked exhausted but headed straight for the kitchen. "I'll make something good for Caleb."

Kyle pulled out his phone, appreciative. "I'll invite him over. Thanks bro."

He ducked into the empty living room and flung himself backwards onto the couch. Kicking off his Vans, he pressed the phone to his ear. He stared at the ceiling as it rang three times.

Caleb answered when the fourth ring began to chime. "What?"

He was starting to get used to his uncle's gruff manner, but it still threw him off sometimes. "Uh— Hey, Caleb. It's Kyle."

"All right? How was your precious class?"

Kyle chuckled. "Boring. I'd much rather have been looking through Hestor's things with you."

"Well, tough shit then, isn't it?"

Kyle sat up, regretting his decision not to stay at his uncle's more than ever. He wondered if Caleb would decline his invitation out of spite, so he blurted it out, asking if he'd come over to eat with them that night.

"I suppose you'll be wanting me to bring Hestor's stuff?" Caleb sniffed.

"Did you find anything useful?" He had tried, but failed to sound disinterested.

"You could say that." Caleb tantalizingly rustled some papers.

"So, will you come?"

After the longest pause, Caleb finally relented. "What time do you want me?"

CHAPTER 16
BE OUR GUEST

At seven-thirty, Kyle opened the heavy front door. Caleb stood on the top step, shoulders hunched and arms hanging, his back straining under a heavy-looking rucksack. He wore the same clothes he'd been wearing earlier—oversized jeans that were torn from overuse, not through fashion, and a stained T-shirt with a faded picture of Superman on the front. His khaki military jacket was slung through the straps of his rucksack, and the hairs on his arms stood up straight in a sea of goose bumps.

"Gonna let me in, or what?" Caleb said.

Kyle stood back and let him pass, the scent of cigarettes and old paperwork wafting down the hall. Caleb headed straight into the kitchen and shook off the rucksack, plonking it down heavily on the table Lance had just laid with neat sets of cutlery and the household's best plates.

"This your boyfriend?" Caleb asked Kyle, pointing at Lance when he turned from the stove.

Kyle laughed, shaking his head. "Housemate. This is Lance. Lance, Caleb."

Lance wiped his hand on his jeans and held it out for Caleb to shake. He seemed brighter for cooking, Kyle noted, unsure whether the healthy flush on Lance's cheeks and the gleam in his eye was from the heat of the pans or from the contentment that being in the kitchen brought him.

"Pleasure." Lance gave Caleb a tight smile, eyeing the rucksack.

Kyle stepped forward and lifted the bag, diplomatically gesturing in the direction of the dining room. "We're eating first, but we'll spread these out on the big table after. There's more room in there." He carried the bag through to the next room and set it down on one of the chairs. He was itching to take a peek inside, but from the looks of it, Lance was just about ready to serve.

He ducked his head back into the kitchen. "Should I grab the others?"

"Please." Lance was ladling his burrito mix from a pan into a serving dish. He'd placed a pile of wraps on the table and prepared a mixed leaf salad and some rice for the housemates to mix and match as they wished. Caleb had popped a beer and was sat in Pete's chair, looking as though he'd never moved out of the house in the first place.

Kyle clambered up the stairs and stood between Cassie and Pete's doors. "Guys? Lance has made burritos."

Cassie darted out a moment later, her face daubed with white gobs of spot cream. "Brilliant! I'm starving."

Kyle grabbed her arm as she passed. "Cass, you might want to wipe your face. Caleb's here."

She looked puzzled for a second, then touched a smear of cream and swore. "I forgot. Hang on."

She disappeared back into her room. Kyle wandered

down the corridor and rapped a knuckle against Tad's door. "Food's up!"

No answer.

Tad was a light sleeper, and Kyle couldn't hear any music coming from his room. Perhaps he'd gone out, he reasoned. He was about to turn away when he hesitated. A sinking feeling plummeted through his stomach. He reached out and yanked on the door handle, pushing it open.

Tad was sitting upright at his desk opposite the door, his laptop open in front of him. His hands were resting in his lap.

"Dude?" Kyle called.

Tad continued to stare forward, his back poker straight.

Kyle felt a tingle of panic in his throat. He stepped forward. "Tad?"

Tad jumped to, snatching off his headphones and turning away from the YouTube video he had been immersed in. He looked startled. "What's up?"

Relief swam through Kyle. He laughed, feeling foolish at his overreaction. "Food's out. Caleb's here."

"Ah, great." Tad slammed his laptop closed and tossed the headphones onto the lid.

Cassie had emerged from her room, face wiped clean and her baggy T-shirt replaced with a ribbed long-sleeved jersey. She was hovering in Pete's doorway, swinging from the jamb, her fingers gripping the lip above her head. "C'mon, lazy-bones." She grinned over her shoulder at Kyle. "He's coming."

Kyle heard the squeaking sounds of Pete's mattress as he hauled himself up. He appeared in the doorway, bleary-eyed, the fading crisscross pattern of a crumpled pillow embedded in his cheek. He wore black sweatpants and no shirt.

"You all right, man?" Kyle asked.

Pete grunted, ducking as Cassie dropped her hand from the door to swipe her palm over his head.

Kyle gestured to his bare chest. "My uncle's here, if you wanna put some clothes on."

Pete grunted again and headed for the stairs.

"That's a no," Cassie informed Kyle, chirpily. She traipsed down the stairs after Pete, a spring in her step.

"You've cheered up a bit," Tad noted. "Made up with Marty?"

Cassie looked up at him and beamed. "Yes, as a matter of fact. I'm going over to his place tomorrow night. We're gonna work it all out."

"That's good."

Kyle followed his friends down the spice-scented hallway. There was an air of casual calm around them, and he savoured the moment. What with Lance's mood lifting, Cassie buoyant at the prospect of making up with her best friend, and Kyle's own relief after thinking something had been wrong with Tad, the world seemed to have reset itself. Perhaps it was something to do with Caleb being there. Regardless of his caustic manner, Caleb had been a resident of the house before and had managed to get out without an attachment. There was a chance Caleb was the key to the oppression waning, at least for that moment.

The housemates milled into the kitchen, greeting Kyle's uncle. Pete looked thrown that someone new was sitting in his usual seat, but Cassie amiably pulled out her own chair for him. She took the spare stool that Lance had squeezed into a tight nook between himself and Tad.

Caleb didn't comment on Pete's naked torso, but his eyes widened when he got a good look at Tad sitting down. He slyly pointed, mouthing to Kyle, "Is *that* your boyfriend?"

Kyle pretended he couldn't understand, grabbing a heated wrap and slopping a ladle of meat and beans into the centre. Lance had set out a plate of grated cheese, and he tossed two handfuls onto the mixture, ignoring the salad completely.

For the first time in a while, the dinner table felt light and at ease, talk of the ghosts forgotten as the housemates quizzed Caleb about his new home and how it compared to Brackenby House. It was as though Caleb could sense the need for the group to have a rare evening without any ghost talk, and he never raised the topic. Instead, he told them amusing anecdotes about DIY issues around the house, old girlfriends, and his time as a roadie for several high-profile rock bands. He listened carefully when each of the housemates told him about themselves, and Kyle sat back and watched his usually gruff and sometimes intimidating uncle morph into the perfect dinner guest.

When they had finished eating, they complimented Lance on the food, and Tad volunteered to clean up. Pete slinked off back to bed, and Cassie announced that she was going to do her *homework*, holding up the first two fingers of each hand in quotation marks, meaning she was going to go and watch a Netflix crime documentary in her room. Lance hung back in the kitchen and helped Tad with the cleaning, even though he'd already spent so much time cooking. Kyle guessed Lance was doing everything in his power to keep himself distracted. He knew that as soon as his friend went to his room alone, he wouldn't be able to stop thinking about the events at the university earlier on in the day.

Kyle grabbed two beers from the fridge and gestured towards the room next door.

Caleb scraped his chair back and followed him into the hall, saying, "Thanks for the meal, Lance. It was good to meet you all."

Kyle grinned to himself as they sat together at the large dining table.

"What?" Caleb asked, giving him a funny look.

"I dunno. I've just never seen you act like that before."

"Act like what?"

"On your best behaviour."

"Fuck off," Caleb sputtered, pink creeping up his neck, but Kyle could tell that he was pleased at the observation. Caleb hauled the rucksack onto the tabletop and began to extract the contents, spreading out the pages with tobacco-stained fingers. "Can we concentrate on the matter at hand, please?"

"Fine."

Kyle fought away a smile and reached out to grab a photo that spun across the slick varnished tabletop. He turned it over and found himself looking down at his great-uncle, Lucius. Lucius stood in a garden, his handsome face tilted up to the sun. He wore a loose white shirt, the top few buttons undone. The skin of his chest was visible in a gaping V. It was unusual to see an old black and white photo depicting such a relaxed scene. It almost looked like a movie shot.

"I don't see a family resemblance." Caleb sneered,

looking at the picture of the attractive Victorian, then eyeing Kyle with scepticism.

"You're a fine one to talk!"

"No need to get personal about it."

"But you just..." Kyle knew better than to challenge his relative's one-sided logic. He let out a grunt of frustration and shook himself. "Forget it. Show me what you've found."

Caleb riffled through the pages and laid out a few select letters. They were yellowed with age, the folds ingrained so deeply into the paper that the sides sprang up, primed to refold with muscle memory. Lucius's beautiful, looping writing spidered over the pages, the quill ink browned with time, splotches spattering the paragraphs. "Lucius talks about his psychic powers. A lot. He's wrestling with his abilities and the fact that he managed to save himself, but all the other people at the séance were killed."

Kyle reached for one of the letters and squinted, trying to familiarise himself with the outdated script. He read the letter aloud. "*What does it mean that I have the power to control a monster such as Po, yet I watched him tear a man asunder before my very eyes. What might God have in store for me if I allow myself to embrace the gift he has given me, rather than succumbing to the fear of it all.*"

"Heavy stuff." Caleb grunted. "Here, read this." Caleb pushed a second letter at Kyle and tapped the bottom paragraph.

Kyle cleared his throat and started reading. "*My darling, I fear that in being close to you I expose you to a darkness you would never have considered to be of this world had I not come into your life. In summoning and disposing of true evil, I* wonder how much devilment is cast into my soul. I fear what will become of me once my time on earth is come to end."

The two relatives sat and stared down at the picture of the smiling young man. Lucius's words lingered heavy in the room. The same room in which he had caused the violent deaths of Grant and his guests a hundred and fifty years prior.

"He's so conflicted." Kyle experienced a wave of compassion for the man. "I can't imagine how he must have felt."

"Have you had any more contact with him? Here, in the house, I mean?"

"Not really. I don't know. I don't even know if it is him. He's not shown himself the way the evil spirits do. It could be that he's not able to."

"A bit ironic if the person who had the power to summon and erase the spirits in the first place is now trapped in a house with them all and can't do anything about it."

"Perhaps that's what he meant when he worried what would happen to his soul. If he is here, it's got to be a bad sign for him...right?"

Caleb shrugged. "I don't know if I believe in Heaven. But I'd rather everything just be black forever than to be stuck between the living and the dead. It freaks me out."

The pair gave a chilled shudder.

"Is it just me, or did it get really cold in here?" Kyle asked.

Somewhere below them in the cellar, a loud thud sounded.

Caleb set sharp eyes on Kyle. "That still happening?"

Kyle gave a slow nod and reached for another letter.

"It's Po, you know. Slamming about down there."

"I know," Kyle admitted, carefully peeling open the pages of the fragile letter in his hands. This one was different than the others, the paper finer, the writing looping and small.

"I saw him once."

Kyle snapped his head up. "You saw Po?"

Caleb shuffled in his seat, his cheeks pinking over his tangled greying beard. "I think I did, anyway. I thought it was a fucking rhino or something. Thought bloody King Kong had started bunking out behind the shelves."

"Wait, you actually saw him? Physically saw him?"

Caleb swigged at his beer and rubbed his eyes. "Look, you know what it's like when you see something in this house. It comes in a flash, then you spend the next few hours convincing yourself what you saw couldn't possibly be real. But sometimes I get little flashbacks to it. He was standing at the back of the cellar, clear as day, wearing a little He-Man outfit."

"What were his eyes like?"

"Not anatomically correct."

"What did you do?"

"Got the lightbulb I was after and went back up the stairs. He didn't move. But later that night, I heard a lot of noises, like..." He pointed to the floor, indicating the thump they'd just heard. "I think he was upset I'd been down there. As if he wanted everyone to know it was his spot. Can't blame him, being stuck down there for nearly two-hundred years."

"But I thought it was our séance that brought them out? I thought they hadn't shown themselves to you when you lived here?"

Caleb looked down at the table. "It was only that once. And just because your séance made them stronger, it doesn't mean they haven't always been hanging around."

Under their feet, the cellar shelving gave a scrape, the contents rattling on the shelves. Kyle held the letter in trembling fingers. "Maybe we should stop talking about him."

Caleb opened his mouth, his expression momentarily defiant. Then he closed it again, relenting. Kyle guessed that even his uncle could feel the shift in the house. The immediate danger of the ghosts now that Kyle had allowed them to break through whatever banishing spell Lucius had placed over them.

"This one wasn't written by Lucius." Kyle pointed to the lettering.

Caleb stretched his neck and peered at it. "Oh, yeah. That's Hestor."

Kyle began to read the letter in his head. *Darling, Mrs. Lawrence saw us walking by the canal last week. She stopped me at the bakers and told me it was improper to be seen in such a manner, so soon after Richard's death. I am filled with such rage toward these busy-bodies, Lucius. I wish we could leave and travel to a place where nobody knows who I am or anything of my life before I met you. I grow so tired of this torrid existence. You talk of leaving soon, my darling. Won't you take me with you?*

He checked the date at the top. Three weeks before Lucius's death. He glanced up at Caleb, who was watching him read. "When she says that he wants to leave and she wants him to take her with him, do you think she's talking about...you know...ending it?"

"I wondered that myself." Caleb stuck a hand into the

rucksack and pulled out a stack of letters written in Hestor's tiny handwriting. "There's a lot of angsty, star-crossed lover stuff in here."

"So, they weren't allowed to be together because Hestor was widowed?"

"And wealthy, from what I can tell. Lucius was penniless by then and had already been centre stage in a Victorian scandal. He obviously spent time in prison during the trial, then a few weeks in a loony bin. Her family didn't want him anywhere near her. The Morello's threatened to cut off her bankroll and take back Richard's house if she got together with Lucius."

"Doesn't sound like she cared too much about that if she wants them to start a new life together."

"It was a different time then, Kyle. You couldn't just grab a couple of plane tickets on your credit card and start working at a beach café in Majorca. They were trapped, and he knew it."

"What happened to her after he died?"

"She remarried a few years later. That's all I know. There's a rumour she used to come and stand outside the house all the time, but it's only a rumour after all. The Victorians were pretty dramatic, I guess, so it could be true." Caleb rolled his eyes. "Women."

"Don't let Cassie hear you say that. Fucking hell." Kyle snorted.

"Maybe she could give us a woman's perspective on Hestor."

Kyle gave him a sharp look. "Cassie'll be the first person to tell you she doesn't understand other women. Let alone a dramatic Victorian widow with a lost love."

"Not her scene?"

"Not in the least." Kyle froze, noticing a sudden shadow in the corner.

"What?"

"I think he's here," Kyle whispered.

"Who, Po?" Caleb whipped around in his seat, terrified.

"No. Lucius." Kyle tried to focus on the shadow, willing it to stick around. He moved to a standing position, his palms out in what he hoped was a welcoming gesture. "Lucius? Is that you over there by the bookshelf?"

They waited.

A small pamphlet fluttered from the shelf, the kind you get with a pack of Legos, which was exactly what it was, Kyle realised as it splayed out on the floor, the gaudy image of the bricks showing on the cover. "Okay, thank you. Are you here because we're reading your letters?"

Beside him, a small gust of breath sent the papers fluttering, scooting across the tabletop. Kyle picked up the letter from Hestor and held it out towards the shadow. "Is this what you want? You want to hear from Hestor?"

Kyle blinked, and the dark shape was instantly a foot away from him. The paper in his hands went as cold as ice and flopped downwards, sodden. The shadow vanished. Kyle dropped the page in shock, and it landed in a wet heap on the floorboards.

"Why is it wet?" Caleb whispered.

Kyle shook his head, stupefied. He thought first of Lisa Vaughan, who was usually associated with water, but then of Lucius himself. "Wait, we originally thought Lucius died by jumping off the cliff into the sea, right? He touched the letter."

"But Hestor says he went back to the house and disappeared in there."

"Maybe she was wrong. Maybe it's both—he went to the house and got the tome, then took it to the cliffside to destroy it, and decided to jump in with it."

"He's still wet?" Caleb bent down and prodded the page. The ink had blurred and run, making Hestor's words of love illegible. "That's a creepy thought."

"Maybe he wanted to destroy it? Maybe it upset him to hear it again."

"My guess is it's Lisa Vaughan. Think about it. If you were in a house with the psychic who'd brought you back only to banish you into the walls of a house for a century, wouldn't you want to destroy the things he loves?"

They looked down at the mulched paper in a puddle at their feet. It reminded Kyle of soaking paper towels as a kid and throwing them against the toilet ceiling at school. "Poor Lucius."

After that, the pair's eagerness to look through Hestor's belongings faltered. Caleb left soon after, and Kyle was consumed with thoughts about the letter. He swept up the remnants and reluctantly threw them in the bin. The paper was too sodden to save.

Kyle felt a heartfelt sympathy for his dead relative. He ran through the possibilities of why the letter had been destroyed and each was sadder than the last. Lucius may have soaked the letter, possibly attempting to destroy it. Or, worse, perhaps he just wanted to touch it and read it but couldn't. Or maybe it *was* Lisa Vaughan, determined to torture him by ruining something he cared so much about, even from the afterlife. There was a chance that Lucius was suffering even more than the housemates were.

He trudged up the stairs, feeling depressed by it all, and froze outside Cassie's room. Droplets of water dappled the floorboards outside her door. He looked up at the doorknob. Wet tendrils of sodden green strands were looped over the handle, as if someone had raked their hands through a patch of seaweed then opened the door, leaving the residue behind on the handle. He shoved it open.

Cassie sat up in bed. "Jesus! You scared me."

"Everything all right?" Kyle scanned the room, wary.

"Yeah, why? What's up?"

Kyle hesitated, then forced a smile. "Nothing. Just checking on everyone."

"Thanks. I'm okay."

Kyle backed out of the room and closed the door. He pulled the strands of seaweed away from the handle and swiped his socked foot over the droplets on the floor. When he carried the greenery to the toilet and flushed, watching the strands get sucked down into the pipes, he heard a harsh female giggle from the hall.

He washed his hands, feeling even more empathy for Lucius. It was obvious to him then that it was Lisa who had destroyed his love letter in an act of malice. And that meant that his great-uncle was trapped in a hellish nightmare of an afterlife, perpetually tormented by The Suffering ghosts.

One thing was for sure, he wasn't about to let his friends succumb to the same fate.

CHAPTER 17
DROWNING

The glow of the lights hitting the blue water revived Cassie as she strode to the edge of the pool, bent her knees, and sprang into a dive. The chlorine scent rushed towards her face, and she sucked in a deep breath that expanded her lungs. Her fingers cut into the cool water. She was tired after a restless night full of dreams of the ocean. She'd sleepwalked once that she knew of and had woken up standing next to Pete's bed. Mortified, Cassie had retreated as quietly as she could, relieved he slept like a log and that Gaia hadn't been sleeping over. Cassie didn't think the couple were getting along anymore after hearing a few terse phone conversations through the bedroom wall over the last couple of days. She'd shoved her earbuds quickly into her ears each time and wondered why her heart had started pounding.

Don't think about it, she willed herself. *You've got enough problems with your own relationships to worry about someone else's.* She was looking forward to seeing Marty after her swim. Couldn't wait to set right the mess that the sleepover had turned into the other night.

Cassie was in the mood to swim as fast as she possibly could. It was important to her to prove she was strong, both mentally and physically. She burst through the depths, kicking fiercely, ignoring counts and breaths. Her mission was to reach the other side as quickly as she could, then turn and get back even faster.

She wanted to lose herself.

And it worked. Her lungs screamed at the blissful chaos of swimming without discipline. Her arms ached from the exertion of moving at double the speed of her Channel pacing, and her mind was blissfully numbed. Her ears were plugged by the swim cap, and the only noise she could hear was the peculiar rushing wind tunnel sound of the water streaming over the rubber.

Elated by the freedom of the movement, she broke the surface and dipped into a leisurely breaststroke. It was the kind of stroke she would use at a public holiday pool, never wanting to seem like a show-off to the hotel inhabitants. She didn't usually like to swim this way, but at that moment, she felt nothing but peace.

The chlorine scent made her smile into the water. It was the only smell she could truly trust now that the house had been infiltrated by the stench of the dead. She exhaled, bubbles pluming up and tickling her cheeks. This was the best she had felt in a long while.

Something wrapped around her leg.

A slippery, coiling scrap of material with a similar rubbery texture to that of her swim cap yanked at her ankle, then released her just as suddenly.

She spun around in the water and found herself in a pool of grey. The chemical chlorinated smell was replaced with the salty brine that followed her at home. She snatched at her foot and lifted a trembling hand that was threaded with seaweed.

She yelped and began to paddle to the side of the pool, trying to keep her face out of the murky seawater that chopped and churned, somehow as rough as a high sea.

Her hand clipped a cresting wave and when splashing droplets peppered her eyes, she squeezed them shut out of instinct. She opened them again and found that she was no longer alone. She was surrounded.

Cassie froze, trying to remain as still as humanly possible whilst keeping herself upright and afloat. Up to their shoulders in the water, each positioned a metre away from each other, dozens of sailors stood still in the pool.

Lisa Vaughan's victims.

The sailor nearest to her peered down at the water, his long dark hair dripping into the pool. He wore a blue felt jacket that was torn at the arms, and his grey cheeks were covered in dapples of green moss. Strands of seaweed draped his shoulders.

Hearing a door close at the far side of the room, Cassie tore her gaze from the sailor and looked across to where Martin was striding for the pool.

"Oh, thank God. Marty! Help!" she yelled, the exertion of the shout sending her chin plummeting. The rancid waters flooded her mouth.

Her friend ignored her, fixated on the pool. He didn't even seem to notice the sailors. His face was set in an angry frown, and he walked with solemn purpose. Cassie felt goose flesh shudder over her arms, and for the third time in her life, she felt afraid of Martin. Every time something happened at the pool, he had been there, a convenient lapse of memory bringing him to the gym. Or had he planned it all along? Had he been the cause?

Marty stepped up to the edge, strode out into the air, and plunged into the depths. Shocked, Cassie watched through a gap in the sailors as Martin flailed to the surface.

He apparently noticed his surroundings for the first time and began to scream. "What the fuck—what am I doing here?"

He can't swim, Cassie realised, her mind reeling. *He's drowning.*

She moved to swim to her friend, the urgent need to save him making her braver than her fear of the sailors. But the moment she moved toward him, the corpses hoisted their heads up as one. Their gaze snapped in Cassie's direction and their mouths dropped open.

She stared at the nearest sailor and her throat let out a constricted cry when his jaw fell wider, broken at the hinges. His dead yellow eyes blankly met hers and seawater gushed from his mouth, dripping shells and stones down the front of his period clothing. Once the water had tumbled out, his tongue hung loose, purple and swollen and pitted with barnacles.

Martin broke the surface and gave a gargling yell. "Cassie! Help!"

She gasped and sucked at the air, terrified at the thought of swimming past the dead sailors. Whimpering, she focused on Marty. She watched his head vanish below the surface and his desperate hands claw at the air, splashing salt water. Her inability to sit and watch her best friend drown again overrode her fear. She dove towards a gap between the dead men.

The nearest sailor moved.

Cassie froze a few centimetres from him, quivering in fear, certain he would reach out and grab her at any moment. Instead, the corpse's chest rose, and its yellow eyes rolled back into its head. She expected more salt water to jet from its expanding lungs. But instead, it expelled a violent gust of air that moaned like a foghorn—a rumbling, pitiful warning that shook Cassie to her core. She covered her ears, kicking her legs to stay afloat, but still the rumbling found her heart, the way a lion's barking roar could cause her to instinctively freeze at the zoo.

She screamed and squeezed her eyes shut.

When she opened them again, the pool was back to normal. The sailors had vanished, and the strip lights bounced crystal sparkles off the gentle crests of the undulating waves. Chlorine masked the lingering scent of an ancient sea.

Cassie stared out at the still water.

It was just a trick, she realised. Some obscene illusion cause by Lisa Vaughan. Martin hadn't even been at the pool at all.

Just as the notion entered her mind, his lifeless body floated to the surface at the far end of the pool, face-down and still.

CHAPTER 18
HOME AGAIN, HOME AGAIN

Pete waited on the porch, sitting on the steps with his hands clenched around his knees. A light rain began to fall, and when the droplets ricocheted off the pathway, they bounced shimmering spatters onto his trainers. He watched the liquid soak into the material, not bothering to move his feet.

The wooden boards of the porch creaked beside him, and the burnt wax scent of candles huffed like a breath past his face. He didn't bother to turn around. He had enough on his hands with his own ghost. He didn't need to take Lance's on, as well. He knew Pile was in a playful mood, having heard all about Lance's disrupted class the previous day. It seemed that all the ghosts were getting bolder, testing their limits. He decided to treat the satanic member of the Hellfire Club like a needy toddler, ignoring him in the hope that he'd get bored and leave. A few moments later, the smoky scent cleared as car headlights illuminated the puddles on the street. The vehicle rolled to a stop by the hedges.

Pete stood up when Cassie emerged from the back seat of

the unmarked police car. She slammed the door and strode up the driveway, her head down, her arms wrapped around her body and her legs so stiff she looked like a wind-up doll. Her swim bag hung from the crook of her elbow, and when she saw Pete, she let it fall to the floor and crumpled into his chest, sobbing.

He held her tightly in the rain, breathing in the earthen wash of the cloud burst. He relished being outside, away from the scents of the house. From their ghosts.

In time, Cassie's shoulders stopped hitching and her crying eased. She turned her cheek into the damp cotton of his hoodie, watching the falling rain. In time, she leaned back a little and stared up at Pete, her expression unreadable. The rain collected against her eyebrows and then rolled a track of water directly into her inner eye.

She blinked and pulled away. "Let's go inside."

Pete led her through to the kitchen and turned on the kettle. Cassie shook her head, reaching for a bottle of red wine and sitting at the table with it in front of her.

"Glass?" Pete offered, but when she shook her head, he snapped off the kettle and slid into the seat beside her.

She unscrewed the cap and took three long swigs, then pushed the bottle across the table. As Pete drank, she began to tell him what had happened, her voice robotic. "There were so many of them. Just standing there. They were real, Pete. And Martin kept turning up at the pool at these weird times, lately. I thought he was playing games because...well, just because. So, when he walked in, I was mad. I thought for a second that it was another prank, even though I knew it didn't make any sense."

Pete nodded and passed the bottle back to her, watching

her swallow a huge mouthful. A plum trickle rolled down her cheek, pinkened by the lingering drops of rain on her skin.

"Then he jumped in the pool," she said. "I knew he couldn't swim."

"He was in a trance?"

"When he jumped, yes. But as soon as he hit the water, he came to his senses. He was screaming for me. I tried to go to him, but the sailors..." She blinked fresh tears from her eyelids and grabbed for the wine, drinking deeply. Speaking fast, as though speeding through the details made them somehow less painful, she told Pete about the foghorn sound, the barnacle-studded tongue. "They wouldn't let me help him."

Pete reached across the table and stroked her hand with his thumb. "It wasn't your fault."

"I've treated him like shit," Cassie whispered. "And I don't even know why. I've been so horrible lately."

"It wasn't you, Cass. It was Lisa."

"But I brought her into his life. He'd be alive now if it wasn't for me." She swigged from the bottle and set it down angrily, the remaining liquid sloshing black inside the green bottle. "I was terrible to him. I made him miserable in his last days on earth, when all he wanted was for me to be happy."

Pete scooted his chair closer to hers, their thighs bumping together. "You're wrong. You may have had a rough few days, but he was always happy when he was with you. He loved you, Cass."

"I loved him, but as a friend. I—Lisa—toyed with him. It was...it was just awful, Pete. You didn't see the things I did."

Pete lifted the thumb from her hand and brought it to

her cheek, smoothing away the tears. "It wasn't you. You're not awful, Cassie."

Cassie looked up at Pete, her expression thoughtful. He gave her a sympathetic smile, and when she opened her mouth he waited for her to say something. But instead her lips pressed against his, cold and a little numb from the rain.

His muscles tightened in surprise, then his hands swept over her sodden back, his tongue swiping between her lips, tasting wine. He moaned as she kissed him ferociously, her lips full and plump, her hands exploring his face and chest.

Pete stood, pulling her with him to the living room, still kissing as they stumbled and felt their way through the door and onto the couch. Ramming into the cushions, Cassie arched her back when Pete pulled up her T-shirt, tugging it over her damp hair and plucking at her bra. Her breasts spilled from the filmy cups, her nipples reacting immediately to the cold and to her desire for Pete. He ducked down and clamped his lips over the left one, sucking it into his mouth.

Cassie groped under the weight of him and found the band of his jeans, thumbing the button from its hole and peeling down the zipper. Plunging her hand into the rough denim, she snagged the thin cotton of his pants and tore them down, his penis springing up into her palm. She squeezed and pulled and smiled when Pete groaned in pleasure.

"Oh, God, I want you in me," Cassie whispered, urgently clutching his cock with her right hand and peeling her pants down over her ass with her left.

Pete raised his hips to give her room to manoeuvre, the tip of his cock tapping against her belly and leaving a glossy pearl of pre-cum against her skin. Cassie tugged her panties down low enough to part her thighs.

Pete began to lower himself down onto her. She angled herself up to meet his hips. He kissed her cheek, bracing himself with his left arm, stroking his free fingers through her hair.

He froze and grunted in confusion.

In Cassie's hand, Pete's penis shrank away, retreating from her wet lips. Surprised, she stared up at him and saw that he was looking at something to her left, his expression aghast. "Pete, what is it?"

Slowly, he pulled back his trembling hand until she could see it. Her hair was snagged in his fingers from where he had been stroking it. Dripping from his palm were strands of sodden green seaweed.

Cassie cried out, reaching her hands up to her hair, pulling clumps of the weed from her head. She bucked, kicking Pete away from her, and bolted for the stairs.

"Cassie!" Pete yelled, following after her. When he reached the bottom of the stairs, the familiar rollercoaster sensation stopped him in his tracks. He clutched the banister and lowered his head, gagging.

Cassie tore up the steps two at a time, barging past Lance who was starting to head down.

"Cassie what's— Whoa!" Seeing his housemate was naked from the waist up, Lance covered his eyes and turned his head. Cassie fled to the bathroom and slammed the door behind her.

"What the hell's going on?" Lance asked from the top of the stairs. He trotted down to the step above Pete.

Unable to speak, Pete held up his hand, showing Lance the seaweed.

"Where the hell did that come from?"

Pete swallowed thickly and croaked, "Cassie's hair."

"Holy shit."

IN THE BATHROOM, Cassie stood before the mirror in horror. She looked like a swamp monster, naked from the waist up, chest heaving, her tangled and sodden curls hanging down past her shoulders and caked in tendrils of seaweed. She lifted a piece of hair and found it crusted in salt, the stench of the open sea filling the bathroom.

She steeled herself, glaring at her reflection, then reached for Pete's soap bag. Inside it, she found his hair trimmer, a circular gadget he used every few weeks. In the cupboard, she found Kyle's nail scissors and began to snip at her locks with aggressive urgency, throwing the strands and the seaweed into the toilet. When she had cut most of it down to inch-long stumps, she flicked Pete's trimmer to the longest setting and pressed it against her scalp.

PETE AND LANCE made their way to the top of the stairs. Twice, Pete had lurched dizzily for the banister, falling heavily into the wood. Both times, a faint giggle echoed down the hallway, Rourke evidently amused by his continuous torture.

They sat down outside the bathroom door and waited for Cassie. When the low buzz of Pete's razor sounded, the two men looked at each other in surprise.

"She's cutting it off," Lance pointed out.

"I honestly don't blame her," Pete said, rubbing his hand against his jeans. He still felt as though his hand was tainted, even though he'd shaken the seaweed off on the stairs.

A few moments later, the bathroom door opened, and Cassie strode past, a towel wrapped around her upper body, her shorn hair stuck out in uneven tufts.

Pete clambered to his feet and reached out to her. "Cassie, wait!"

She spun around, her tearful eyes and clenched fists stopping him in his tracks. "I think you should call Gaia," Cassie said, her expression full of warning and regret.

"But Cassie—"

"Pete!" She held up a palm, silencing him. "I can't do this right now."

She disappeared into her room, and shut the door in his face. Pete could hear the soft squeak of Cassie sitting on her bed, followed by sniffling.

"What the hell is going on with you two?" Lance asked, stepping up behind him.

"Martin died," Pete said, softly.

"What? How?"

Pete turned to look at him, his expression bleak. "Lisa Vaughan."

Lance let his mouth fall open in shock. "Is Kyle home?"

Pete strode to Kyle's bedroom and knocked, then opened the door.

· · ·

KYLE WAS LYING on his bed, scrolling through his phone with earbuds in. He snatched them out and looked at them in confusion. "What's up?"

"Something's happened." Pete told him.

Kyle sat up, hearing gentle sobs from down the hall. "Is that Cass?"

"Lisa drowned Martin tonight."

Kyle felt the air punch out of his lungs. Guilt washed over him, sickening him. If he hadn't called out the ghosts on Halloween, Marty would be alive right now. He'd be hearing him laughing and joking with Cassie through the walls, instead of hearing her crying in grief.

"Are you sure it was Lisa?" he stammered.

"Cassie saw the sailors. And then, after she came home, Lisa messed with her again. I saw it. She had seaweed in her hair," Pete's cheeks grew flushed, and Kyle guessed he wasn't telling them the full story. "She had to cut it off."

Kyle's cheeks tingled as the blood drained from his face. He kicked off his bedcovers and scrambled to his feet. "She cut the seaweed off or her hair?"

Lance spoke up behind Pete. "She cut off her hair, man. The whole lot."

"No, no, no!" Kyle moaned, balling his fists up against his cheeks. He had to see for himself.

He shoved past Pete and stumbled to Cassie's room, throwing open the door. His friend sat on the edge of her bed, holding a pillow to her front, tears streaming down her face. Her hair was clipped close to her head, sticking out in blunt, irregular tufts, just as it was in the old woman's drawing.

Kyle staggered backwards, tripping over Lance's feet. He

wordlessly rushed back to his own bedroom and grabbed his phone, yanking his hoodie over his head. Bracing himself at the foot of the bed so his friends didn't see what he was doing, he groped under the mattress and pulled out the strip of parchment and stuffed it into his pocket. Then he dashed past his bewildered housemates, thundered down the stairs, and ran out into the street.

CHAPTER 19
REVELATIONS

Caleb yanked open the door and scowled. "How did I know it would be you, you little fucker?"

Kyle stood dripping on his uncle's doorstep, panting and shivering.

Caleb's furious expression turned to one of puzzled concern. He tugged the belt of his blue dressing gown tighter around his middle. His hair was on end and Kyle's frantic knocking had obviously dragged him out of bed, but he stepped back and let him in.

Kyle tripped through the hallway, trying to get his breath back so he could explain. He tugged the damp parchment from his hoodie pocket and thrust it to Caleb, who caught the page and stared down at it in confusion.

"It's Cassie..." Kyle struggled to get the words out. "The old lady in Peru had a premonition about how she'd die. But I always thought she might be wrong...because Cass has long hair."

"Okay." Caleb looked at him warily, as though he thought Kyle might have finally lost the plot.

"But she doesn't anymore." Kyle bent down and braced his hands on his sodden knees, heaving in a shuddering breath. "Lisa made her cut it off. She killed her friend and made her cut her hair."

"Cassie killed her friend?"

Kyle shook his head, frustrated but beginning to catch his breath. "No. Lisa Vaughan killed her friend. Then she put seaweed in her hair, so she cut it all off and now she looks like that."

Caleb glanced down at the drawing.

"We have to do something. We have to get rid of them, Caleb. Or this is going to happen."

Caleb swallowed, looking nauseated. "What a way to go."

"Po's gonna kill her in the same way he killed Cillian Waverley. And I'll be standing there watching it happen like a fucking idiot." Kyle was shivering wildly now, both from the shock of seeing Cassie with short hair and the midnight dash through the freezing rain.

Caleb exhaled and put the paper down on the sideboard. "Right, first things first. You've got to get dry. I'll grab you some clothes. They'll be a little big, but that's tough shit. Come on. Let's get you a towel."

He led Kyle up the stairs and opened his wardrobe, tossing Kyle a fresh beige towel and grabbing a pair of maroon sweatpants and a long-sleeved grey jersey. "Here. Go get changed and dry. I'll put the fucking kettle on."

Caleb had been right about his clothes. The pants hung precariously from Kyle's hips even after he cinched the waist in as far as it would go. The shirt gaped and hung over one of his shoulders, the way Cassie liked to wear her dance gear. He rubbed the towel through his hair and felt the chill in his bones start to ease.

The pipes in the bathroom clicked and groaned, and when Kyle put his hand to the radiator, he could feel that his uncle had turned the heating on for him, the metal beginning to warm to the touch.

He went downstairs and found Caleb at the kitchen table with his laptop open in front of him, the curled parchment resting on the tabletop. Caleb had made them each a mug of tea, and Kyle sat down and picked his up with a grateful smile, wrapping his chilled hands around the scorching porcelain. He shuddered.

"You'll warm up soon. The heating's on."

"Thanks." Kyle sipped at the tea. Caleb must have put at least three sugars in there. It was far too sweet for Kyle's usual taste, but he swallowed it gratefully, soon growing accustomed to the sugar.

"I don't know where you want to start looking, but I figured we could go back to the good old internet since the library wasn't much use."

"It's worth a try."

Caleb typed a few words into the keyboard and jabbed at the mousepad. "I knew that bitch was the one to watch."

"Cassie?" Kyle looked up in confusion.

"Lisa Vaughan." Caleb corrected. "She got another one. All this time later."

"Looks like she's not going to be the only one." Kyle peered down at the drawing of Po killing Cassie, distraught. "And I just stand there like a lemon and watch it happen."

"Looks more like Lucius than you," Caleb pointed out.

Kyle peered at the sketch. His uncle was right; with the

white shirt and wide features, the drawing did look like Lucius. "Family resemblance, I guess."

"Fuck that. I never got it." Caleb squinted at him. "And neither did you."

Kyle managed a laugh at his uncle's usually catty humour and sipped at his tea. "What are you searching for?"

"Images of Brackenby. I don't know, I thought if we could find pictures it might lead us down another route, instead of looking for articles and getting nowhere all the time."

Kyle scooted his chair to sit next to Caleb and looked at the screen. It was strange seeing rows and rows of pictures of his own house. Some were photographs taken through the years. Others were engravings and watercolour prints, little changing about the appearance of the house itself, but the landscape around the grounds morphed from orchards and grasslands to the built-up townhouse on the busy road that it now was.

"That's cool." Kyle pointed to a moody-looking oil painting of the house as it must have looked in the seventeen-hundreds. The front of the house showed through a copse of winter-bare trees, dark and ominous in the moonlight. A ghostly figure stood to the right beside the trees.

Caleb clicked the image and followed the link to the webpage. "It's hanging in the museum in town."

Kyle reached for his tea and took another swallow as his uncle skim-read, scrolling through the page. A cold droplet of rain dripped from his hair and trickled down his neck. He slapped it with his palm and swiped it away.

"Guess who painted it. The Prof's wife, Lyla Grant."

Kyle snapped his fingers. "I thought it looked familiar! We still have a lot of her paintings stored in the basement."

It says here the Grants donated the picture to the museum before Lucius bought the property. It's been in storage for a while, but it's currently on display in the *Local Legends* exhibit."

Kyle looked at the picture, thoughtfully. "Well, it's pretty cool and all, but it doesn't really help us."

Caleb squinted at the picture, apparently lost in thought. "I suppose not."

"What? What's wrong?"

"I don't know. It's probably nothing. Let's keep looking."

Caleb went back to the main search and clicked on a few of the photographs. He jotted down the names of the people who had taken the pictures, just in case, but nothing seemed to be of any use.

Kyle found himself scrutinising the windows of the house, expecting to see the shadowy face of Lisa Vaughan beside the curtains, or the hulking handprint of Po on the ground floors. It was ridiculous, he knew, but he couldn't help but check the panes, half a hope that he might see a pair of eyes looking back at him in one of the shots.

"Wait a minute..." Caleb scraped his chair back, snapping his head towards Kyle with a sudden look of distracted excitement. He jumped to his feet and ran from the room.

Kyle went after him, padding barefoot down the hallway, stepping around the lingering puddles and muddy footprints he had made upon arrival. He followed his uncle into an office room, the desk and floor covered in cardboard boxes, presumably the items he had bought from the Morello family. Caleb was hunched over one of the boxes, rummaging through the contents.

A moment later, he pulled out a small tan notebook. "Yes! This is it, I think."

He leapt to his feet and bustled past Kyle, carrying the book back to the laptop and flicking through the worn old pages. "Here it is. *Mists at Brackenby*."

Kyle followed Caleb's finger as it jabbed at the title of Lyla Grant's moody oil painting that was currently hanging in the local museum. "What is it?"

"This is one of Hestor's diaries. She was worried about Lucius, thinking he was starting to go mad. She says here he asked the museum for the painting back, but they wouldn't give it to him because the Grant family had donated it. I only skim-read up to here. I wonder if she talks about it again…" Caleb flicked through the next few pages and read a passage, then lowered the book. He stared at Kyle with stunned excitement.

"What? What does it say?"

"She thought he was losing his marbles, but he told her there was a rhyme written on the back of the painting that would get rid of the ghosts for good."

"You've got to be fucking kidding me."

"Exactly."

"And you're sure it's that painting?"

"It says right here on the museum page, same as the diary. *Mists at Brackenby*, it used to hang at Brackenby House but was donated to the museum following the tragic death of Josiah Grant. And in Hestor's diary she says Lucius was obsessed with getting the painting back and talked about little else. He even tried to break into the museum the night before he died. He got taken to the jail, but they released him with a warning because they knew who he was and what he'd been through."

"We've got to get that painting."

"Good luck," Caleb snorted. "The museum wouldn't even give it to Lucius when he bought the house. I hardly think they're gonna hand it over to a runty little uni student."

"Hey!"

"You know what I mean. It's all very well and good knowing where it is. Getting hold of it is another matter."

"Well, wait a minute. We don't need the whole painting, do we? We just need to lift it up and get a photo of the rhyme on the back. Right?"

"I suppose. But again, the general public can't usually go manhandling the goods on display. That painting looks heavy as fuck. And lifting it up without anyone noticing is going to be difficult."

"We have to try. This is it, Caleb." Kyle gawped at the painting on the screen, the cold in his system completely eradicated by the heat of his excitement. "This could be exactly what we need."

"Great. Now can we get some fucking sleep?"

GAIA'S PHONE lit up on the bedside table, a third message from Pete. Sitting hunched up on the edge of her mattress, she craned to read the text before her screen went black. She closed her eyes at the sensation of lips pressing against her naked back, a scuff of stubble on her shoulder.

"Are you ready?" Jonah breathed on her neck, one hand snaking around to cup her breast.

"Yes." She closed her eyes, trying to push all thoughts of Pete from her mind. She leaned back against Jonah and squirmed, tilting her head to one side as his tongue slid over the tendons in her neck. He inched closer, his erection nudging her lower spine.

Shifting to sink back into the pillows, Gaia licked her lips with desire. Jonah clambered on top of her, his fingers parting her lips with rough haste before he plunged into her, aggressive and eager. She winced and bit his shoulder as he drove deeper into her. Pinned beneath him, she let him rock her whole body with the movement of the bed, enjoying the feeling of being dominated. He grunted when he thrust, staring down at her with furious lust in his eyes, his teeth clenched and animalistic.

She tilted her head back and closed her eyes, the head of Jonah's cock plunging and probing against her G-spot, tantalisingly pulling back before ramming into her wall over and over. Her nipples stood at attention, tingling and tight.

She opened her eyes, wanting to stare into Jonah's eyes while she came. Concentration forced his dark brows together, and his tangled black hair tumbled forward, the lilac-dyed tips swinging against his sweaty cheeks.

Her eyes darted to his shoulder. A grinning spectral face with wide, black eyes and grey skin stretched over high cheekbones perched on Jonah's shoulder like a grotesque, disembodied parrot. It leered at her.

Gaia screamed and kicked her legs, pinned by Jonah's body and unable to do anything to get away from the ghoul.

It grinned wider, swiping a blackened tongue over its upper teeth, then vanished.

Gaia bucked under Jonah, screaming again, tears springing from her eyes. Finally, she managed to push him away from her.

"What the fuck!" Jonah gasped when his cock slipped out of her at the crucial moment. He snatched it in his fist and pumped, releasing the jet of cum that had almost spilled into her before she started screaming and kicking. He gaped at her, wiping his hand on her sheets, furious. "What the fuck did you do that for?"

"There was a man behind you." Gaia cried, shivering uncontrollably.

Jonah spun round, taking in the room with a panicked expression. "There's nobody here."

"I think...I think it was a ghost," Gaia stammered.

Jonah slammed his fist into the mattress. "Oh, for fuck's sake. Not you too! You've been spending too much time with fucking Pete and all his crazy ghost shit."

"Don't talk about Pete," Gaia whispered, tugging the sheet up to cover her breasts.

"Well, it's a bit late to get sentimental now, babe." Jonah sneered.

They sat for a moment in silence until he sighed and let his shoulders drop, his frustration visibly ebbing away.

She knew it was wrong to start up with Jonah so soon after she and Pete had broken up, but it had been a long time coming. Pete had been growing more and more distant for a long while. Since Halloween, if she really thought about it. She had a sneaking suspicion his decision to end things had something to do with Cassie. When she'd asked him straight out, he'd hesitated. She deserved better than that.

She wasn't sure that Jonah really was better, and deep down she knew she'd be kidding herself to think so. But he was there, and she needed someone.

He looked at Gaia, his expression suddenly sympathetic. "It really scared you, huh?"

She nodded.

"Will you be okay if I take a shower?"

"Be quick."

He stroked her cheek, smudging the tear up into her hairline with fingers that smelled of sweat and sex. Then he got up and left the room, not bothering to clothe himself. Gaia was home alone that night, but even if her family had been there, she doubted he would have covered up. It was one of the things she liked about him, his carefree, devil-may-care attitude. This was the main reason she gravitated towards him, knowing that she was often too uptight for her own good. Pete was like her in many respects. And Jonah, with his course attitude and rough sex, was a breath of fresh air, despite his flaws.

Gaia picked up her phone and read Pete's messages, then opened her Instagram feed. Thumbing through the posts, she deleted any that showed her ex. It was time to move on.

She lay down, still feeling a little vulnerable. She skimmed through her friends' feeds while she waited for Jonah to finish his shower, liking and commenting on a few posts to keep her mind from roaming to the fiendish face she had seen looming over his shoulder.

Gaia went to roll onto her left side, but was yanked back,

her hair snagged. What the fuck? That was Pete's usual trick. But Pete wasn't even here...

She tried to jerk her head, but the hair was stuck.

Easing down onto her back, she painfully turned her eyes to the far right and saw the leering face of the ghoul beside her in the bed, its thin hand lying flat on her hair, holding it down against the mattress. She let out a piercing scream, frozen to the bed, unable to do anything but stare at the grinning maniacal face right beside her.

Gaia heard Jonah rush down the hall. He slammed open the door and barged into the room wearing a towel around his waist. The creature released her, but sped right at Jonah in a blur, the pattering sound of rapid footsteps thundering across her room. The white blur smashed into Jonah in the doorway. He staggered at the top of the stairs, windmilling his arms, his heels teetering back over the edge of the top step.

With a shriek, Jonah tumbled backwards.

CHAPTER 20
SHARING IS CARING

Pete jumped awake in the dimly lit room and instinctively reached for his phone. Gaia hadn't replied. He sat up against his pillows and hefted a sigh, absently scrolling through her Insta feed. Her photos, usually showing multiple images of the two of them, had become decidedly solitary. She'd deleted him.

He leaned his head back against the bedframe and whacked it heavily a couple of times against the wood. He'd been an idiot. But at the same time, he couldn't ignore the soft fuzz of relief somewhere deep inside. He had always had feelings for Cassie. Gaia knew it, all along. He had just been slow to catch on himself.

Knowing he wouldn't be able to get back to sleep unless he peed, Pete swung his legs from under the covers and stood, reaching for his bedroom door. Although Rourke could strike anywhere, the landing was his main hunting ground.

Fear of what might be lurking on the other side of the

door exacerbated his need to pee, so Pete grabbed the handle, gradually revealing the landing.

It was dark, with silver shadows cast by the open bathroom door streaking across the end of the corridor. He stood still for a moment, listening, waiting for the faint stampede to patter towards him. All was quiet. He realised he was clenching his teeth, anticipating the wave of nausea that usually threatened to overwhelm him when Rourke was near, but there was nothing. His ghost didn't appear to be home.

His mind goaded him; *not only are you being ghosted by your girlfriend. Even your* ghost *is ghosting you*.

He chuckled softly at the ridiculousness of the idea and strode for the bathroom, not letting his guard down for a second. Although it seemed as though Rourke wasn't around, he knew the ghost was a trickster. He anticipated him jumping out at any moment.

Pete reached the bathroom and stepped into the silvery light, grateful for the frosted window. He didn't want to turn the light on and wake himself up completely, but there was enough light from the moon to give him the vague illusion of safety.

Yawning, tiredness hitting him, Pete stepped sleepily to the toilet, peeling down his pyjama pants and sitting down on the seat. He couldn't be bothered standing when he was so ready to go back to bed. He hunched forward and rested his chin on a palm, elbows propped against his thighs, and listened to his stream hitting the porcelain. He didn't want to stand right away when he was finished, enjoying the sensation of sitting in the cool room. He told himself he was letting himself drip dry, rather than simply being lazy.

A hand reached up from inside the toilet and clasped his balls.

Eyes jumping wide, Pete leapt from the seat, feeling the quick, wet fingers probing his butthole. He stumbled over his pooled pyjama pants and landed heavily on his forearms, bare ass in the air, water trickling down his thigh from where the hand had stroked his skin.

He flipped over, scrambling back to the door, eyes staring at the toilet bowl, expecting whatever had grabbed him to rise out of the water.

Everything was quiet and still, the moonlight glinting off the stark white porcelain.

He panted, trembling, goose flesh sticking up all over his bare, skinny legs.

Not daring to take his eyes from the rim of the toilet, he reached down and began to tug his pyjamas up, hoisting them up to his waist. It felt better to be covered.

"Rourke, you bastard," Pete whispered, his violation making him suddenly brave with rage. "Was that you?"

He clenched his fists at his sides, his cheeks hot with anger and humiliation. Standing, he could see more of the toilet. There didn't appear to be anything inside it. From where he stood, he could see the curve of the back of the basin, the greyish waterline and a glimpse of the liquid that pooled there.

He stepped closer.

Movement made the slightly damp fabric cling to his butt where he had been touched. He plucked at the cotton and shivered.

Craning his neck, he stopped two feet from the porcelain and peered into the water.

A large, iris-less eye with feminine lashes stared up at him. It blinked.

Pete screamed and raced backwards, hitting the door with his shoulder as it was pushed open from the outside. Lance stood stunned in the entrance, reaching out to catch him.

"Sorry man." Lance gawped at him, then followed his gaze to the toilet.

"Lisa Vaughan," Pete stammered. "Lisa Vaughan just touched me."

"But she's not your ghost," Lance blurted, sleepiness and surprise making him curt.

"I know what I fucking saw!" Pete yelled.

"All right, all right," he soothed, reaching for the light and pulling the cord.

Amber light flooded the stark white bathroom.

"I'll check," Lance reassured his friend, moving over to the toilet. He peered down into the water and looked back at Pete, horrified.

"What's going on, guys?" Tad grumbled from the landing, his hair sticking right up on end and cascading forward into a point like a cartoon character. "I've got my pitch presentation tomorrow, so can you keep it down?"

Lance turned to him and stepped back. "Look..." He gestured to the water in the toilet.

Tad stepped past Pete, who stayed put by the door, rubbing the red line that had bloomed on his forearm after crashing into the door. His jaw was clenched, a pulsing muscle appearing in his cheek.

The boys looked down into the water. Lance reached out

and pressed the flush. They watched the strands of seaweed swirl and get sucked away down the drain.

"I fucking told you," Pete cried. "I fucking told you it was Lisa. She touched me."

"So now you're getting messed with by Rourke *and* Lisa?" Tad asked.

"I think they're getting even stronger," Lance said. "Maybe that's why."

Tad gawped at him. "What chance do we have if they're ganging up on us?"

"I don't think Rourke's even here," Pete said softly. "I don't feel him."

They all listened for the tell-tale footsteps that were often ready to prove him wrong, but none came.

A vibrating sound pulsed into the room. They all looked at Lance as he took his phone from his pyjama pants pocket, a dazed look on his face.

"Who's calling you at 3 a.m.?" Tad asked.

Lance read the name on his screen, looking perplexed. He turned to Pete. "It's Gaia."

Puzzled, the housemates watched Lance swipe the screen to answer and lift the phone to his ear. "Gaia?"

He listened, his eyes on Pete. He paled, and his eyeballs went glassy as they swamped with tears. He pinched the bridge of his nose and bent over, a tear squeezing loose and tumbling to the tiles.

Pete snatched the phone from his hand. "Gaia, what the hell's going on?"

Gaia's breath hitched. "Pete... I'm sorry. It's Jonah. He's dead."

～

KYLE WOKE up on Caleb's couch at nine-fifteen, far later than he'd intended. He swore, realising his phone with his alarm set was still sitting on the kitchen table. He threw back the covers and rushed to the kitchen, tugging his clothes from the dryer and quickly clambering into them. His mobile was chiming softly with an alarm, and he snatched it up and swiped the screen.

He frowned. He had three voicemails from Pete. "What the fuck?"

Without waiting around to listen to the messages, he jabbed the call button. Pete picked up on the first chime of a ringtone. "Where the fuck are you, man?"

"I'm at Caleb's. What's up?"

"Didn't you get my messages? Jonah's dead."

Kyle's head swam and he sank to his knees. "What happened?"

"Rourke fucking happened. He threw him down the stairs. Gaia saw it."

"Rourke killed Jonah?" Kyle shook his head, bewildered. "Why was he with Gaia?"

"They were at her place. I don't know...maybe Rourke thought Jonah was me. We're not... We broke up yesterday."

"Shit, man." Kyle didn't know what to say. Instead, he snapped his attention to the matter at hand. "Look, get everybody together and I'll meet you at home. Me and Caleb, we found something that might get rid of the ghosts."

"Nobody's here," Pete hissed.

"What? Where the fuck is everybody?"

"Well, Lance is with family since, y'know, his fucking

cousin just died and all. Tad is at that interview for his shit-machine grant, and Cassie's at the doctors getting a flu jab. I'm the only one here."

"Shit. All right, Pete, listen to me..." Kyle ran to the hallway and started tugging on his shoes. "Meet me at the museum in town. There's an exhibit upstairs called *Local Legends*. There's a picture of our house and on the back of it there's some writing. We need to get a photo of it. I'm heading there now. Meet me there?"

Pete was silent for a moment, thinking. "Okay. I'll set off now."

"You might get there before me, but I'll be as quick as I can. Head straight for the exhibit and get the picture."

"Okay."

"And Pete? Be careful."

CHAPTER 21
COLLATERAL DAMAGE

Tad cleared his throat and moved to the project board. The panel of three watched him with curious expressions. From the way they kept staring at his face, then to the machine and back again, Tad guessed that, like most people he'd shown his prototype to, they were confused about why someone who looked like him was 'wasting time' worrying about turning sewage into fuel. The woman closest to him, a pinch-featured sixty-year-old wearing Armani, raised her chin and sniffed at the air.

Tad smelled it, too. There was no waste in his prototype model. This was mould. The dark, fuzzy stench of decay lingered on the back of his tongue when he swallowed, and the heavy presence of Jarvis Rice loomed behind the panel's table. It was the first time he'd been out alone since the incident at the hotel, and after he woke up that morning he'd had a sinking feeling that something bad would happen. He'd tucked his grandparent's talisman into his suit pants pocket and said a little prayer before leaving the house.

"Let's start with some introductions," the woman said,

warmly "I'm Vanessa Shylock. On the panel with me today are Hayden Bates, divisional manager of our renewables faction."

The broad, redheaded man sitting beside her lifted a large hand and gave a small nod.

"And we also have Walt Templeton here today. Mr. Templeton oversees the financial side of these grants and where the money is distributed."

Walt grinned. He was an older man with liver spots dappling the top of his bald head, but he had a youthful glimmer in his eyes that Tad immediately warmed to.

He began to relax and told them his name.

"Whenever you're ready, Mr. Oyama," Hayden Bates said softly, scribbling on the pad in front of him without lowering his eyes.

"The item I have brought for your perusal today is a simple construct that aims to turn household waste into viable fuel. It is a project I started working on three years ago. I believe in that time I have managed to perfect a solution to some of the urgent needs of the planet."

"How old are you, Tad?" Vanessa interjected.

"Twenty-one."

"So, you came up with this idea when you were eighteen?"

"That's correct. I've been processing similar ideas from the age of about thirteen, but that was the age when I finally moved closer to achieving the results I had intended."

"And would you say that— Oh!" Vanessa shot back in her chair, slamming her hands down on the top of the table. Beside her, Walt placed a steadying hand on her shoulder, his eyes glittering with startled amusement.

"I'm sorry." Vanessa laughed, her neck and cheeks streaked with red. "I felt like my chair was tipping over, but I wasn't even leaning back in it!"

"I hate it when that happens!" Walt roared with laughter.

"Really? Oh, I've never experienced it before. Certainly not like that. I do apologise, Tad."

Tad shifted his weight from foot to foot and hooked his finger under his collar, sweat prickling the back of his neck. He had no business remaining in the meeting, that was clear. Jarvis was taunting him. Seeing how far he could push it. The ghoul was going to ruin his big chance. Or worse, he might hurt someone.

"It's fine, Mrs. Shylock," Tad said.

"Please do go on. Explain your mechanism in more detail." Hayden waved his large hand, gesturing for Tad to disregard the bizarre antics of his co-panellist and cut to the chase.

Trying to ignore the ever-increasing stench of mould in the room and the way Vanessa kept shooting looks over her shoulder towards the dark mass Tad knew only he could see, he began to explain the intricacies of his prototype. He held up the plastic model and described the internal functions with rehearsed diligence.

Vanessa held up her hand and Tad motioned for her to speak. "That stench—is that because the prototype has been used in practice?"

"That smell isn't from my machine, ma'am. It's not from me at all," he added, quickly.

The panel shifted in their seats, surreptitiously sniffing at their shoulders and casting accusing glances at each other.

Jarvis appeared behind Vanessa and gave a wild-eyed,

rotten-toothed leer. Tad sucked in his breath, but the ghost simply stood and stared at him, daring him to make a move.

"Are you all right there, son?" Walt asked.

"Yes, sir." Tad turned away and blinked, focusing on his presentation board. His heart was hammering. It was bad enough keeping his nerve to conduct the presentation in the first place. After the hotel incident, he was terrified for his life. He willed himself to remember what Kyle had said, that they'd never attack in front of witnesses. He exhaled, trying to calm his nerves, hoping his friend was right. "Here we have the figures from my last fifty-four attempts at converting—"

A sudden squeal jolted him from his speech. He spun around, dropping the board marker he had been using as a pointer, and saw Vanessa's feet fly up into the air, her chair falling backwards. Her head smashed against the back wall with an audible *thunk*, and something—Tad assumed a neck bone—cracked.

Walt leapt to his feet. From the way his body slowly rotated, his arms reaching first toward Vanessa's chair and then toward the door, he seemed torn between attempting to grab the woman and running from the room to get help. Hayden scooted his chair back and covered his mouth with his hand, staring down at her.

Tad hesitantly stepped closer to the table. He ignored the hammering thud in his chest and craned his neck to see over the woman's notes, his own name elegantly scrawled at the top of the page. She gawped up at him, her head crushed against her chest, her tongue snagged between her teeth and turning ashen in colour.

With a snarl, Jarvis rushed through Tad and shoved him into the table. Tad's body crashed against the plastic edge, and he yelled out. Unbalanced, he braced his hands on the surface and watched in horror as the whole table began to topple forward under his weight. The table tipped slowly, then slammed down, taking him face to face with the dead woman as the wooden edge crushed her already broken neck into the back of her chair. Her windpipe popped and gurgled next to Tad's ear.

Behind him, Jarvis chuckled and murmured in a thick Scottish accent, "Just the way I like 'em."

Tad staggered to the side, his palms sliding over the table, causing a piercing screeching noise. Hayden shoved his shoulder, forcing him away. The tabletop whacked Vanessa's chin as it flipped back into an upright position. Her teeth audibly clashed together. The tip of her tongue lingered for a moment on her bottom lip, then slid down her chin, guillotined clean through, a smear of already congealing blood mixing with her pearlescent pink lip gloss.

Hayden retched, his eyes bulging in horror. He pushed his hands into bent knees and pitched forward, depositing his breakfast onto the tight-weave carpet. His face was as grey as Vanessa's.

Behind Tad, the receptionist ran into the room, surveyed the carnage, and let out a scream. Still, nobody touched Vanessa. She remained hunched against the wall, her head sunken into her chest, the purple slug of her tongue resting in the bow collar of her Armani blouse.

CASSIE STEPPED into the nurse's room and scanned the walls, taking in brightly coloured posters, charts, and plastic bins marked with various warning signs. The nurse had already laid out the inoculation on the desk, a small vial that looked unimposing enough. Nonetheless, Cassie was irrationally nervous, as she often was when it came to needles. She knew it wouldn't really hurt much, that it would be over within seconds. For someone who'd already sat through three tattoos, getting panicky at the thought of a flu jab seemed silly. But, she reasoned, they had been under so much pressure lately. It was no wonder she felt extra jittery.

The nurse widened her eyes when she saw Cassie. "Wow, I love your hair! I've always wished I had the guts to go short, but I don't know if I'd suit it. Then I see girls like you and really wish I'd done it a long time ago!"

Cassie patted her palm against her shorn hair. She was still getting used to it, sometimes forgetting she had cut it at all. That morning, she'd reached for a hair bobble without even thinking about it. The band still sat on her wrist, digging in and leaving a pink wedge in her skin.

"Don't like needles?" The nurse was a young woman with a broad, tanned face and a wide mouth. She smiled in practiced sympathy.

"It's okay. I'm not usually too bad."

"You'll be fine. Over with in two seconds." The woman smiled again and handed Cassie a small clipboard. "If you can just complete the checklist for known allergies and pop your signature down there, we can have you out of here in no time."

Cassie took the pen and paper and stared down at the questionnaire. A droplet of water landed on the top of the page. She glanced up, scrutinising the ceiling. There didn't appear to be any leaks, but it was raining heavily outside. She swiped a hand over her hair, wondering if she had brought a dapple of raindrops into the room with her.

"Everything okay?"

Cassie snapped to attention and quickly checked the box to confirm that she didn't have allergies to the trigger items on the list then scribbled her signature. She trembled as she handed back the clipboard, the scent of the seaside wafting through the room.

"Left arm?" the nurse asked, skim-reading the form.

She rolled up her sleeve, watching the nurse spray antibacterial lotion onto a cotton ball, then swipe it against her upper arm.

Bracing herself, Cassie tried not to look when the nurse unwrapped the needle and inched closer. "Just relax your arm," she said, gently.

Cassie held her breath.

"Little pinch..."

The little pinch was more like a bee sting, but Cassie was relieved it would soon be over.

The nurse gasped, jerking her arm. The needle snapped clean off in Cassie's muscle, a sliver of metal dotting her skin.

"Oh my God!" the nurse stammered, both women staring at each other in shock. "It felt like someone shoved me. I don't understand... I'm so, so sorry. I'll have to run and get the doctor. I am so sorry!"

Cassie tried to smile in an attempt to make the nurse feel better, her arm throbbing dully around the metal spike. She looked at the clipboard, at the droplet that had grown into a sludgy puddle.

. . .

AN HOUR LATER, Cassie charged into the house and shrugged off her coat, wincing at the ache in her upper arm. "Anyone home?" she yelled.

Tad stepped out of the kitchen.

"You are not gonna believe what just happened to me." She paused, taking in the sight of her friend. "Hey, Ugly, what's wrong? Didn't it go well?"

Tad looked ashen, his eyes pained in the way they had been after Rice's attack at the hotel. "He killed one of them."

Cassie rushed towards him. "Are you talking about Rice? Rice killed one of your interviewers?"

Tad gripped his hair, strands sticking up between his fingers. "Yeah. I shouldn't have gone. We...*we* shouldn't be going anywhere. It isn't right."

"Lisa shoved my nurse. The needle snapped off in my arm." Cassie tried to imagine how she'd feel if Lisa had attacked the nurse instead, if the nurse had been killed right in front of her.

"Kyle and Pete are headed for the museum. Anything could happen to the people around them." Tad looked stricken.

"The museum? It's hardly time for a bit of a sight-see."

Tad gave her a courteous half-smile. He knew that joking was Cassie's favourite coping mechanism, and she was glad he was humouring her despite the tense situation. "Kyle texted. He thinks he may have found something that might help us. It's a rhyme written on the back of a painting in one of the exhibits."

"I'll call them." She slipped her phone from her jeans pocket. The screen bubbled with water, the large droplets moving with the angle of her hand like a spirit level. She swore and marched into the dining room, heading for the old rotary phone on the wall. Tilting the mobile until she could read Pete's number under the grey water, she started painstakingly turning the dial on the wall. "Fuck, how tedious is this..."

Tad stood in the doorway and watched as Cassie twisted in the final number and waited for the dial to spin back to the start, rolling her eyes in irritation.

Cassie listened to the strange static on the other end of the line. There were a few moments of silence, then a click, as though someone had picked up at the other end. "Pete?"

The foghorn noise that had tumbled out of the dead sailor's mouth burst from the receiver at a deafening volume. She screamed and dropped the phone. It clattered against the wall, then swung from side to side, the coiled cord stretching with each swing. Letting out a shuddering breath, she grabbed the neck of the phone and slammed it back into its cradle.

CHAPTER 22

WORK OF ART

The museum was busy, filled with locals and visitors taking respite from the rain. Mingling with the browsing tourists who left trails of raindrops on the pale wood floors, three classes of students ambled through the corridors, trying and failing to keep the noise down.

Pete climbed the stairwell to the gallery, peering down at the foyer below. It crossed his mind that he shouldn't be there, that the stairwell was the perfect place for Connor Rourke to strike. But the painting was displayed on the upper floor. He had no choice if he wanted to help Kyle defeat the ghosts.

He plucked his phone from his back pocket and fired off a text: *Heading up now. You close?* He hoped Kyle wasn't far away.

The museum felt oddly claustrophobic even with its open plan, pale wooden layout. The stairs creaked under his feet, and the droplets that had scattered down from soaked umbrellas had caused a murky wet mush to pool in the centre of the walkway. He held the railing tightly as he climbed, forcing his weight into his arm as a ballast. He reached the top and scanned the signs on the walls. There were three rooms off the balcony that overlooked the entrance hall. To his immediate left, a modern sculpture exhibit depicted the seasons. Over the centre door the sign read "Monet, A Reflective". An art student whose hands were dusted with pastel chalks carried an A5 pad from the entranceway and trotted past him down the steps.

Across the landing, the far door had a small plaque beside it: "Local Legends: Tales of the Town". Tales. If only that were true, Pete thought. The landing had cleared of patrons. He had more than enough room to stay next to the inner wall as he walked over the platform, as far from the railing above the two-storey drop as possible.

He took a step forward. Dizziness swam through his mind, fogging his vision. He gritted his teeth, determined to fight the effects of his ghostly oppressor. *Not today, Rourke*, he said to himself, recalling Eldon's advice. If you don't show them your weakness, it's less likely they can harm you. But he felt the oppressive weight of the ghost all over him, no matter what he told himself.

Pete cleared his throat against the constricted sensation Connor inflicted on him. He took another step, just as a group of kids came surging out of the seasons exhibit. He stepped out of their way, an instinctive move, but his shoe slid out from under him on the sodden walkway. He felt his body teeter to the side, saw the railing swimming up towards his chest. The metal bar caught him in his ribs and his legs shot out. His momentum sent his upper body pitching forwards.

His eyes widening in terror, he saw the blurred spectacle

of the entrance hall below, the ticket counter and the gift shop. The people milling in from the street to get out of the rain. Panic shot through him like a rocket going off, tingles flooding his entire body as gravity failed him.

A pattering of footsteps scurried up behind him.

His feet shot up off the ground and the bar slid down his torso as he tipped forward. He waited for Rourke to deliver a final push.

Hands gripped his upper arm, and he was tugged back, his feet eventually finding purchase and scrabbling against the wet wood. His fingers clasped the silken duffel coat of the woman who had saved him.

She held onto him for longer than was necessary, her expression probably more shaken than his own. She was a middle-aged woman with short dark hair and long, horse-like features. She bared her oversized teeth and exclaimed, "My Goodness! Are you all right, young man?"

Pete nodded, unable to speak, his heart thundering in his chest.

"I'm going to tell them to mop up this rainwater. It almost killed you!" she continued, finally letting him go.

He felt the familiar rush of vertigo consume him like a tidal wave, stronger than ever. His near-miss had fed the urge in Rourke, and Pete's salvation had only enhanced the ghost's frustration. As soon as the woman let him go, the fear of falling turned into something else, an ill-advised primal need to regain some control. Pete wrapped his hands around the railing and hoisted himself up on straight arms. Before the woman could react again, he swung his leg up over the barrier and pitched himself forward over the side. He regained his senses the split second he launched himself into the air, the sickening realisation that he was falling straight down into the museum lobby striking him dumb. He would have screamed, but his breath was stuck fast.

The pale wood floor flew up to meet him.

A woman screamed. People ran.

His foot connected with the ground, and he heard three sharp snapping sounds as his leg crumpled under the weight of his body. His back slammed the wood, punching the remaining air from his lungs. His skull cracked into the floor, and his head snapped forward, a whiplash effect. Black swam across his vision as unbearable pain began to pulse through his leg, pushing through the blissful numbness of shock.

Above him, a dark shape scurried along the railing. It stopped where he had thrown himself over, then it too leaped on the same trajectory. Halfway down, the black smudge morphed into a slender young man with overly long forearms, wearing a white work shirt that billowed out behind him. Connor Rourke landed on Pete's chest, his spectral feet somehow digging into his solar plexus, cutting off what little air Pete was managing to breathe.

Rourke leaned forward and leered in Pete's face.

KYLE HURRIED down the street to the museum, splashing through the growing puddles and soaking the backs of his jeans in his rush to get to Pete. It felt wrong leaving him alone outside of the house. They needed to find the painting, check the back of the frame, and get back to Brackenby as quickly as they could.

His phone rang, and he tugged it from his pocket,

expecting Pete. He was surprised to see it was the house phone, and answered hesitantly, bewildered about who might be calling from the old dial-up. "Hello?"

"It's Cassie."

Kyle squirmed with relief. He had a horrible feeling it might have been one of the ghosts, as much he knew that would be insane. "Hey, what's up?"

"Shit's hitting the fan. Rice killed one of Tad's interviewers and Lisa attacked my nurse... Well, me, really, but she shoved my nurse."

"Wait, he killed one of the interviewers? Is Tad okay?"

"Not really. Look, you and Pete need to watch out for the people at the museum. We've got no fucking business inflicting these ghosts on other people. Get in, get whatever it is you need, and get the fuck out. Okay?"

"Okay." Kyle felt numb, processing Cassie's words. She was right. If the ghosts were harming the people around them—*killing* them, even—they definitely needed to get in and out as fast as possible.

The squeal of a passing ambulance turning on its sirens sent Kyle's heart hammering. He felt foolish when he visibly jumped and put a hand on his chest in shock. A woman walking towards him on the path smirked a little, and his cheeks reddened.

He watched the ambulance turn the corner, and the siren ceased almost immediately. A crowd of people huddled on the street corner, facing the museum.

A sensation of dread washed over Kyle, and he broke into a run.

The ambulance crew were heading through the double doors, green medical bags at the ready. Kyle followed them through, hearing a girl outside sobbing into her phone. "He just jumped! It was awful."

In the foyer, Kyle skidded to a halt. He saw a flash of red and knew it was Pete's hoodie. Another smear of red was streaked along the pale wood floor, coming from under his friend's legs. One of them was bent at an unnatural angle, in more than one place.

Pete thrashed his arms against the floor, gasping for breath. His chest sounded constricted, and his shirt had been yanked open to show his skinny chest.

"Tension pneumo," one of the paramedics—a broad, middle-aged woman with bobbed blonde hair—muttered.

She tore open a packet and stuck a large-bore needle into the skin between two of Pete's ribs. He squealed and bucked, and the other paramedic shifted position, moving to hold his shoulders. It was then that Kyle saw the real reason Pete couldn't breathe. It was the spectral man crouched on his chest, leering into his face, unseen by all but the two residents of Brackenby House.

"No good... Sorry, Peter. Let's try that again." Looking puzzled, the paramedic adjusted the needle and plunged it into Pete's chest a second time. They listened for the usual gush of trapped air that simply wouldn't come.

"Why isn't it working?" the second medic, a young man with a Geordie accent asked.

"I have no idea, but it better work, this time..." She jammed the needle between his ribs once more, and Pete gave a strangled cry.

Rourke let out a delighted giggle, then leapt into the air and vanished.

Pete sucked rapid sips of air through blue lips, finally able to breathe. He choked and cried, his eyes rolling as he fought to stay conscious.

"Got it!" the medic cried, although the confused look on her face told Kyle that she knew something was amiss.

Torn between the desire to comfort his friend and the need to complete their mission, Kyle sidestepped in the direction of the stairs as staff began to head into the foyer with rolls of yellow cordon tape. He had to move fast. If he didn't, Pete's injury would be in vain. As quickly as he could, Kyle bolted for the stairwell.

"Hey, we're closing!" an attendant yelled.

Kyle ignored him, his trainers sliding on the wet steps. He dashed to the top, trying not to think about how high they were or the fact that this was the spot that Pete had fallen from.

He spied the sign for the "Local Legends" exhibit and dashed into the room.

The exhibit was larger than he had expected, with glass cabinets displaying artefacts and excavated jewellery that had been pulled up from the moors. A fake wishing well had been built in the centre of the room, depicting the singing well on Riley Hill. Rumour had it that something in the well sang at the full moon, and if you sang along with it, your heart's desire would come true. The artist had created a small imp-like creature that clung to the inner wall of the well. It was painted in greys and browns and reminded Kyle of Tad's description of Jarvis Rice.

The walls were covered in antique paintings with ornate frames. He skimmed over them, wracking his brains to remember what Grant's painting looked like. On the far wall, just past the well, he found it. He darted forward, swerving around the installation. It burst into an eerie song and the imp creature danced jerkily from side to side, making him jump out of his skin. For the second time that morning, he placed a hand on his racing chest, feeling foolish.

He stood in front of the picture and stared up at it. A copse of shadowy trees lined the road in front of Brackenby House. Peering out from one of the tree trunks, a painted spectral figure was emerging, casting white light onto the leaves at its feet.

Behind him, footsteps sounded along the corridor.

"Shit!" He placed his hands on the base of the picture and prised it away from the wall. He hunkered down and twisted to look upwards, seeing neat black writing scrawled over the brown paper backing. The picture was far heavier than he'd anticipated, and he struggled to hold it with one hand as he scrabbled at his pocket with the other, sliding out his phone.

"Hey! What the hell do you think you're doing?"

He looked over his shoulder at the museum attendant standing in the entrance, the roll of restriction tape in her hand. She looked wary and annoyed.

"Just a second. It's for a school project," Kyle stammered, bracing the weight of the frame against his forearm. His back ached, the weight of the picture and the unnatural angle making his muscles scream in protestation.

"Get your hands off it! You need to leave. There's been an accident." The woman hovered in the doorway, looking unsure of how she should proceed. She seemed to be a little frightened of him, and Kyle felt guilty.

He finally managed to lift his phone, jabbing the camera icon. He angled it as best as he could, firing off three pictures in quick succession. He just hoped he'd captured the rhyme, or all of this would have been for nothing.

He dropped the frame back into place and hurried past the woman, tightening his lips in an apologetic expression. He moved out onto the platform, hearing Pete moaning below. Kyle rushed for the stairs and grabbed the handrail, flicking to his phone's gallery. Holding his breath, he checked the pictures.

The first image showed nothing but brown paper and gum tape on the back of the frame. His heart lurched. What if he'd missed it completely? He swiped across, feeling relief when the next picture showed black ink. It was half of the verse, the first few words of each line cut off. He couldn't bring himself to breathe, even though his lungs were starting to burn. He swiped again. His last chance.

In the centre of the image, the words of the rhyme were intact and clear. Kyle felt like crying with relief.

Pete's scream disrupted his elation, and he plunged the phone into his pocket, running down the last few steps. He ducked under the tape that had already been wrapped around the end of the staircase and headed for the paramedics.

The attendant had followed him downstairs. She called out, "Hey! You need to leave, young man!"

Kyle ignored her and landed on his knees next to Pete's head. "He's my housemate. My friend."

The attendant gave him a strange look, glancing at the paramedic for guidance. When Pete reached out blearily and grabbed Kyle's wrist, she backed away.

The paramedic smiled at Kyle, reassuringly. "Okay, we need to move him. We've given him some pain relief, but it will still be unpleasant for him. Keep him calm for us. Stay near his head and move when we tell you."

Kyle crouched down and brushed his fingertips through Pete's cropped brown hair. He leaned close to his ear and whispered, "It's okay, man. He's gone. And I got it. I got the rhyme."

To the side, a horsey-looking woman spoke frantically to a policeman. "He slipped, and I grabbed him. He looked so relieved."

"So, he slipped on the wet floor?" the policeman confirmed, writing in his notepad.

"The first time, yes!" The woman cried. "After that, he just...jumped. It was like he wasn't even there anymore. His face went completely blank until he was over the rail."

"And then?"

"And then he woke up. But by then it was too late."

Pete let out a strangled scream as the paramedics started to stabilise his leg. Two pink circles rose up on his ashen cheeks.

"The morphine will kick in soon," the paramedic told Kyle, regret in their voice.

"Can't you wait until it does?" He placed his hands against Pete's cheeks, willing him to keep still.

"No time. He's going into shock."

Pete's bones crunched like a bag of gravel as the woman straightened the leg, and he slumped into unconsciousness in Kyle's hands.

CHAPTER 23
HOSPITALITY

"As soon as you find out how he is, you have to get back here," Tad said, his accent strong, stress causing his words to blur into one another.

Kyle slumped against the waiting room wall, the antiseptic-scented public phone gripped tightly in his hand. There was no cell reception in the hospital, and he felt ominously detached from his housemates without his phone on hand. "We can't leave him here. They'll come for him!"

"What choice do we have, Kyle? He's just got out of an operation. We can't exactly storm the hospital and wheel him out of there."

"I know, you're right. I just think... I feel like Rourke's already here for him."

"If that were the case, would he even have made it out of the operating room?" Tad asked, solemnly.

Kyle sighed into the phone, his breath fizzing through the mouthpiece. First Martin and Jonah, then Tad's interviewer. Almost Pete. It was getting to be too much. "I don't want to leave him here alone."

"You need to go to Caleb's with the rhyme. Then you need to get your ass back here as fast as you can."

Kyle looked down into his empty coffee cup, the peach plastic streaked with drops of brown liquid. It reminded him of his first meeting with Caleb at the library. It had only been four days, but it felt like weeks. He heard squeaking footsteps and saw the nurse moving briskly along the corridor, raising her eyebrows as she approached.

"Peter Moseley's friend?" she asked.

"Yes," Kyle slammed the phone down and tossed his cup into the waste bin.

"You can see him now, but only for a very short time. He's still sedated. Don't be alarmed by the tubes. He is doing as well as could be expected after that type of fall."

Kyle hurried along beside the petite nurse, his mind racing. He had to make sure Pete was taken care of. "I think he's in danger," he blurted.

The nurse gazed at him, her brow furrowing in concern. "What makes you say that?"

"I don't think he fell. I think he was pushed. And I think the person who did it might come back for him here." The words tumbled from Kyle's mouth in a frantic stream. It wasn't lies, he told himself. Not really.

"That's a strong allegation. I can arrange for the police to come and chat with you?"

Kyle raked his fingers through his hair, his heart thumping. He thought of Caleb and shook his head. "No, I have to go. Can you please make sure someone keeps an eye on him, though?"

The nurse gave a small shrug and smiled. "He's in intensive care. That's the best we can offer. People can't just come and go."

Kyle lowered his hand and felt the bracelet pluck his wrist hair. He scratched the sharp sting with his other thumb, then stared down at the tan cord. "If I give him something, can you make sure it doesn't get taken off?"

The nurse stopped at the doorway to the ICU and glanced down at the bracelet. "We don't allow jewellery. It can get snagged. Cause problems... I'm sure you understand."

Kyle peered through the glass and saw Pete lying in the nearest bed, a ventilator lifting his skinny chest with unnatural rhythm. He felt tears of frustration prick his eyelids, his cheeks growing hot. "Please! It's just...it's just this thin cord and some stones. It won't hurt him."

The nurse looked from the band to Pete, then back to Kyle. Her eyes widened in sympathetic understanding. She reached out and touched her fingers to Kyle's wrist. "He's in the best hands, honestly. We're doing everything we can for him."

She thinks he's your boyfriend, Kyle suddenly realised. Well, what the hell. It would have been laughable if not for the circumstances. Even if Pete *had* been gay, there was no way he and Kyle could ever be compatible as a couple. Still, if it helped him to get the damn talisman onto his friend's arm, he was more than willing to pretend. "Please, nurse. I couldn't bear it if he woke up when I'm not here. At least if he sees this, he'll know."

The nurse chewed the side of her lip and opened the door, gesturing towards Pete's bed. "You can go see him, now. I need to go and check on something. I'll be back in two minutes."

She shot Kyle a look of collusion, then hurried off down the corridor.

Kyle rushed to Pete's side, took the cord from his own wrist and tied it quickly onto Pete's. As soon as the bracelet left his skin, he felt the threat in the air around him increase. His lungs tightened with oppression and a strange sand-like scent clouded the room. He tucked the stones underneath the edge of Pete's plastic identity wristband, peering down at him. "It's the best I can do for now, buddy," he whispered. "They won't get you, so long as you're wearing this."

He wished he'd been able to give it to him that morning, before he'd set out to the museum. Kyle grimaced at the blue shadows under his friend's eyes, at the alarming cage that housed the pins and brackets that were holding his leg together. At the tubes snaking from his mouth, from his arms, and stuck to his bare, bruised chest.

"I have to go and see Caleb, now. We're going to fix this, Pete. We're going to get rid of them once and for all."

KYLE HURRIED from the hospital grounds and felt his phone vibrating in his pocket. The hospital was a service dead-zone, and when he lifted the phone and checked the screen, he discovered he had missed a call from Caleb. The voicemail symbol filled his screen, and he thumbed it and put the phone to his ear.

After the beep, his uncle's gravelled voice filled the speaker, sounding breathless and hurried, his words over-pronounced in his efforts to keep calm. "Runt, I think I've got what we need. In Hestor's things there's a fancy crate marked *Back from Whence They Came*, but it's locked and I don't see a key anywhere. I'm pretty sure it's connected to the poem Lucius was so obsessed with."

Kyle pumped his fist at his side, elated at the news. They really were getting somewhere.

Caleb continued, his speech quickening. "But there's something else. I got it wrong. We've been fooled this whole time. I found Holgrove's diary in Hestor's things. He's not the good guy in this!"

Static shuddered through the speaker, causing Kyle to flinch and pull the phone away from his ear. Through the screaming static, the halting consonants of his uncle's words occasionally broke through, followed by a grunting chuckle.

The line went dead.

"Shit!" Kyle exclaimed, earning a tut from an old man sitting on a bench. He called Brackenby's landline. "Come on, pick up pick up pick up!"

Lance answered after the fourth ring, his oddly cheerful voice a peculiar contrast to Kyle's panic. Although his cousin had just died, Lance was unable to shake his natural warmth. "Hullooo."

"Lance! I need you to go in the cellar."

"No fucking way."

"Listen to me— I don't think Po's there."

"He's always lurking down there. No way, man."

Kyle raked his hands through his hair in frustration, hurrying his pace. "I'm on my way to Caleb's. He left me a voicemail just now and I heard Po in the background."

"That's impossible."

"So, can you help me out? Just run down and see if you can feel him. Please!"

Lance heaved a reluctant sigh, then muttered, "Hang on."

Through the receiver, Kyle heard his friend wander out of the kitchen, the squeak of the cellar door opening, and the receding thud of Lance's footsteps.

Instinctively, Kyle looked to his wrist, proof of his protection from the pre-Incan monster, but found his skin bare and remembered he'd left his talisman with Pete. If Po was on the loose, Pete lying helpless and unconscious certainly needed it more than Kyle did. All the same, Kyle experienced a sudden sense of intense danger with a ferocity he hadn't felt since his return from Peru.

Impatient, he hurried along the road, almost running in his need to get to his uncle's home. After what felt like eternity, Lance creaked back up to the phone and spoke into the receiver. "You're right. I don't think he's down there. It just felt normal. I even called him out, and I didn't hear a breath or anything."

Even though Kyle had been certain, he suddenly doubted himself. "Are you sure?"

"Put it this way, if Cassie needed a nap right now, I'd feel happy with her bunking down there and saving herself the sleepwalk. He's gone, Kyle."

"Shit."

"What, is that not a good thing?"

"Caleb!" Kyle cried.

He hung up and dropped the phone into his pocket then broke into a sprint, dashing across a road without looking, a furious honk from an oncoming car blasting behind him. He ignored the swearing motorist and pounded on, his trainers pinching his toes as his feet slammed the pavement. Kyle turned onto Caleb's cul-de-sac and stumbled to a halt outside his front door, breathing heavily. He rapped on the door and waited.

Nobody came.

He pounded again, harder this time, and the door sprang open beneath his curled fist.

Kyle paused on the doormat, his chest rising and falling. "Caleb?" he hissed. He stepped carefully over the threshold of the home and strained into the silence of the hallway. "Uncle Caleb?"

A sound like rolling glass came from the office room. Kyle turned to the door. It was mostly closed, a crack of light pooling on the hallway floorboards in front of his feet. He took a soft step closer to the study, held out a trembling hand, and gently pushed his fingers against the door.

The door crept open and a wash of red burst into Kyle's vision. He threw his arm over his nose and mouth as the metallic shit scent of gore assaulted him. Staggering back, he let his eyes dart around the scene, his brain running sluggishly, trying to make sense of what he was looking at.

The desk was covered in letters and notebooks pulled from Hestor Morello's boxes which were piled to the side of Caleb's office chair. Red splodges coated the cardboard, dripping down the desk and pooling in sticky daubs on the open pages of the books. Ink smudged into watery brown fluid, and hunks of what looked like gobbets of chicken were scattered across the desktop.

Kyle lowered his gaze to the mass of red on the floor. It

soaked the round rug, a tiny sliver of white wool still visible on the right-hand side. The rest was sodden with gore.

Caleb lay in the centre.

Kyle stepped forward to see if there was any hope in hell that he could help his relative, then recoiled when he realised what he was looking at.

Only half of Caleb lay in the centre of the rug. It was as though someone had laid him down in front of a circular saw and pulled him through it, the blade tearing through the centre of his face, the middle of his ribs, cleaving the length of his spine and hacking his hips down the middle. The only difference if it had been a circular saw was that the cuts would have been relatively clean, the line drawn evenly. Here, something had torn through the bone and flesh, triangles of gaping skin draped over crushed and jagged hunks of bone.

One leg. One arm. Kyle stepped gingerly closer and saw that Caleb's missing half had been flung carelessly to the other side of the room. It had evidently hit the wall before sliding to the ground, a human-like smear of blood and viscera painted down the wallpaper. Caleb had landed with his left leg bent and his left arm resting over his knee, as if he was casually observing at the scene. It was a pose that made Kyle half-expect him to lift his head and say through half a mouth, "What do you think of all this, then?"

He almost laughed, overcome by the bizarre madness of grief and fear that makes a person gravitate towards the inappropriate.

Then he felt a cool breeze blow against the nape of his neck, and a rough grunting sniff sounded directly behind his shoulder.

Kyle grabbed for the bracelet, again forgetting that he no

longer had it. He whipped around, expecting to come face to face with the three-eyed beast, but there was nothing there. Kyle reversed, his heel squelching into one of his uncle's dispelled kidneys, and he slipped, grabbing the desk for support before he hit the ground. Caleb's phone, already smashed, crunched under his foot.

He looked up at the desktop. An ornate box was in the middle of the reams of bloodied letters. It was beautifully crafted—polished wood with jade green edging and copper fixtures, and a rounded lid that was locked with a simple keyhole. The side of the crate was marked with looping painted scrawl: *Back from Whence They Came.*

A book lay open next to the box. The pages were spattered with fresh blood congealing over a diary entry written in familiar Victorian script. He flipped the book closed and scanned the cover. Green leather, the same colour as the crate, embossed in gold print: *From the Desk of L. Holgrove.*

Kyle heard his uncle's voice in his head, the phone message that had been interrupted by Po's attack. *"I got it wrong. We've been fooled this whole time. I found Holgrove's diary... He's not the good guy in this..."*

He grabbed the book and shoved it into the waistband of his pants, hoisted the crate under his arm, and ran from the house.

CHAPTER 24
POETRY IN MOTION

"I've...I've never seen somebody die before," Tad stammered, sat upright but curled in a ball on the couch. He was barefoot, clad in baggy grey cotton sweatpants and a loose sage-coloured jersey, his arms wrapped around his knees and tugging them into his chest. He rested his chin, his cheek, then his forehead on his knees, sinking further into himself.

"Me either," Kyle mumbled. He had Lucius's diary on his lap and occasionally flicked through the pages half-heartedly.

Cassie rubbed Kyle's arm and heaved a world-weary sigh. After Kyle had brought the crate back to the house and set it down in the kitchen, the housemates had been overcome with a solemn need to congregate together and commiserate. To recharge their batteries before even attempting to unpick the rhyme. They needed the break, though they all knew it would be short-lived.

Cassie tensed her arm, flexing the sore muscle. After some excruciating prodding and poking, the doctor had managed to pull the flu jab needle out with tweezers. The nurse was distraught, and neither of them could quite understand Cassie's calm acceptance of the incident. It wasn't the nurse's fault, there was no doubt about that. And, judging by what had happened to Tad's interviewer, Pete, and Caleb that morning, both she and the nurse had gotten off lightly.

Lance handed Kyle a glass of whiskey and crouched down in front of him. Like Tad, he was wearing sweats, as though each member of the household was striving to find the smallest comfort. "I'm so sorry about your uncle, man."

"He just wanted to help us, you know? I feel like such a shit; he moved out of this house to get away from the ghosts. He didn't even experience them like we have. Then I go and fucking release them, and he tries to help us, and they kill him. They literally tear him to pieces." Kyle's cheeks turned scarlet, and he screwed up his eyes, tears pooling and spilling from his lids. "If we'd listened to him, none of this would have happened."

"If your mum had listened," Tad said, softly. "Remember, it was your mum who said he was making a drama out of nothing. It was your mum who told us the house was safe and the legend was bullshit. Who are you gonna believe?"

"But I *didn't* believe her! I wanted a cheap house to live in through uni. And if it was haunted like people said, all the fucking better." Kyle glanced at his housemates.

"He's right," Cassie murmured. "We all knew the history of the house. Even though I didn't want to believe, I was a little scared to move in, deep down. But I couldn't pass up the chance of knocking two-hundred quid off the rent each month."

"I wasn't scared," Tad told her. "I didn't believe at all."

Lance shook his head. "Me either."

"But Pete did," Kyle recalled. "I remember one night after we'd first moved in. We put the empty boxes down in the cellar, remember?"

Cassie smiled. "I remember. He shouted at me for having three whole boxes for makeup."

"Well, we dragged them all down the steps and then started unfolding them to flatten them against the wall. All of a sudden, Pete looked into the back corner and froze up. He said he felt like there was a bear or something hiding in the shadows."

Tad unfolded his long legs and stretched them out, crossing his hands over his chest. "That's weird."

Kyle nodded. "I know. I keep thinking about it, now. Like, we *could* feel them before, just like Caleb could. I know we could. The more I think about it, the more I wonder whether all this would have happened regardless of the séance."

Cassie frowned. "Before Halloween my stuff got wet. I thought it was me being ditsy because I swam all the time. But I remember whenever I had a bath in the house weird stuff would happen."

"Like what?" Lance asked, swirling his whiskey. The ice cubes clattered in the glass.

"Like, I would lay out a towel on the rack, but when I went to grab it, I'd find it on the floor. Or I'd put my cleanser on the side of the bathtub, but when I reached for the bottle, it wasn't where I'd left it. I thought I was being paranoid because the house was so big and old. I grew up in a council flat, for fuck's sake. You couldn't lose anything in my bathroom as a kid—everything was all at arm's length. I just thought I was creeped out because of the size of the room."

"I get that." Lance grimaced. "I was used to things being a lot smaller and newer. I got spooked in the front hallway when I first moved in, and that's where Pile usually jumps me now."

"What about you, Tad?"

Tad shrugged, closing off to the group as he thought. They knew not to bother him, but to wait. Lance and Kyle drained their glasses. When Lance got to his feet to refill them, Cassie motioned that she wanted one, too.

Eventually, Tad sucked a lungful of air and said, "I woke up being choked. But not choked; it was a feeling like something had fallen on my neck. I can't help but think about my interviewer. How when the table landing on her throat, Rice said it was *how he liked them*."

The group looked at the floor.

"I get it, now. That's his M.O. The executions. Whether he was cutting off heads with axes or hanging people from gallows. Whether he was strangling women in their beds to frame their husbands or slitting men's throats in dark streets. He went for the neck. I thought I had reflux, from being stressed about the prototype. I thought the stress was giving me acid in my sleep. And I could hear him smacking the axe handle again his hand at night, but I rationalised it. I told myself it was just the old pipes, but it was his axe." Tad hunched over, shuddering.

Cassie leapt from Kyle's side and hopped up beside Tad on the couch, wrapping her arm around his shoulders. By comforting the others, she didn't have to face the fact that Pete was miles away, unconscious, already vulnerable to harm. By acting as the remaining boys' protector, she could pretend she was halfway tough enough to deal with this herself.

When Lance passed her a glass, she reached out and took it, gulping at the tan liquid. It burned her tongue, but she gritted her teeth so as not to show it.

Kyle sipped his whiskey and looked at Lance when he sat down beside him in Cassie's place. "I remember you saying it, too. That you felt like something wasn't right."

Lance looked dazed for a moment, then slapped his hand against his forehead. "It's the year."

The others stared at him, blankly.

"It's the fucking leap year!" Lance jumped up, suddenly animated, the mood in the room dragged from its sombre heaviness by his enthusiasm. He rushed to the bookshelf and yanked a local history book from the shelving, flipping through to the chapter on the house. "What do all the ghosts have in common?"

"February 29th." Tad sat forward.

"They all died on the same day," Cassie shrugged, looking to Kyle.

He shrugged, as baffled by the sudden excitement as she was. "Except Po, as far as we know. We knew that already."

"It's the leap year." Lance insisted.

"Well, obviously. But it's not February 29th now," Kyle protested.

"But it was. This year is a leap year. Our séance brought them out again...*because* it's a leap year." Lance clicked his fingers and pointed to Kyle. "When did Caleb move out?"

"Umm, two years before we got the place."

265

Lance grinned and shut the book with a theatrical snap. "That, my friends, was a fucking leap year."

Tad nodded. "They're stronger on the leap year. That must be why Professor Grant summoned them in 1876."

Kyle leapt to his feet and rushed to the kitchen, standing over the blood-stained crate he'd left on the table. He placed Holgrove's diary down next to it. The others followed him and crowded around. "Caleb thinks this box is linked to the verse on the painting. He was talking about it when Po killed him."

"Are we definitely, one hundred percent sure it was Po?" Lance asked.

"He was torn in two."

"But could it have been something else? An accident?"

"Aside from Caleb swallowing a hand grenade, I'm pretty positive it was Po," Kyle barked, leaning heavily against the table.

"So, they really are even stronger when they leave the house," Lance mumbled.

Tad narrowed his eyes. "I told you that. After the hotel. I told you they were stronger away from home, but you didn't believe me."

Cassie shot Lance an accusing look.

"It wasn't that I didn't believe you. It's just, it's a haunted house, right? Things aren't supposed to happen away from home. You didn't believe it, either, Cassie. That night you had that fight with Martin..." He caught himself and trailed off.

"It's us that's haunted though, remember? Even more so than the house itself," Kyle said.

"And nobody's safe when we leave," Cassie murmured.

"So, we're trapped." Lance put his hand on the crate and narrowed his eyes, as though concentrating hard enough to see inside. He shook it, trying to prise up the lid. It remained tightly locked.

"What about Pete?" Cassie looked to Kyle.

"I gave him my bracelet." Kyle pulled back his sleeve to reveal his bare wrist. "He should be safe, for now."

"I wish we could break him out of there." Cassie said, miserably.

"Believe me. He's in the right place."

Only Kyle had seen first-hand the extent of Pete's injuries.

The room fell into solemn silence. Upstairs, mocking footsteps pattered faintly across the landing.

"So, what next?" Cassie asked. "Apart from locking ourselves inside for the rest of our lives."

"We eat," Lance insisted. "Let's just get some take-out, then we'll look at the rhyme. We'll need to get our strength up if we're to stand half a chance of facing the ghosts."

CHAPTER 25
INVENTORY

Although the housemates had been reluctant to eat at first, the food they ordered had gone down surprisingly well. Once they were all finished, Kyle bundled up the wrappers and paper trays and dumped everything in the trash, keen to get back to business. The others waited for him, standing around the table looking somewhat less weary than they had been before the meal.

Kyle reached for his phone and accessed his photos. "I got the verse, but I don't know how helpful it is. I haven't really had chance to look at it."

The housemates leaned over the table as Kyle expanded the image and spun the phone towards them:

A third eye for the untamed beast, not amethyst but black as pitch.

Baptism by the Light of Dawn will quell the wrath of the siren's song.

Bake your bread and silver hide, placed inside the axeman's loaf.

Hell's fourth circle's guardian sits and banishes with Eucharist.

Show the steps of the fallen fiend, doomed to plunge with eternal scream.

"Well, that clears that up," Lance quipped.

Tad grabbed a pad and quickly wrote out the words, tearing off the paper and putting it in front of them so that Kyle could put his phone away. They read the verse through in silence.

"Damn it." Cassie struck a hand across her shorn hair.

"No, it has to make sense," Kyle gritted out in frustration. "Let's think."

"Who wrote the verse on the painting?" Tad asked after a while.

"Lucius."

Tad frowned. "Are you sure?"

"Who else?"

"It didn't look like his writing. From what you've shown us before, I mean."

Kyle dug out his phone and focused on the lettering rather than the words in the picture. He grabbed Lucius's diary and opened it to a random page. Tad was right. Lucius wrote with looped letters and wide, arching strikes. The writing on the back of the picture was joined close and tight, by a more restrained hand. "Perhaps he was writing with the painting already up on the wall, so it looks unusual...or maybe he changed it on purpose. That's the only thing that makes sense, right? I mean, who else would have written about getting rid of the ghosts?"

Tad pointed to the wording on the side of the crate. *Back*

from Whence They Came. It was the same handwriting as the rhyme.

A strange sinking sensation poured ice down Kyle's belly. He thought back to the last words of Caleb's call. Words that he'd temporarily forgotten at the sight of his friends in mourning.

"What is it?" Tad scrutinised his face, never missing a trick.

"Caleb said something else when he called me. He said something about Lucius not being what we thought he was."

"In what way?"

Kyle shook his head and looked around the kitchen, trying to see Lucius's tell-tale shadow in the one of the corners, but he was nowhere to be found. He hoped Caleb had been wrong, that Kyle hadn't been pinning hopes on a family member in the other realm who may well be as dangerous as The Suffering ghosts. He opened the well-worn leather diary and started to flick through the pages. His thumb pressed against something hard inside the back sleeve. He flipped to the back, slipped his fingers under the binding, and pulled out a heavy gold key.

"Yes!" Lance cried, snatching it from Kyle's fingers and inserting it into the box's keyhole. He twisted it to the right. With a mechanical clunk, the hinges popped away from the lid. Lance's eyes shone as he looked up at Kyle. "Well, he can't be that bad if he had the key to the box that might stop them."

Kyle nodded slowly, but he couldn't shake the ominous feeling that Caleb was right. He looked back to the diary and opened it to the pages that had been lying open on Caleb's desk when he called.

They were soaked in dark blood, the dried edges browning. Apart from a few illegible words here and there, any remnants of ink had been dissolved in the puddle of blood from the attack. Whatever secrets the diary may have held, Po had made sure they'd never be seen again. He dropped the book onto the table, disheartened.

Tad had been watching him and caught his eye. He looked hopefully at the box as Lance made a show of lifting the lid. Kyle gave him a short smile in response. He was right; there was still some hope.

Lance stared into the crate, his brow creasing in concentration, then snatched up a piece of dark glass. "Hey, look—*not amethyst but black as pitch*? What is this? Coal?"

Kyle plucked the stone from his fingers and held it up, dawning realisation quickening his heartbeat. "It's onyx."

"Isn't that a Pokémon?" Lance smirked at his joke.

Kyle looked at the group, stunned excitement in his eyes. "It was used to make sacrificial blades in Incan rituals. Selestino told me it was one of Po's weaknesses."

Lance matched his sudden excitement. "Amethyst is the stone that links to the third eye."

Cassie raised her eyebrows.

"I worked in the spa for that godawful summer, remember? It was on a poster in the reception."

"So...what, it wants us to ram the onyx into his middle eye?" Cassie asked.

Kyle grinned, palming the stone in a triumphantly balled fist. "I think that's exactly what it wants us to do."

Tad lunged for the crate and began to unpack it. Dust plumed into the kitchen, filling the room with a musty, chalky scent. He pulled out a mould-speckled shoebox and an oblong package wrapped in age-yellowed muslin.

"If that's a mummy's head, I'm out of here," Cassie quipped, pointing at the fraying material.

Tad gathered up the strange bundle and pressed his fingers into the white residue it left on the table.

"Cocaine?" Kyle guessed.

He rubbed his fingertips together. "Looks like...flour."

They watched as Tad gently tugged at the binding and unwrapped the parcel. In the centre of the wrapping a half-empty hessian sack of King Arthur flour lay crumpled. "Antique flour?" Tad read from the sack, looking confused.

"Well, that's not something we need for the ritual," Kyle said.

"Unless we need it for the bread?"

"Isn't this for the bread?" Cassie delved into the crate and pulled out a dull silver coin. *"Bake your bread and silver hide, placed inside the axeman's loaf."*

Tad dusted flour from his hands. "Perhaps we need both?"

Kyle frowned. It seemed to make sense, but a niggling voice in the back of his mind told him that they had missed something. He reached for the shoe box and carefully prised open the spore-dappled lid. "Oh, hey. I'm guessing this is yours, Cass."

Cassie handed the coin to Tad and moved around the table to stand next to Kyle. She peered apprehensively down at the contents. "It's all stuff from a ship." The mildew scent from the box made her nose twitch. She reached down and lifted a coffee-stained letter from the top, a ship's emblem emblazoned on the header.

"The SS Daybreak," Kyle read. "What does it say?"

Cassie read the letter aloud, her voice cracking in the quiet room. "I, Captain Jonathan Fairbrother, do proclaim the launch of my vessel, the SS Daybreak, a success. Here, on 6th June 1802, I bid her fair seas and guiding winds."

Tad plucked a small glass bottle from the box and gave it a little shake. Murky water sloshed inside the glass. "What's this? Poison?"

"I doubt it," Cassie said. "It's all just stuff about giving the crew good luck in here." She dropped the letter back in the box and looked thoughtful.

"Perhaps it's sea water," Lance suggested. "I read that sailors used to carry sea water from the maiden voyage and store it on the ship to keep it from sinking."

"Is that true?" Cassie questioned.

"Well, I read it in a novel, but it sounds about right."

Kyle slipped his phone from his pocket and quickly typed into his search engine. "Yes! It was supposed to keep the ship safe."

"Can you find anything about the ship? The...uh...SS Daybreak?" Tad asked.

Kyle chewed his lip and typed swiftly with his thumb. He scrolled, then read out loud, "It just says it launched on the same date in the letter and was decommissioned in 1873. It had a good run from the looks of it."

Cassie took the bottle from Tad. "So, I guess it worked."

"But why did Caleb have it?"

"He bought crates of rubbish from the houses of people whose ancestors knew Lucius and Professor Grant. It was how he discovered the truth. He's been doing it for years."

Kyle grew pensive. The name Jonathan Fairbrother rang a bell. He just didn't know why.

"Do you think I can use this to get rid of Lisa Vaughan?" Cassie peered at the tiny bottle, sloshing the water inside.

"Lucky sea water? Maybe. It's better than nothing." Kyle smiled. "All of this stuff is here for a reason, after all. Thanks to Caleb"

The group stood in reverent silence for a moment, and Kyle knew they were each thinking of his gruff uncle with gratitude.

Kyle's memories drifted back to the library, to the moment he and Caleb pulled out almost identical note-books. He recalled Caleb's fear of Lisa Vaughan, and his warning not to underestimate her. "Wait! That's where I know that name. Jonathan Fairbrother testified against Lisa at her trial. He was the only person who'd ever stopped her from killing his men. He'd heard the rumours about her—when he found out his men had been to see her, he tied them to their bunks. They ended up in asylums."

Cassie held the bottle to the light. "That explains it then. Water from the one ship's crew she couldn't drown."

"Caleb said Fairbrother was more than just a ship's captain. He was some kind of demonologist."

"So, this is like holy water, but for demons?"

Lance hoisted a shoulder in a shrug. "Isn't that just the same thing?"

"Either way. I'm glad we have it." Cassie placed the bottle back in the box and peered down at the poem.

"I vote that we try and get rid of Rourke first," Tad said softly, pulling the page towards him and underlining the words with his finger.

"Right. Pete'll never get better if Rourke keeps on at him in the hospital." Cassie peered over Tad's shoulder, bracing her arm across his back and resting her cheek on her hand, concentrating on the words. "So, Rourke must be the 'fallen fiend,' I guess. It wants us to *show his steps*.'"

Lance grabbed the sack of flour. "Hear me out. He worked at a grain factory, right?"

"Yep. That's where he died, falling through a trapdoor in the rafters." Cassie confirmed.

"If you scatter flour on the floor, what can you see?"

"Footsteps." Tad took a pen from the counter and circled the line. He drew an arrow and wrote Rourke's name, then labelled the first line with Po's. "A siren's like a sea witch, right? That has to be about Lisa Vaughan."

Cassie leapt from Tad's back, suddenly animated. She snatched up the tiny bottle of seawater. "Baptism by the Light of Dawn!"

The boys stared at her, blankly.

"The SS Daybreak! Daybreak is Dawn. I reckon I have to soak her forehead with this, like a baptism." She shook the bottle, then placed it carefully in her pocket and patted it.

"Yes!" Kyle exclaimed, then pointed at the poem. "The axeman is obviously Rice. He needs the silver coin in the bread. But how in the hell would we get him to eat it?"

"Perhaps we just leave it upside down on the side?" Tad scrolled through Wikipedia on his phone. "It says here that the executioner would always know which was his loaf, because it would be left upside down. That way nobody took it and he'd always get fed."

"Maybe..." Kyle wasn't convinced. It seemed far too easy.

"That only leaves Pile," Lance told them, looking dejectedly into the now-empty box.

"Wait, you don't have anything to use?" Cassie looked at the selection of objects, four items that appeared to correlate with the poem and link to each ghost.

Lance shook his head.

"Wait, what does the poem say for Pile?" Cassie asked.

"*Hell's fourth circle's guardian sits and banishes with Eucharist.*" Lance read.

"What the fuck is a eucharist?"

"It's like communion, you dummy." Lance wearily sat down on the nearest stool, then shot to his feet. "Jesus Christ!"

The others watched in stunned silence as Lance picked up the stool and threw it across the kitchen. It landed against the back wall, clattering to a halt.

He rubbed the back of his jeans and shuddered, then turned to them in explanation. "It's all to do with Pile and the Hellfire Club. That's the extra stool. The one we only bring out for guests. He keeps putting it out to fuck with me. It's a setting for the Devil. The seat's always fucking freezing. My ass is frozen."

Kyle looked to the stool on the ground, then back to Lance. "Pile's trying...to give you piles."

The housemates stared at him for a second, then dissolved into laughter that started half-heartedly, like titters in a church, then grew into amiable guffaws.

Cassie wiped tears from her eyes and nudged her elbow into Kyle's arm. "I needed that."

Lance choked back the last of his laughter and held his

arms out wide. "Hey, me too, but I still don't have a weapon, you guys. Let's get serious for a sec."

Kyle looked at the empty box regretfully. "Well at least we know who the guardian of the fourth circle of Hell is."

Lance nodded. "Pluto."

"So we know it's the right ghost," Tad pointed out.

At Cassie's confused look, Kyle explained. "The Hellfire Club worshipped Pluto. When you were at Martin's that night, we got a voice through the spirit box. We think it was Pile. He said things that linked to Pluto."

"Like what?"

"*Why do you hoard*. It's from Dante," Lance told them. "The people in the fourth circle of Hell push boulders back and forth with their chests. They go one way and ask why you hoard. When it gets pushed back the other way, the other person says, '*Why do you waste*?' Pluto watches over them. It all fits."

"But if the Hellfire Club worships Pluto, why would Pluto be the thing to defeat him?" Cassie asked.

"I guess we're about to find out," Kyle deadpanned. "Are we ready to do this?"

CHAPTER 26
MORTAL COMBAT

The housemates slowly climbed the stairs, Kyle carrying the antique sack of flour. On the third step, he felt a wave of nausea.

"Anyone else feeling ropey all of a sudden?" Lance asked, shaking his head sharply and leaning down to press his fingertips against the edge of the step above him.

Cassie placed both hands on the banister and closed her eyes, her body weaving a little. "Jesus. Is this how Pete felt all the time?"

Tad gripped his thigh and swallowed. "Ugh. The fucker's here with us, at least."

Kyle looked at Tad incredulously. He could feel his cheeks losing colour, his skin tingling the way it did whenever he had to go on a boat and seasickness kicked in. "At least?"

"We know he's not with Pete," Tad explained.

They clambered up onto the landing and scrambled back against the wall. Kyle placed the sack of flour at his feet, his hands trembling as he untied the frayed rope cord.

Footsteps pattered towards them and Kyle felt a sudden, sharp shove in his side. He lurched forward and stumbled into the banister, kicking the sack. Tad wrapped an arm around his waist and hauled him back, and Kyle's skull collided with Tad's chin. Kyle heard his friend swear in Japanese and he apologised quickly, untangling himself and moving to the flour.

"Shit." He looked down at the mess. Rourke's shove had caused him to flip the bag, leaving a thick triangle of scattered white across the floorboards.

"Well, we needed it on the floor," Cassie pointed out.

"I dunno, I thought it needed to be a thin layer. He might not run through it."

In mocking response, Rourke's footsteps pelted for them at breakneck speed from the direction of Pete's room. As they watched, the flour puffed into the air, two small depressions stamping into the blanket of white. Three shoe-shaped white marks appeared ahead of the spill. Then the footsteps paused.

Before their eyes, Rourke materialised. He stared down at his feet in puzzlement, then looked back at the spilled flour. His overly long arms receded, the spindly fingers morphing into those of a regular human. He raised his head, the sickly green pallor of his skin pinking, the sagging flesh tightening, until he looked like a normal young man standing on the landing in front of them.

He regarded the flour footsteps and began frantically panting, his eyes widening in terror. Something under his feet shifted, and an unearthly creaking sound reverberated around the landing. Although the floorboards of the house remained solid, Rourke's left foot plummeted, his whole body twisting as if something had given way beneath him. He lifted his eyes to Kyle's and let out a terrified scream, reaching out a hand for him to grab.

Kyle ducked away, refusing.

He watched as Rourke shot downwards through the landing, his scream fading. There was a sudden, sharp crack, and he was silenced.

Tad stood up straight. "I don't feel dizzy anymore."

"I think he's gone." Kyle said.

"We did it." Tad grinned, then the smile fell from his face and he ducked and cowered as an axe whistled through the air. The sharp blade sailed over his scalp, ruffling strands of his hair. "Shit, it's Jarvis— Run!"

Kyle had never seen Jarvis Rice materialise before, and the sight of the spectral executioner solidifying on the landing was terrifying. The gore-covered man pulled back the axe, furious that he'd missed his mark.

They all rushed to the stairs, traipsing spilled flour in their wake. As they thundered down the steps, a fearsome knock came at the front door.

"That's Pile!" Lance cried when the tell-tale glow of a candle flame floated through the window and into the hallway in front of them.

Kyle leapt off the bottom step and went flying, sliding in a puddle of water and seaweed.

Cassie swore. "They're all coming at once!"

Kyle clambered to his feet, dripping, and fell on the front doorknob, forcing it open and tumbling out onto the porch. The others dashed through the door beside him, piling onto the driveway. The heavy antique oak door slammed shut behind them.

Trembling, Tad leaned forward, gingerly pressing his fingertips to his scalp. "Did he get me? Am I cut?"

Cassie peered through the section of hair that had been caught by the executioner's blade and shook her head. "You're good."

Lance braced his hands against his knees and huffed deep breaths. He looked on the verge of tears, his eyes wide and glassy. "We have to get out of here."

Cassie rounded on him. "And go where, exactly?"

"I dunno. We got Rourke, so Pete's safe."

"So, fuck everyone else we might come into contact with? I love Pete. You know I do. But I don't see why he's more important than anybody else in our lives."

Kyle ignored the blush that spread over Cassie's cheeks when she said she loved Pete, and he instead turned to Lance. "She's right. We have to finish this."

"We can't! They'll kill us," Tad yelled. He looked as frantic as he had in the car the night they picked him up from the hotel. His skin had gone the colour of off cream, and a sheen of sweat glistened on his high cheekbones.

Kyle gripped his friend's wrist and squeezed, trying to ground him. "They'll kill us if we leave. Sooner or later. We don't have a choice."

"Oh, fuck!" Lance squealed, pushing his hands into his curls and spinning around on the spot.

"We've got the upper hand, here! We know how to defeat them." Kyle insisted.

"We don't even know if it's going to work!" Tad cried.

Cassie stepped forward and jabbed her finger at him. "It worked for Rourke. And that's good enough for me." She turned to face the house, her eyes narrowing determinedly.

She rocked on the balls of her feet and clenched her fists, looking the way she did at swim competitions before the starting whistle blew and she sprang into action.

Kyle met Tad's eyes, feeling numb. His heart sank when his best friend stared at him helplessly and mouthed, "I don't want to die."

"You won't." Kyle mouthed back. He wanted to believe it.

"Fuck this," Cassie snapped. "You can stay out here and wait for them to come to you if you want. I'm going to face this bitch."

Kyle watched with admiration as she bolted for the porch, leaping up the steps and shoulder-barging the door. She disappeared inside the house. "I'm going with her," he called to Lance, who still clasped sprouts of his curly blond hair between his fingers and gazed longingly at the road.

Kyle reached the door and was relieved to hear Tad's footsteps directly behind him. They slipped into the hallway. When Kyle held the door open, Lance stepped inside.

CHAPTER 27

SHOWDOWN

Kyle looked down at his feet, expecting to be standing in the puddle of seawater that he had skidded on at the foot of the stairs, but the floorboards were dry. Pile had been standing near the door, but now the hallway was completely empty.

The walls of the entrance hall appeared somehow taller and whiter, the path leading to the rooms ahead wide and empty. It was a place Kyle had stood hundreds of times, taking off his coat or getting ready to step out. But the house seemed alien to him now. It didn't feel as though he belonged there at all.

Beside him, Tad shivered and rubbed his arms. His breath came out in little curls of steam when he spoke. "Where have they gone?"

"They're still here," Lance whispered. His eyes darted around, scanning the stairs and the kitchen entrance at the far end of the hall with jerking movements of his head.

Kyle felt a slight brush on the back of his neck and flinched away, expecting to find one of the ghosts standing directly behind him. It was just their coats, hanging on the hooks. He let out a shuddering breath, trying to keep his cool, even though his heart was hammering. "I don't know why they aren't coming for us."

"Maybe they're scared," Cassie suggested, raising an eyebrow and smirking as though she was making a joke. But the steely look of determination in her eye made Kyle wonder if she might be right. He assumed the ghosts knew they'd managed to get rid of Rourke. Perhaps they were waiting until they could regain the upper hand.

"We need to draw them out," Kyle whispered. He opened his mouth to speak again, then froze.

Jarvis Rice materialised in the hallway, emerging from under the stairwell. He floated, his filthy feet hovering an inch away from the ground, the festering crater in the back of his head exposing his moulded brain. The axe dragged along the floor, scraping a channel into the wooden floorboards and leaving spatters of brown gore in its wake. Inside the living room doorway, he turned and leered at Tad. The door slammed closed in front of him.

Tad heaved a sigh and moved closer to the living room.

"Wait, we didn't make any bread!" Kyle grabbed for Tad, stopping him in his tracks.

Tad stared down at the silver coin in his left palm. He closed his fist around it and glanced back at Kyle. "I will just have to make do."

There was a sudden crash from the living room. The housemates staggered back against the front door, startled. It sounded as though the room were being ransacked, the bookshelves splintering to pieces, the television thrown into the wall, and the couches overturned. In the silence that followed, there came the noise of something metallic reverberating, accompanied by a soft *whump*—an axe handle being slapped into a palm, over and over.

"He's ready for me," Tad said through gritted teeth.

Kyle felt a wrenching urgency to protect his best friend. He grabbed Tad's wrist, but Tad shook him off and strode to the living room. Kyle pictured the monster executioner on the other side of the wall, standing with his legs wide in the carnage he'd made of the room, menacingly slapping the axe down as he waited for Tad to appear. Tad held the coin—a coin that might be completely useless without the loaf of bread—to his ear. He shook his closed fist, and the coin jangled against his silver ring.

The slapping of Rice's axe stopped.

Tad nodded to himself. He stepped into the living room and closed the door.

A waft of smoke filled the hallway. Lance trembled. "I still don't know how to fight Pile," he whispered.

Kyle wracked his brains for an answer. "How about the things he said in the EVP?"

"It's worth a try." Lance puffed out his chest, ready for battle. Outside, a cat yowled.

LANCE'S KNEES quaked with fear. He knew all-too-well what it was like to be in close-proximity to Pile and still hadn't fully recovered from his antics during economics class. Then, Pile hadn't even come close to hurting Lance, but he'd sensed the threatening danger emanating from the spirit in waves. Somehow, Abina had sensed it, too. He recalled the advice she had given him after the attack: *Call it out. Never give it the upper hand and you'll stay one step ahead.* It was easier said than done for someone as anxious as Lance, but he knew she was right. If he made it through this, he decided as he steeled himself, he would finally pluck up the courage to ask her on a date. Now that prospect was almost more terrifying than facing his ghost. Bolstered by Abina's words, Lance cleared his throat and called in a challenging voice that surprised him, "Why do you hoard?"

Through the heavy front door, Pile materialised, his black robes flailing, the hood pulled up over the horns that stuck out on either side of his temple. He strode forward, and as he stepped his heavy boots shifted in shape, becoming narrowed hooves. "Why do you *waste*?" the spirit yelled, then rammed his body full force into Lance's.

Lance flew backwards down the hallway away from the spectre and felt his back slam into the kitchen table. He lay dazed and in pain against the table leg. The empty *Back from Whence They Came* crate rocked noisily above him. It tipped and slammed down over his head. The key slipped from the lock and clattered against the tiles next to his foot.

Lance peered down at the key, the gold glinting in the light. He looked over at the spare stool, mercifully still lying on its side at the far corner of the kitchen. He thought about what he'd learned when he researched The Hellfire Club and their customs. What he'd learned about Pluto from *Dante's Inferno*.

He reached out and palmed the golden key a moment before Pile fell on him once more. The ghoul grabbed his collar in both fists and hauled him up onto his feet, slamming his already bruised back against the tabletop. Pile shoved his chest against Lance's, re-enacting the eternal physical joust that Pluto forced the fourth circle of Hell inhabitants to perform. The hood hung low over his face, but Lance could see eyes that glowed like scorching embers through the black material.

Struggling, Lance tried to reach for Pile's hood. He needed to pull it back, to see the creature's mouth. His fingers grazed the material, but it was snagged tight on the horns and wouldn't budge.

Behind Pile, there was a blur of movement. Cassie leapt at them, seeing what Lance had been trying to do. Straining, she reached out with what looked like her best front-crawl motion and tugged the hood away from the horns, yanking it back. She tumbled away and rolled to the side, slamming into the kitchen cupboards.

The hood hadn't come fully away but was plucked far enough for Lance to see the monster's mouth. The curls of a gentleman's powdered wig hung down by his chin.

Struggling against the force of Pile's chest, Lance wheezed in a breath and managed to speak the words again. "Why do you hoard?"

Pile grinned, surprised at the challenge. He opened his mouth. "Why do you—"

As his mouth dropped into an oh shape, ready to holler the word "Waste" and strike Lance with a final crushing blow to his chest, Lance struck up between his arms and plunged the gold key into Pile's mouth.

This was Pluto's eucharist, Lance recalled from his research—the placing of a golden key on the tongue of the sinner.

The Hellfire Club member let go of Lance's clothes. He shrank back away from his chest, the key held against his tongue. His eyes were still shrouded in the black hood, but Lance could see the panic on his lower face. Smoke began to plume from his mouth, and the key started to sizzle, growing as red as his eyes had been behind the hood.

From somewhere in the kitchen, a cat yowled.

A second feline scream sounded, followed by a third, until the whole room was flooded with the noise of dozens of cats caterwauling. Lance cupped his hands and covered his ears, watching in horror as Pile's robes began to move. Dozens of lumps under the black material began to scurry around his torso, and Lance realised the yowls were coming from Pile himself. The cats he had tortured and sacrificed in life shot around his skin. Black blood dripped from the robes and Pile let out a strangled cry as the key dissolved into his tongue and the cats tore him to shreds, their claws ripping into his flesh.

With a final scream of "Do What Thou Wilt!" that sprayed blood in Lance's face, Pile disappeared. The horns tumbled to the kitchen floor.

Cassie clambered to her feet and looked down at the horns. She gave a cheer. "That was amazing!"

Lance rubbed his chest and staggered towards her. "Thanks to you. You saved my ass."

"It was nothing." Three of Vaughan's sailors materialised and stood around the kitchen table. They stared down at the ground, unmoving. Waiting. Cassie took a deep breath. She looked solemnly from Lance to Kyle, who had been watching helplessly from the hallway. "I guess my fight's in here, too."

Kyle agreed, staring at the sailors with an anxious look on

his face. "And I'll be...down. Whatever you do, Cassie, don't follow me into the cellar when I go, okay?"

Cassie gave him a nod.

Lance breathed heavily, his shoulders heaving. He kicked at one of the antlers, dazed and beaming. He looked toward Cassie and the goofy grin tumbled from his mouth. "Um...Cass?"

~

CASSIE SPUN ROUND.

Directly behind her, Lisa Vaughan stood, close enough to touch. She wore a sodden green dress and a dripping white apron, her weight on one hip, her arms hanging down by her sides. Her chin was lowered and framed with soaked red hair. She stared at Cassie with a look of pure hatred in her wide, iris-less eyes. The small dots of black in the sea of her whites dilated. She lunged at Cassie with her palms up, arms waving as though she was ministering a spell.

Cassie dropped to her knees, clutching her throat. Stagnant seawater rushed up from somewhere inside her, a never ceasing stream that clogged her throat, pouring down between her knees, the water murky grey and laced with greenery. Through her panic, she recalled her sea swim training, remembered how to stay calm if she was caught too-long under the battering waves. She firmed the muscles in her chest, preventing the urgent need to inhale. Her vision swam with little black dots.

Lisa Vaughan stepped into the puddle, towering over her, the corners of her eyes crinkled in mirth.

Cassie's mind cleared of everything but the poem, the

line repeating over and over. *Baptism by the Light of Dawn will quell the wrath of the siren's song.*

Salt water gushing down over her chin and soaking her top, Cassie looked down and patted her jumper. Frantic, she realised that when she'd grabbed Pile's hood, the vial had fallen from her pocket. She turned to look at the ground where she had landed, putrid water still gushing from her throat. Her vision doubled, lack of oxygen shutting down her senses.

The bottle lay smashed on the kitchen tiles.

Blinking through tears, Cassie watched as Lance crouched and snatched up the remnants of the bottle, a teaspoonful of the water mercifully cradled in the base of the glass. He reached out and passed it to her. Reflexively, she jerked her arm up at the fortune teller's face.

The sea of the Daybreak's maiden voyage hit Lisa Vaughan's forehead like a spatter of spring rain.

The ghoul screamed and dropped to the ground.

Her spine split open like a cockleshell, revealing a core of coral, seaweed, and sand. The spell broken, the water stopped pouring from Cassie's mouth and instead bubbled up from inside Lisa, spilling out over her sides and washing her body away in a tidal stream until all that was left were a few grains of sand in the puddles on the tiles. The sailors that had acted as her sentries opened their mouths, the foghorn wail sounding for a split second before they too vanished, collapsing into puddles of salt water.

Her lungs completely free of Lisa's sorcery, Cassie turned her attention to getting rid of the taste of the deep sea from her mouth. She worked saliva around her cheeks and spat on the tiles. When Lance pushed a glass of water into her hands, she took it gratefully, swilling and spitting until the briny taste had been diluted enough to stop her from gagging. Her clothes were soaked, and the puddles made by the dead sailors had run together, a slew of water flooding toward where Kyle stood in the hallway.

Kyle appraised she and Lance with an impressed expression. "Good job, guys."

AT THAT MOMENT, the living room door burst with a splintering of wood, a rectangular axe blade punching through the panel. Tad was flung through the shattered door. He tumbled heavily into the stairwell and lay for a second. Dazed, he rose into a tabletop position, his elbows holding him up. He lifted his head. Blood spilled down his face, a huge gash running from just under his eye to his top lip, which was split so violently Kyle could see his front teeth and gum through the cut.

Kyle rushed to his friend's side, throwing an arm under his and helping him to sit up. Dark blood pattered the floorboards. Bubbly spit mixed with crimson dripped from Tad's mouth. His left eye was bruised, and he struggled to keep it open as he looked at Kyle. "Help me up," he muttered.

"No! You can't..."

"Have to...finish this," Tad insisted, bracing himself against Kyle's shoulder.

The pair stood together.

Tad reached into his back pocket and pulled out the yakuyoke. The small pouch now looked like it had been mauled by a dog. As they studied the talisman, the final threads snapped on the side, as though Jarvis Rice was raking his axe blade against the silk. It split into two pieces, small blocks of carved wood and kanji-stamped paper tumbling to the ground with the two sides of worn and faded silk.

"Shit!" Kyle wailed, but Tad just shook his head, blood drops tumbling from his chin.

"Take me to him," Tad murmured, his open eye more determined than ever as they stepped over the remnants of the protection spells that had been frantically working their ancient magic inside the silken bag.

We don't have the loaf... We don't have the loaf... Kyle thought, over and over, helping Tad walk shakily towards the living room.

Behind the disintegrated remains of the door, Jarvis Rice stood, his legs spread wide and his stance showing he was ready for action. He patted the neck of the axe down into his gloved palm. He looked thrilled.

Kyle held Tad close to him, feeling his friend tremble with the shock of his injury. "You don't have to do this, Tad!"

Tad turned to him, his blood-soaked mouth hanging open. He smiled blearily, the loose cleft of his lip parting over crimson teeth. "I know what the poem means, now."

He placed his right hand against the doorframe, leaving a bloody smudge. From his cupped palm, Kyle could see that Tad held the silver coin in the other hand.

"Leave me," Tad grunted.

Kyle glanced at Cassie, who knelt shivering in the puddle Lisa Vaughan had left on the kitchen floor, her hands still clasped around her throat. She shook her head, terrified. Lance stood beside her, his eyes glassed in terror, his skin blotchy.

But Tad grinned, his torn lip flapping. "I'm going to put it in his loaf." He shoved with his elbow and Kyle stumbled back, his arms falling away from his friend. Tad tripped forward into the living room, dripping blood.

Rice leered and swung the axe.

CHAPTER 28
THE CELLAR

Tad fell to his knees.

Kyle thought it was accidental, that he had succumbed to the injury and fainted.

But when Tad's kneecaps hit the living room carpet, Rice overswung the axe, missing his target and twisting with the weight of the heavy blade. He spun to the side, his shoulders pitching down, his body bending at the waist. The back of his head became visible when he turned, putrid brain sloshing inside the open cavity.

Tad rose, lifting his hand up high. He held the coin between his index and ring finger and let himself fall forward. He slammed his arm down, the silver disc driving into the monster's open scalp, fingers delving past the shattered skull and into the mouldering mush of Rice's brain.

Jarvis Rice screamed, and the axe tumbled from his hands, cleaving straight through his own foot. He began to fall perilously close to landing on top of Tad, but the executioner disappeared halfway down in a puff of foul green smoke.

Directly below them, someone hollered in rage, the force of the voice rattling the floorboards under their feet. Kyle looked at the cellar door under the stairwell, expecting it to swing open at any moment to reveal Po on a thunderous rampage.

But nothing happened.

Cassie rushed forward and slid on the wet floorboards in her haste to reach Tad. She crawled to him and gently turned him over into her lap.

"I did it." Tad went to smile, then frowned, lifting his fingers to his cuts. Kyle guessed since the adrenaline of the fight was wearing off, his injuries were beginning to throb. He touched a fingertip to his torn lip and jerked his hand away.

"It's all right." Cassie winced in sympathy, assessing his wounds.

Lance grabbed a ream of kitchen towels and began to tear sheets from the roll.

Kyle stood still, his mind racing. Something was missing —a piece of the puzzle that had left a gaping hole in the picture. He thought back over all of Caleb's clues. The crate Caleb had found just before his death that held the key to the rhyme. The phone call about Lucius. *"He's not the good guy in this..."*

Then it dawned on him.

"I get it now!" Kyle yelled. "It's in the cellar."

"We know he is!" Cassie distractedly smoothed Tad's hair back, her hands already soaked with his blood.

"I don't mean Po."

"What then?" she asked, sounding irritated. Blood oozed

from Tad's wounds, smearing across her shirt as his head lolled against her.

"The tome. The fucking spell book— Lucius hid it there all along. And he didn't banish Po to the cellar to get rid of him. He's there to protect the book. Caleb learned the truth, so Po went to kill him before he could tell us. Po's a fucking sentinel, you guys. The spell book is in the cellar!"

Lance stared up at him, wild eyed, his chest heaving. "You shouldn't go down there alone, man."

"I think I have to," Kyle told him, firmly. He checked that the onyx stone was in his jeans pocket, then reached for the small flashlight hanging from a key hook by the cellar entrance. Tad had drilled it into the wall and hung the light beside the door soon after Cassie's last late-night visit to Po. "Wish me luck, I guess."

The others watched him, saying nothing. They'd done all they could—had vanquished their own ghosts, after all. It was up to Kyle, now.

Kyle didn't want to go into the cellar. Every nerve of his body screamed for him to stop, but he reached out and tugged the door. It swung open, the scent of dust pluming up to greet him, taking him back to his time on the red road in Peru.

Steeling himself, he dashed forward, descending the steps in a jog. It was the only way he could summon the courage to go down at all. He had deployed the same tactic when he and Lance did a bungee jump on holiday in Spain the previous year. *Don't think about it, just take a run up and go.*

He hopped down the last step and planted both feet on the ground, shining the flashlight around the room. He saw the usual—dank brick and cinderblock, the earth at his feet grey and chalky. Open rafters lined the ceiling, and ramshackle wooden shelving held random tubs of screws and old, dusty paint tins.

A shadowy figure stood looming large at the back, just visible behind the shelving.

"I see you, you cunt," Kyle called, his voice surprisingly firm.

There was a grunt and a shuffling of feet.

He spun the light, illuminating the shelves as the monster moved from its tenuous hiding place. Kyle gasped and staggered at the sight of it, tumbling back into the steps, fear shrivelling his muscles. His eyes grew so wide his lids felt strained. His brain struggled to comprehend what he was looking at, his train of thought shuddering and stuttering like a chewed VHS tape.

Po was the size of the back of a truck. Slabs of muscle draped his arms and chest, his orange-tinted skin straining under the leather straps that criss-crossed his body and held a brown loin cloth at his waist. The lobes of his ears were stretched, housing two flat discs of jade. A bolt pierced his nose—not just the septum, but the nostrils and bridge, too. With a sick squirrelling sensation in his stomach, Kyle realised the adornment was made of sharpened human rib.

Po was bald, his face large and blockish, his jaw square, mouth open to reveal slab-like teeth shaded with brown staining. Unable to resist, Kyle let his gaze climb over the cheekbones to where a normal man's eyes would be. The sunken planes were disconcerting, but the forehead was the worst. Above the creature's hairless brows sat Po's eyes. One on either side of the forehead, blinking out of time with each other. And one eye directly in the middle, staring continuously, locked on Kyle—a nightmarish vision from a Ray Harryhausen classic. Except it wasn't a Sunday afternoon movie. It was in Kyle's cellar. And it was moving towards him.

He snapped out of his stunned freeze and pelted for the far side of the room, kicking up plumes of grey dust. Po didn't run, but one of his strides were worth four of Kyle's.

Kyle slipped his fingers into his pocket, the jeans tight and resisting his hand. His fingertips brushed the onyx stone.

Po's hand wrapped around Kyle's shoulder and before he could pluck the stone from the tight pocket, he found himself hurtling for the damp grey bricks of the far wall. Kyle threw his free arm across his forehead a moment before he landed on the other side of the floor to where he'd just been, his arm twisting painfully with his fingers still trapped by the band of the pocket, his back wrenched and aching.

He braced himself up on an elbow and plunged his fingers deeper into the pocket. Kyle snagged the smooth stone between his knuckles and began to withdraw his numbing fingers.

Po strode closer, grunting in fury. The ghoul leaned his shoulders forward, his arms spread wide, chest muscles flexing. His lips curled in a sneer, his middle eye narrowing. He began to charge.

Kyle rolled to the side at the last moment, spitting dust and sneezing as he scrabbled away.

Unable to stop his momentum, Po crashed into the wall. Brick crumbled and burst from the structure as though a car had just driven into the house, and Kyle scrambled back in fear of the rafters tumbling down. Po let out a furious scream, throwing slabs of brick from his shoulders as he rose to stand.

Kyle clambered to his feet and made it to the far shelving, ducking around to the other side. It was a makeshift, flimsy shield, but it was all he had to protect himself from Po's growing wrath.

Po moved forward, kicking Lyla Grant's paintings and scattering them across the ground. The creature moved slowly this time, lumbering to the row of shelves, searching for Kyle. He grunted and sniffed, the bone twitching in his nose. His two outer eyes blinked in succession. They were red and watery, the dust apparently irritating him, which seemed crazy. How could a ghost get an allergy? That was the problem, Kyle now realised. The ghosts of The Suffering ritual had grown so strong after causing the sequence of deaths, they were no longer spectres. They were fully formed. Hard to the touch. Even more deadly.

Po's huge arm swung forward, knocking boxes of spare screws and nuts from the shelf. Kyle ducked back, leaping over a tray of wrenches that slid down and hurtled towards his feet. He clambered up onto the lowest ledge of the shelf, peering through the clutter. Po's huge arm snaked through the gap, almost grasping his shirt, and he leaned his weight back, barely avoiding the huge groping hand.

Willing himself to be nimble, Kyle shimmied along the shelving, working his way to the edge. The stone was clasped in his right hand, his thumb securely clamping it against his palm. To gain purchase on the shelving, he painfully pressed his weight into his balled fist.

Po roared, the sound shrivelling Kyle's guts. The monster

grabbed the whole case of shelving and shook it in frustrated fury.

Kyle almost slipped, one of his feet losing its setting and plummeting down, his ankle striking the shelf below. He grunted, swallowing the cry of pain, and regained his composure.

Po had cottoned on to the semantics of the issue. He pivoted his huge body to the side and craned his tree-trunk neck to spy around the corner. Locating Kyle, seeing a clear pathway to him, the beast squealed in petrifying delight. Po lurched to the edge of the shelving, his hulking body taking time to turn the corner and bring him directly into Kyle's path.

It was now or never.

Kyle swung at him.

He used his left hand to brace the end post of the shelves, pushed off with his legs, and let himself fly, hurtling around to meet Po. The grotesque creature fixed him with a look of pure, insatiable desire.

Kyle pulled back his right arm. He extended his fingers and let his body twist in a circular motion, his hand directed at Po's middle eye.

For the first and only time Kyle had witnessed, it blinked.

A millisecond later Kyle slammed the onyx stone into the bulbous ball of jelly.

Po clawed at his face and squealed, staggering. Red smoke began to billow from his middle eye. His body tumbled backwards like a tree being felled. He shuddered and bucked on the ground. He roared, the power of his scream sending dust scattering from the rafters, more bricks tumbling from the gaping hole he had made in the far wall.

Kyle slammed back into the edge of the rack and crumpled to the ground. "Oof!"

Dazed, he shook his head and pulled himself upright, bracing his hands on his knees and staring down at the humongous body in case Po suddenly came back to life.

Po twitched. His hands fell from his face. In the centre of the monster's forehead, between two wide and glassy eyes, the onyx stone sat deep in his skull, yellow ooze pouring from the edges of the burst eyeball. Po's skin began to bubble and blister, his whole body breaking out in the smallpox that had infected him all those years ago.

As Kyle watched, the beast faded and disappeared.

Kyle let out a gasping whoop. Despite his exhaustion, he was elated. "I did it..." he whispered. Then louder, he cried, "I did it!"

Kyle began to limp for the stairs, calling for the others. He had done it. He had beaten Po. In disbelief, he realised he'd beaten the prophecy of the old woman's picture. *He'd saved Cassie's life.*

He was almost at the steps when a slow, echoing clap began to ring out of the shadows and a man stepped forward into the light.

Lucius.

CHAPTER 29
IT'S ALL RELATIVE

Kyle froze, dazed and winded, staring at the familiar face.

Lucius was tall and slim, elegant in his damp-looking white shirt and black suit trousers, pointed dress shoes buffed and shining in the dim light. His face was handsome, with large, deep-set eyes and the heart-shaped mouth Kyle recognised from the family photograph Cassie had fawned over. His dark hair was smoothed back, similar to Kyle's in length, hanging low to his collar at the back.

"Did you say you beat Po?" Lance yelled down from the top of the cellar steps.

"Don't come down here!" Kyle managed to cry out when he heard the creak of his friend beginning the descent.

"Is Po dead?" Cassie yelled, her voice distant.

He guessed she was still cradling Tad in the hallway.

"Yes," Lucius answered for him, his voice low and ominous. "I have to say, I'm not very happy about that, Kyle."

Kyle shouted up the stairs, "Lance! Shut the cellar door. Do not come down here!"

With a reluctant groan, Lance did as he asked and retreated.

The door thumped shut above them.

Kyle turned back to Lucius and raised an eyebrow, suddenly furious. "Fuck you," he spat, lifting his chin.

There was a rushing sound and Kyle's vision blurred as his great-uncle shot across the room at breakneck speed. The blur instantaneously morphed back into his relative at the same moment a long-fingered hand clasped Kyle's windpipe.

Kyle shuddered at the proximity of his dead relative's face. This close, the illusion of handsome ethereality was shattered. The skin was sagging and grey, hanging loose under the eyes and hollowing under sunken cheekbones. Blue veins like Tube maps sprinkled the layer underneath his chalky skin. When Kyle blinked, he saw Lucius's skull, cracked and decaying, the eyes barely hanging by a thread, the whites as yellow and malleable as a newly hatched lizard egg.

Despite the deathly shambles of the creature before him, the fingers squeezed with the strength of any living man, the bony tips sinking deep into his windpipe, causing Kyle to rapidly swallow at the sensation of something lodging in his throat. His mouth swam with saliva, his brain confused at the sudden contusion in his throat.

With nothing to lose, he tried to lash out, but his arms and legs couldn't find purchase. It was as though Lucius could shift dimensions with each limb, his face and left arm fully fixed in Kyle's world, lifting him higher off the ground as he bucked and kicked. His lower torso and legs remained ghostly. Untouchable.

If he was going to die, he at least had to learn the truth. He croaked, "But...you wanted to help us. The verse and the crate. Why?"

Lucius looked puzzled for a moment, then exhaled with a breathy laugh. "The verse and the crate of objects were created by Professor Grant before the séance was even begun. Grant suspected the dangers, had little trust that I was as innocent as I portrayed myself to be. I masterminded the entire séance, not he. With my cousin's help, of course. Grant would have done anything for her, imbecile that he was. Alas, I regret that she fell at the hands of the spirits we unleashed, but she knew the risks. I found the box after the carnage and hid the key in my diary for safekeeping. I requested that a friend of mine destroy it after my death. Sentimental though she was, I thought she would do as I bid her."

Angered at the mention of his friend, a friend that Kyle knew had to be Hestor, Lucius's fingers clenched tighter around his throat. Choking, Kyle wilfully held the remaining air in his lungs and tried to think past the horse race kicking of his heart; his screaming amygdala; his frantic will to survive. *Think, think*, he begged himself, casting his mind back over the clues Caleb had brought to him. He couldn't let his real uncle's death be in vain.

"It was Hestor, wasn't it?" he eventually choked out, his voice a peculiar gurgle that sounded nothing like himself.

The spectre tilted his head, one half of his mouth twitching. "What?"

Kyle repeated the name, then clutched at his throat, sputtering and spitting when Lucius let go and he fell in a pile at his translucent feet.

"Go on, distant nephew. Consider me intrigued. What of Hestor?"

"She knew the truth about you," Kyle croaked. "You thought she didn't, but she did."

The ghost's expression faltered, his eyes widening. As Kyle watched, the skin changed, moving from almost human, to blue and bloated, to skeletal, and back to fully human in the blink of an eye. "How do you know this?"

"Caleb discovered her diaries. He read them all." Kyle rubbed his Adam's apple, the nodule tender, his throat feeling as though he had swallowed a jagged crisp.

Lucius's shoulders sagged. "So, she knew."

It appeared to have touched the nerve Kyle hoped it would. Apparently, there was some remnant of humanity left in him, after all. "She did. And she didn't care."

Lucius gave a snort of laughter.

"Honestly. She knew you were still a good man. She still..." Kyle hung on the words a moment, hearing how insincere and cheesy they sounded in his mind. "She still loved you."

The ghost stood over Kyle, tall and menacing even with his slender figure. He reached down a hand.

Bewildered, Kyle tentatively reached out his own. Could his plan have worked? "Uncle?"

Lucius snatched his hand and yanked him to his feet with such force, Kyle felt his shoulder wrench in its socket. Nose to nose—his great-uncle's no more than two gaping holes—the skeletal form came back for a second, then shifted to the blue, sagging, bloated corpse flesh that Kyle could smell.

When Lucius spoke, maggots skittered from the corners

of his tongue, a putrid waft of rancid vegetation and rotten meat flooding Kyle's senses. "You contemptable fuck!"

Kyle blinked, horror dawning on him as the ghoulish vision of his long-dead ancestor leered in his face.

"What would you know of love? The asylum I stayed in was full of filthy sodomites like you." Lucius clasped Kyle's chin, wrenching it to the left. Kyle's feet skidded through the grey dirt, trying to gain purchase as he was thrown mercilessly from side to side. Eventually, Lucius pulled Kyle millimetres from his face, his weeping yellow eyes narrowing, the blue thread veins stark in his ashen cheeks. His face gradually returned to normal once more. "And as for Hestor Morello? Who do you think killed Mr. Morello for her?" He gave a fiendishly charming smile.

Lucius pitched Kyle's chin like a baseball.

Kyle flew across the cellar, memories of the bungee jump flooding back to him once more as he rammed into the hole made by Po during their fight. His shoulder took the brunt, skimming under the broken bricks, taking off a layer of skin but lessening the momentum of Kyle's descent as he skidded back into the open wall cavity.

He knew that, ironically, Po had probably saved his life. With the force that Lucius had thrown him he would have no doubt snapped his neck had the hole not been there. As it stood, he assessed, lying in the hole and staring up at the house's internal foundations and gasping for air, he had a dislocated shoulder and a couple of cracked ribs. Hot blood pulsed down over his chest from where the sharp brick had cut his collar bone.

Groaning, he sat, using his good hand to brace against the bricks and haul himself up. His right hand was useless, dangling in his lap, his whole arm had gone numb and felt like the physical equivalent of television static. He would need to use his left to shuffle forward out of the hole before Lucius decided to join him in the tiny crawlspace.

He put his palm flat to the ground and pressed against something rectangular and smooth. Too dark to see, Kyle groped with his fingers until the tips pressed into the cold curve of padded leather. He slipped his fingers underneath it and felt pages riffle against his palm. "No fucking way."

He dug into the chalky earth and scooped his hand under the book, lifting the tome and cradling it against his chest. His heart leapt with exhilaration. He had nothing to fight Lucius with, no verse for him on a museum picture frame. No trinket found in a mildewed box in a Victorian woman's attic. But now he had the tome of spells. The very reason Lucius had returned to the house in the first place.

"Oh nepheeeew?" The ghoul called, his voice echoing through the foundations of the house. A secondary whisper continued on after he had finished speaking, "*Nephew, nephew, nephew, nephew.*" The echo chilled Kyle to the core. "I know you're alive in there."

Feeling like a little kid with a slight upper hand in a game against an older sibling, Kyle held the book and willed himself to think of something. Aside from somehow battering Lucius to death with it, he really had nothing. He started to panic. He tilted his head back and banged it against the foundation timbers, then opened his eyes.

A half-naked Jonah sat in the foundations directly opposite him, a cocky grin on his face and a towel around his waist, leaving little to the imagination.

Startled, Kyle's mouth fell open.

Lance's cousin tongued his lip ring and nodded at Kyle's waist. "You've got something of mine, dickhead," he winked, then vanished.

Gritting his teeth, Kyle wriggled his hips, scurrying out of the hole, the tome held tightly against his chest with his good arm. He sat up on his knees surrounded by Lyla Grant's oil paintings. Lucius was still standing where he had thrown Kyle from, lazily waiting for him to come out. The spectre turned cockily to him, gazing over his squared shoulder. He locked eyes on the tome.

He was visibly surprised, a mean feat for a ghost, Kyle thought. His great-uncle's mouth opened slightly, his narrowed eyes widening. Then, he regained his composure. He spun round and took three long strides towards Kyle, his face twisting in rage.

"Wait!" Kyle held up Jonah's cigarette lighter and flicked the flint wheel, a tiny blue spark bursting into a full orange flame.

Lucius breathed through his nose, a conceited snort. "You think the book will burn? Honestly, I was led to believe you twentieth century children were far advanced."

"I'm not a child," Kyle told him, then dropped the book down into the centre of one of Lyla's landscapes of Brackenby. He lowered the Zippo to the paint-slathered canvas and watched the blue glow begin to spread. The flame danced over the picture, spreading out to meet the ornate frame.

Lucius stared, unperturbed.

As Kyle had hoped, the frame worked to contain the fire, the flames eating through the linseed oil and paint-soaked canvas and quickly surrounding the book. The curling pages of the tome caught, just a gentle singe at first. Kyle held his breath, willing the book to burn. The flame ate into the pages, sparking yellow for a moment before burning green in the darkness from the copper sulphate used in the old ink. Contained within the inferno of the painting, the pages combusted with an audible *whumph* that to Kyle sounded like Po's exhalations in the shadows of the cellar.

Lucius shrieked and broke into a run, dashing to where Kyle lay prone.

Kyle was so exhausted he couldn't even bring himself to try and move, the destruction of the spell book his final, *only* option.

Before he even reached the book, Lucius's shirt caught on fire, despite its sodden appearance. The spectre screamed, twisting to pat the flames. His hands caught the green fire, spreading it rather than muffling it. He fell to his knees, screaming as he burned, his face bubbling, the blue flesh sliding down over bone.

"Nephew!" he cried, his voice a guttural wail. This time, there was no reverberating echo.

With a groan, Kyle managed to stand, and stepped closer to his suffering ancestor. "Here," he said compassionately. "Let me help you."

Lucius's half skeletal, half ghoulish and burning face somehow managed a grateful expression. He reached up, his fingers on fire and dripping fat, the tips showing bone.

Kyle snatched Lucius's wrist bone and yanked him downwards.

Lucius let out a shriek that shook the house and toppled to land on his knees in the flames. Now burning from head to foot, he calmly opened his mouth and began to chant in a low, calm voice. The words whispered around the room, reverberating in Kyle's ears. He cringed away from the unnatural sound.

Lucius stopped chanting and took a deep breath, intentionally sucking smoke into his lungs, then vanished before Kyle's eyes. The fire instantly died.

Kyle blinked against the plumes of acrid smoke, searching for the ashen remains of the tome. But he was stunned to find the book laying intact at his feet, a new chain secured around it as it had been when Professor Grant came into possession of it, its pages re-grown and stark white.

Dazed, Kyle let his eyes skim the room, unsure of exactly what had happened. Although the book and chain had rematerialized, there was no sign of Lucius.

Above him, the door creaked open, and Lance spoke tentatively. "Kyle? You down there?"

Kyle cleared his throat. "Yeah, I'm here."

Lance carefully started down the steps, closely followed by Cassie. They both peered over the banister, watching him with pensive faces. "Is it over?"

Kyle moved to the tome and picked it up. He couldn't feel Lucius in the room anymore. That heavy, inexplicable sensation of darkness in the cellar was gone. Still, he didn't trust his great-uncle, and the chant he had uttered the moment before he disappeared unnerved him.

He shoved the book back into the foundation of the house and turned to the others, pleading, "We need to brick this back up."

Wordlessly, his friends descended the steps.

Lance found a tub of mortar that had been kicked from the shelving and began stirring it with a trowel. Cassie set about gathering up the broken bricks and putting them in a pile. She rooted at the back of the room, telling the others she'd spotted a jumble of old junk upon waking from one of her nightmares that might help. Moments later, she hauled out a couple of breeze blocks that would take the place of any bricks that had been pulverised.

All the while, Kyle held his dislocated arm steady and watched the tome, distrustfully.

They began to reassemble the wall. Even Tad managed to come down and help, crusted blood streaking his swollen face. He looked awful, and Kyle couldn't help but admire the fact that his determination to encase any evil that was left in the house was overwhelming his obvious need to rest. Tad slathered mortar onto the stones before Cassie and Lance jammed them into place, building a haphazard barricade around the book.

When they slid the last stone into place, Cassie rubbed a hand against Kyle's back, shaking him from his vigil. "It's okay. We did it."

Kyle looked around the cellar, waiting for Po's tell-tale grunt. After a few moments, he realised they truly were alone. "You're right. It's over."

The housemates ascended the creaking steps.

"So, what are we going to tell the hospital?" Lance asked, holding the door open as the wounded clambered out.

"Skateboarding incident?" Cassie suggested, pointing down at the gash on her knee that could have easily come from a spill on the half-pipe.

"Skateboarding incident," Kyle and Tad agreed at the same time as they headed for the door.

CHAPTER 30
HALLOWEEN ONCE MORE

Kyle wasn't too surprised the household had opted for a quiet Halloween this time. Although Cassie filled two large buckets with packets of sweets and stood them next to the door ready for trick-or-treaters, and Lance had selected a movie marathon of horror classics to watch as the evening rolled on, this year there were no costumes. There were no parties.

There were no ouija boards.

They took turns at the door, and before eight o' clock, the first bucket was almost empty. "We might run out at this rate." Lance frowned, shaking the last few gummy bear packets.

Tad got to his feet. "I'll go to the shop."

"You're sure?" Lance looked grateful. He seemed way too comfortable to head out into the cold night, and Kyle knew his favourite scene in *The Texas Chainsaw Massacre* was about to come on.

Tad smiled, his lip twisting downwards. The new scar across his face had somehow made Tad more confident, and

Kyle had watched him settle into his skin in a way his undisturbed beauty had never allowed. Of course, Tad was still handsome, and he still attracted countless attentions. But he'd been thrilled to find that women seemed to have fewer preconceptions about who he was. They found him inexplicably intriguing, *even* when he started talking about sewage, a fact that was just as much of a surprise to Kyle. In turn, Tad's confidence had blossomed since his injury.

"I don't mind going," Tad said. "I need to pick up a couple of bits, anyway."

Lance gestured to the coffee table. "There's a few quid on there. Take that for the sweets."

Tad looked over to the table. "Where?"

"Right there..." Lance stared at the empty glass tabletop and patted his pockets. "That's weird. I know I emptied out my change before the movie started."

"Maybe Cassie took it?" Pete suggested, earning a punch on the arm.

"Hey, I'm no thief!" She had kept her hair short, finding it far easier to swim without having to wear a cap, and the shorn bristles stuck out in all directions.

"Watch it!" Pete grimaced, rubbing his arm. His left leg was propped up, a material splint applying pressure to his latest set of sutures. Although he was well and truly on the mend, he still had three more scheduled ops to completely set the bones and strengthen his shattered joints.

Cassie rolled her eyes. "It's your leg that's broken, not your arm."

"Such a loving, caring girlfriend, I have." Pete pretend sulked, then acquiesced as she leaned forward and gave him a lingering kiss until his lips curved into a smile.

She laughed and pulled out her phone. "Hey, Tad. Before you go, I'll order the pizzas. What are you having?"

"Margarita," Tad requested.

"Of course. Boring." She flicked her thumb over the screen, bringing up her delivery app.

Lance was still scowling at the coffee table, distracted. He muttered, "I'll have pepperoni."

"Done. Pete?"

Pete thought for a moment, then pursed his lips, looking queasy. "I dunno. I might just pinch one of Tad's slices."

"You okay?"

"Yeah...just a little unsettled tonight." He laid a hand over his stomach and sank back against the cushions.

Lance turned to him, pensive. "Like, dizzy?"

"I guess. It'll be the meds." He lifted his leg in explanation, then lowered it carefully, his complexion paling.

"That hasn't happened for a while," Lance told him, thoughtfully.

Kyle caught Lance's eye and gave him a sharp look. Things were finally starting to get back to normal for the residents of Brackenby. He'd known Halloween would be tough for them all, but Lance was acting like a startled deer all of a sudden. He watched him as he walked out to the hallway to return the sweet bucket, then clicked his fingers at Cassie. "I'll have Hawaiian. Twelve-inch."

"Gross," she mouthed. She placed the order, then scrubbed the phone against the front of her baggy sweatshirt. "God damnit. It's doing that stupid condensation thing again."

"Let me see?" Kyle moved to the couch and craned over

to look at the phone screen. A grey dribble of water snaked over the inside of their order confirmation.

A hammering knock at the door made Kyle jump out of his skin, causing Cassie to laugh. "Steady on, jumpy."

"I'll go," he said, feeling foolish.

Lance was lingering in the hallway, staring at the front door.

"Aren't you going to answer it?" Kyle asked.

Lance just shook his head, then ducked back into the living room.

Kyle grabbed the full bucket of sweets and turned the handle.

He immediately recognised the little girl bouncing from foot to foot on the doorstep as the kid who had worn a Lisa Vaughan costume the year before. This time, she had chosen to dress more mainstream as a tiny Carrie, her white dress sloshed with fake blood, her red wig repurposed. Her little brother hovered behind her, taller than before, a bored Han Solo carrying a Wookie cuddly toy.

"What do you say, Emelia?" The mother coaxed from where she stood at the bottom of the steps, distractedly looking at her phone. She gave Kyle a weary wave of acknowledgement, then turned back to her screen.

"Trick-or-treat!" the girl called, grinning up at him.

Kyle smiled back and tossed a handful of sweets into each of the kids' pillowcases. The little boy eyed him warily before hopping down the steps and clinging onto his mother's leg.

Emelia looked back at them, then moved closer to Kyle, beckoning for him to lean in.

Humouring her, he bent down, placing his ear close to her mouth.

"I did my own séance today," she whispered, eagerly. "Lucius says hi."

Kyle stood up, a heavy feeling of dread washing over him as the little girl skipped down the steps, waving. Trembling, he closed the front door. Immediately, it knocked again, three sharp raps that thundered through the hall. He stepped back, his heart thudding.

A flickering light shone outside the windowpane, moving past the door.

Above him, quick footsteps pelted across the landing.

"No, no...no!" he cried.

Lance and Cassie ran from the living room, staring at him, aghast. "What the hell?" Lance's eyes darted to the landing as the footsteps sounded again, running back the way they had come.

Under their feet, from somewhere deep in the cellar, something thudded.

The cellar door flew open, and Cassie was sucked inside.

THE END

ABOUT THE AUTHOR

MJ Mars is a horror enthusiast living in Lancaster, UK. MJ has been published in a number of horror anthologies, including Dark Peninsula's *Negative Space*, and Colors in Darkness' *Deadly Bargains*. *The Suffering* is MJ's debut novel, and it was inspired by a love of horror monster icons and their backstories.

Join her on Twitter: @MJMars, Instagram: @mjmarsauthor, and her Facebook page, MJ Mars Author.

Printed in Great Britain
by Amazon

23100166R00184